Joy and Felicity

— SARAH MEYRICK —

Sacristy Press

Sacristy Press
PO Box 612, Durham, DH1 9HT

www.sacristy.co.uk

First published in 2021 by Sacristy Press, Durham

Sacristy Limited, registered in England & Wales, number 7565667

British Library Cataloguing-in-Publication Data
A catalogue record for the book is available from the British Library

ISBN 978-1-78959-176-7

In memory of my beloved mother, Elizabeth Meyrick (1934–2020)

PREFACE

Endue her plenteously with heavenly gifts; grant her in health
and wealth long to live; strengthen her that she may vanquish
and overcome all her enemies; and finally after this life she may
attain everlasting Joy and Felicity; through Jesus Christ our Lord.

The Book of Common Prayer

PROLOGUE

January 1942

The cry of the baby, little more than a kitten's mewl, stirs her awake.

She feels herself being dragged unwillingly into consciousness, swimming upwards from the fathomless depths. Dark green, the colour of oblivion. She opens her eyelids, to be met by pitch black. Night, then. Her eyes are gritty, stinging with dust. She blinks and reaches for the light-switch, but her hand flails in the void. She realizes she's cold. Very cold. She needs to get up, to reach the child who is summoning her, but her legs don't seem to be working. Her head is lower than her feet, and something heavy is pinning her to the mattress. Pain shoots up her left thigh.

Mother of God, have mercy. Her leg is on fire.

It is all she can do not to retreat into the foetal bliss of unconsciousness. She drifts off for what may be seconds. Or it could be minutes. Hours even. She has no way of knowing. But then the cry becomes more desperate, the mewl cranking up a gear into a wail. Fear? Hunger? Pain? At barely two weeks old, it could be any of the three, poor wee mite. And surely she can smell burning. Gas? Did she leave the ring on? As the wail becomes louder, she feels a lurch of fear. A tug as strong as a dockside hawser is yanking her awake. She must find the baby, take her in her arms, soothe her distress.

This time, she forces herself to keep her eyelids wide, to give her vision a chance to adjust to the gloom. Deep breaths; count to ten. Yes. She's in her bed. She recognizes the candy-striped pillowslip she stitched herself from a worn-out sheet of Veronica's that was beyond patching. Veronica! She's on duty tonight, patrolling the streets. She doesn't recall hearing her key in the lock. Perhaps she's still out there, bless her soul?

An air raid. They've been bombed, wouldn't you know it? There was no warning, or surely to God she'd have bundled the baby into a blanket and made her way down to the Anderson shelter. Despite the nuisance of her neighbour's wandering hands, she wouldn't have risked staying put. Somewhere in the distance she can hear the clang of fire engines. Are they getting nearer? If there are fire engines, perhaps help is on its way.

For the love of God, would you look at those Jerries? After last year's hammering, you'd have thought the city had had its share. Bloody Fritz must be after clobbering the docks again. But he surely has no business dropping bombs on innocent women and children.

The room looks all wrong. In the normal way of things, her bed is tucked under the sloping ceiling. Not only is the bed listing drunkenly, but from what she can make out, the eaves are no more. The roof has collapsed, and surely to God her legs are trapped under a beam. The skylight—no, the entire *wall*—has been blown out. No wonder it's so cold! A blast of arctic air is blowing straight into her face. And if it seems a little lighter now, it's because she can glimpse starlight through the dusty haze.

She manoeuvres herself upright. Her arms are functioning, at least. As are her hands. She feels down her body, to work out what's what. She's pinioned to the bed and no mistake. She can just about move her right leg, but the left is stuck fast under the weight of the shattered roof. But the obstruction is not as thick as you'd expect of a beam. Rafters, then? Yes, she can feel the splinters in the wood. Wooden struts, chunks of plaster, broken roof tiles. She attempts to shift the rubble, to free her poorly thigh, but she's trapped fast. Well, she's in a pickle, so she is.

Weh, weh, weh! The baby's cry is drilling into her brain, propelling her forward.

All of a sudden there's an almighty crash, and the bed teeters to the floor as one of its legs gives way, opening up a cavity an inch or two between the mattress and the remains of the roof. With a strength she didn't know she possessed, she swings her right leg out of the covers and then uses both hands to lift her injured left thigh free from the debris before any more rafters have the chance to come down on her. Adrenaline surges through her body. She is giddy with relief.

Weh, weh, weh! The baby is sobbing now, great gulps signalling her rising distress.

"Sure, there's no need for all that," she calls out. "I'm coming as fast as I'm able." Shards of broken glass glisten on the floorboards. Oblivious to the pain, she carves a path towards the sound, crawling on her elbows and right knee and dragging her useless left leg behind her. It's only a few feet, but by the time she reaches the crib she is sweating with the effort. Her hands are grey with grit and streaked with blood.

Miraculously, bar a thick layer of plaster dust, the crib is untouched. The infant's tiny arms are waving indignantly, a picture of fury. She's kicked off the covers and will be feeling the chilly January air. Otherwise, there's not a scratch on her, thank the Lord.

She scoops the furious baby into her arms. "Enough, *a stóirín*," she murmurs, holding the child to her breast, desperate to shield her from the icy blast. "Enough, my treasure. Shush, now, shush . . . "

She can feel her own tears burning hot on her cheeks. "Will you let me get my breath back, now, my lovely? And then we'll see what's left of the stairs, and go and find your mammy, so we will."

BRIDIE

2019

When I open my eyes, the sun is streaming in through the window, like the yellow sunrays in a child's drawing. Have I overslept? Likely as not my Da'll take the strap to me if so. But just as I'm asking myself if it's school or Mass I'm late for someone comes in, and it's not my Da at all, nor my Mam for that matter, and I don't know who she is, but I know she's kind.

Morning, Bridie. And how are you today, my darlin'? says she. And I'm not sure how to answer because, so help me God, this woman isn't family, and I can tell you that for sure because she's big and fat and black as your hat. You're not supposed to say that, are you, but the boys tell me I can't say *coloured* either, so what's a body to do? Racist, apparently. But one thing's for sure. I don't know her name, even if she knows mine.

Let's be getting you all spruced up, shall we? she says and suddenly my head is rising without me moving from the pillow and I'm wondering about another topsy-turvy bed that wouldn't stay flat, but memory's a slippery thing, and I can't place it for the love of God. Except I think I can smell fireworks, so perhaps it's Bonfire Night, though we don't really hold with any of that, Father Joseph and I. Nasty Catholic persecution, he calls it. But I never liked the girls to miss a wee bit of fun, because fun is thin on the ground, and no one wants to be the odd one out now, do they?

And now she's washing me, and the flannel is warm, and that's grand, but I don't much care for the smell of the wet cloth on my face. How do I know she won't hold it over my mouth and nose, and I won't be able to breathe, so?

Steer well clear of a nun with a face cloth, says Mary-Pat, and she should know. Sisters of Mercy; mercy my arse. Not much mercy shown to the likes of our Mary-Pat in that steaming laundry, let me tell you. Slave labour and no mistake, with a dollop of shame and humiliation for dessert. So now I'm in a terrible twit, and I'm starting to twist my head and fight back, and herself with the flannel says, *Bridie, my darlin', calm down, I'm not about to hurt you, am I now? You know me, my darlin'. Abayomi. Your very favourite nurse.*

Then I remember Abayomi isn't a nun, so perhaps I needn't watch myself. Now I see she has a uniform, and she's probably telling the truth about being a nurse, for all it looks like pyjamas she's wearing. *Where am I?* I ask, but the words sort of slide out of the side of my mouth in a jumble, not at all as I meant.

So you are speaking to me today, after all! says the big black woman, and when she smiles I see she has a wide mouth with a pink tongue and big white teeth with a gap at the front. She has a sing-song voice, with a hint of laughter bubbling underneath the words. And my heart lifts because I remember she is cheerful and kind, and she doesn't seem to mind that I slur my words and I dribble when I speak.

You're in hospital, she says. *Do you remember? You had a little stroke, and we're lookin' after you until you're back on your feet, bless you.*

She says this as if it's the most natural thing in the world. *Little stroke* sounds such a gentle thing that I think of stroking a kitten. Or a puppy. The rag-and-bone-man's horse, who liked his nose petted. What was his name, now? *Ginger.* The horse, not your man.

When my girls were little, I always wanted to stroke their dear little cheeks. The very smell of them, so help me! Like bread from the oven or spring sunshine after rain. The freshness of clean sheets, wet from the wringer, flapping in the wind. How could a body resist? Joy didn't put up with that for long, mind. She had a way of shrugging me off if I came too close. I had to wait for her sister to come along because she loved being babied and was so much more biddable.

But I'm not at all sure this *little stroke* is as gentle as Abby . . . Abba . . . the nurse-nun would have me believe. The memory is a bag of fragments, like cracked glass. A blinding headache, the worst pain ever. Worse even than childbirth, so help me God, and that's the kind of agony that rips you in half from head to toe with the force of it. *Abayomi*. That's herself with the flannel. Abayomi.

Little stroke, I say, or try to say. It sounds more like *Ick . . . oke*. But Abayomi seems to understand.

That's right, Bridie, bless you! A stroke. And now shall I brush your hair for you? Make you all beautiful before that handsome doctor comes on his ward round?

I'm about to say no, I'll be grand, when I catch sight of my arm lying useless on the bed cover, and I remember I'm not so clever with my right hand. The little stroke has put paid to that. And I think again that this is a kind woman, and I wonder why she is looking after me when I'm not her Mam. Where are my own girls? Shouldn't they be here? Perhaps they're at school. But why don't they come? Now there are tears leaking down my face.

The last time anyone else brushed my hair . . . well, that would be my Mammy, now, wouldn't it? I remember the feel of her, even if I can't see her face. Sitting on her lap before the fire, the smell of stew in the pot and tatties in the stove. Her crooning a song in my ear, brushing out the tangles after a wash. A sense that all was right in the world, for that one moment at least. I've not thought of that for years and years and years. Oh, but there's comfort in the recollection.

I feel the brush on my scalp, gentle as anything, and Abayomi's soft voice, though I can't catch the words. But she is so pleased, and the morning sun is still shining through the window, that I let her carry on and try to smile, too.

JOY

1949

Joy is hovering at the school gate. She's been waiting and waiting for Mammy to fetch her home, but there's still no sign. The school is at the top of Coronation Road, and the playground wall offers the perfect lookout to spot her mother's approach.

For the first few minutes after the bell, she simply waited for Mammy to materialize out of the crowd. She has developed a way of standing completely still. She imagines she's wearing magic shoes with magnets that fix her to a secret spot on the ground that nobody but she knows about. It's like extra gravity, pulling her down to the earth and keeping her safe until Mammy arrives and undoes the spell. All Joy has to do is stand still as a statue. But today there's no sign of Mammy.

At first, she kept completely calm, even when Sylvia Jenkins barged into her with such a shove that Joy dropped her satchel, and then said in a sing-song voice: "Sorr-*ee*, Joy, I didn't *see* you there," which was a mean sort of joke.

Sylvia and her friend Irene have been making Joy's life a misery ever since she started at St Anthony's Infants last year. To begin with, it seemed to be something about the way she spoke that made Joy stand out. It was the same with horrid Aunt Marjorie who kept asking her to repeat herself. When they first moved to Northampton, her aunt spoke to her very slowly, as if she was hard of hearing like Vera Watts in Class 2. In the end, Joy decided it was easier to stop talking altogether. Now she speaks only when necessary.

She still hasn't really got any friends. Unless you count runny-nosed Rita, who's happy to pair up with Joy for PE and once lent her a hair ribbon. But Rita hardly counts, because she misses lots of school. She disappears for days at a time, leaving Joy stranded, then silently reappears in the classroom, her face all pinched, and won't meet anyone's eye.

Mammy says Sylvia's a silly so-and-so, and to take no notice, but it's not always that easy. Today when Sylvia pushed her, Joy dropped her precious satchel in a puddle which means it's wet and muddy, and so is her reading book which was sticking out of the top. She loves her satchel. It's smooth and shiny like a conker and still smells all leathery, even though she's had it a whole year. There are pockets at the front, and you close it tight shut with two shiny silver buckles. She will have to find a way of hiding it from Father until it's dried out, because otherwise he will be cross. She hopes the mud won't leave a mark.

Joy is also getting very cold. It's a gloomy November afternoon, the sort of day where it's never been properly light. A blustery wind is buffeting the last few dead leaves around the playground. They gather in grubby corners of the netting fence, before taking off with the next puff.

She shifts her weight from one leg to the other, barely aware that she's doing so. What she does know is that she needs the lav. The trouble is that if she goes back inside, Mrs McLeod will want to know the reason why, and then Joy might miss Mammy altogether. What if her mother comes and can't see her in the playground? She might go away again without her. Also, she'll be worried sick, because the rule is that Joy always waits by the gate and Mammy always comes.

Mammy is never, ever late. Some of Joy's class—like horrible Sylvia and her brother Kenneth—walk home on their own, and that's one of the things that she gets teased for. "Baby Joy's waiting for her Mummy to take her home in the pram!" shouts Sylvia. "Bye, baby bunting!" And she uses another word that Joy knows is so rude that she's not even going to say it in her head.

She's beginning to worry that Mammy is ill again. Last term she kept being sick in the bathroom, and sometimes Father used to bring her to school in the mornings. When that happened, she had to scuttle to keep up, because his legs are so long and he walks so fast. It's the total opposite with Mammy, because her poorly leg plays up in the damp, and then Joy is scared they'll miss the school bell, and she'll be for it with Mrs McLeod.

In the end, she summoned her courage and asked Father to leave her at the foot of Coronation Road. That way she could catch her breath for the last bit up the hill.

She thought Mammy was better now, but perhaps she's fallen ill and is in hospital? There's a heavy feeling at the pit of Joy's stomach, as if she's gobbled her dinner too fast or swallowed something lumpy. Can people get hairballs, like cats? Blackie next door is always sicking them up, and it's disgusting. The thought of a hairball makes her panicky. What would Sylvia do to her if Joy sicked one up at school?

Or maybe Mammy's had an accident. Been hit by a car. Or a bomb left over from the War. Joy worries a lot about bombs, ever since Aunt Dolly wrote to Mammy all about Uncle Ron being called in to help get rid of an unexploded bomb that turned up in Bootle, even though it's years and years since the War ended. Joy had no idea that bombs could be dropped and *not* explode.

If there were leftover bombs in Liverpool, why not in Northampton? Even worse, would people here even know a bomb if they saw one? Father is always saying that Northampton people haven't the first idea about the Blitz. They might walk past an old bomb without any idea it was dangerous. Like Red Riding Hood going to visit her Grandma, not realizing she was actually the Big Bad Wolf in disguise.

On the other hand, they would surely have heard a big bang during lessons if there was a bomb. Mammy talks about the terrible racket during the air raids, how they never had a good sleep from one night to the next, even when the bombs were miles away. It sounds frightening, but Mammy always makes it sound like an adventure.

"We stood up to Herr Hitler in Liverpool and no mistake!" she says. "He may have tried to hammer the living daylights out of us, but who's laughing now?"

Now Joy is desperate. She has to go to the lav, or she'll have an accident. She decides to make a run for it and use the WC that only Class 5 and 6 are supposed to use, because it's nearer the entrance. This feels very naughty, but the Class 3 WC is right down the far end of the corridor. If she dashes in and out as fast as she can, she'll be back in no time. She is hurtling towards the school building at the very moment her mother appears at the gate, red in the face and puffing with the exertion of climbing the hill. Joy changes direction and hurls herself towards her mother.

"Oh, my best beloved, I'm sorry I've kept you," says Mammy, enfolding Joy in her fleshy bosom. She smells of a comforting mix of lavender soap and fresh bread. "I'm here now, though, so I am." And just as Joy is giving in to the heady relief of seeing Mammy alive and well, she is simultaneously consumed with shame as she realizes she's wet her knickers.

Later, when they're safely home in Number 12 and Joy's had a wash and changed her clothes, they sit at the kitchen table. Mammy puts a cup of milky tea in front of her and passes her a bit of bread and dripping on her favourite plate which has rabbits round the edge. "All better now?" she asks, and Joy nods, mute with misery.

"Nothing to worry about, my lovely," says Mammy. "I'm sorry I kept you waiting, so I am. But there's something important kept me. I had to go to see Dr Sheen, and he was running late, or I'd have made it in time for the bell."

Joy swallows too quickly and splutters into her tea. If Mammy's been to the doctor, she's ill.

"No, no, no!" says Mammy, and Joy sees she's smiling a smile that reaches right up into her eyes. "It's nothing to worry about, my lovely. It's happy news, so it is. We're to have a baby. What do you make of that? A brother or sister for you to play with. Dr Sheen was just checking me over to make sure everything's as it should be. That's a happy reason to be late, if ever there was one. Though I'm still sorry I kept you waiting and worried."

Joy doesn't know what she's meant to say. She looks at her mother in silence, and notices for the first time that she is changing shape. Joy knows that babies come from their Mammy's tummies, and that they get fat. Mammy's friend Mrs Hooper had twins before Christmas, and she was as big as an elephant beforehand.

"Will it be twins, Mammy?" she asks.

"I surely hope not! Why would it be twins, in the name of all that's holy? Oh, you mean like little Fred and Stanley Hooper? May the Lord preserve us!" she says and laughs.

"But talking of those two, Shelagh's promised me her lovely Swan perambulator, because it's already on the small side for two. So that's a saving as should please your father.

"We'll still need a layette, mind, so I was thinking I should teach you to knit. How about that? We'll take the bus into town on Saturday and see if we can't find some pretty baby wool in Woolworths and then we'll make a start on bootees and bonnets."

"Where will the baby sleep?" asks Joy.

The new house that's scarcely new anymore has two bedrooms and a tiny box room that's full of her father's books and papers, as well as his desk that Joy's not allowed to touch. The memory of their old house is fading fast. She pictures big, dark rooms, always just too cold for comfort. It was tired and shabby whereas Number 12 is almost brand new. It has a friendly face and Mammy loves it.

"We've fallen on our feet here, so we have," she says almost daily. "So much lighter than that dreary old presbytery. A little garden, all of our own, and that grand park just over the road. My stars, but we've fallen on our feet!"

Mammy tells her that the baby will sleep in her parents' bedroom to begin with, although at some point it will move into a cot. "We'll cross that bridge when we come to it, my lovely. But there's no room to swing a cat in that box room, books or no books." She frowns. "What do you say to helping me make space in your room?"

Joy considers for a moment. Her mother often gets very tired; Father likes his meals on time and the house just so. He is what Mammy calls *a handful*. "My Joseph has his standards, and no mistake," she's fond of telling Mrs Wilkie over the garden fence, though she always speaks as if this is a good thing.

"Do babies make a lot of extra work?" asks Joy.

"I'd say they do. Lots of washing of nappies, for one thing. But to be sure they bring great happiness as well."

And Joy suddenly sees that her mother is going to need help, and that she is the one to provide it. Joy is so sensible, everyone says so. Even

Uncle Norman has started praising Joy when she helps clear the dishes after Sunday lunch.

Their monthly visit to her uncle and aunt is torture. It's as if Aunt Marjorie is just waiting for her to break one of her precious ornaments. She collects china figurines of ladies in swirly ball dresses in different pastel shades. The fabric looks so real that Joy longs to reach out and stroke the folds, just to see what it feels like, but she is under strict instructions not to touch. If she can just about contain the urge to stroke them, she can't avert her gaze. What she really wants to know is whether the dresses are as cold to the touch as they look.

Aunt Marjorie has a cleaner called Ruby who likes to move the ladies into different positions around the sideboard, which makes Aunt Marjorie tut and move them back again. Every time they visit, Joy silently checks who's winning: Aunt Marjorie or Ruby.

"I think he'd better come in with me, so I can watch him for you, Mammy," she says now.

"He or *she*, my lovely. You might have a sister."

"I'm not sure Father will be happy with that," she says. 'I'm not sure he likes little girls very much."

"What's all this?" Her father sweeps into the kitchen. His long overcoat is wet with raindrops. The kitchen is small, and he has a way of crowding a place. "What won't Father be too happy about?"

"Oh, Joseph, you caught us by surprise, so you did!" says Mammy, suddenly flustered. "You're home early and your tea's not ready! I was just telling Joy our happy news. She's got it into her head you'll be wanting a son."

"And so I might, Bridie," says Father. But he's smiling broadly; he's in a good mood. "Though I'll be happy with whatever the good Lord sends us," he adds, bending down to kiss her mother. Mammy blushes and reaches up for his hand.

"We'll be quite the little family, won't we?" she says, squeezing his hand. She looks at him with an expression Joy can't quite read.

"Quite the little family," he echoes.

BRIDIE

2019

I must have been dozing because I find myself waking up again. These days all I seem to do is sleep a little, wake a little. All my life I've been busy on my feet. Floors to scrub, messages to run, meals to cook. One thing after another. Now someone else washes and feeds me. And then I doze off again with the exhaustion of it all.

Imagine! All of a sudden I'm Lady Muck. When once upon a time I was Bridie O'Leary, dragged up in a ditch in the back of beyond. A hovel.

Not that it was always a hovel. My Mam did her best to keep the five of us fed and watered and her house clean and tidy, but it all fell apart when she died, God rest her. My Da didn't know his arse from his elbow when it came to keeping a home. Free with the back of his hand, especially when drink had been taken, but not such a master of the housework. Ah, sure, my sisters did their best, and Aunty Norah looked in from time to time, but things were bound to slide, without a woman in the house, weren't they?

No one ever asked Darragh or John-Joe to lift a hand to keep the place clean, God help us. Housework was for women and girls. Mary-Pat and Ellen and me, for all we were not much more than children ourselves.

To be fair, the lads were out all the hours God sent scouting for odd jobs, until Darragh found steady work helping our neighbour with his milk round. John-Joe, though, he could never stick to anything. He was always getting the heave-ho for eyeing up the girls. Yet somehow he still landed on his feet. Until he went off for a soldier, and we all know how that one ended.

Now Her Majesty Queen Bridie lies in bed and can summon the servants with the press of a button. If my Da could see me now! He said no good would come of me, and now look at me. Though I suppose it doesn't amount to much when it's hospital and the best the staff can fetch me is a bedpan. It's not as if I can ask them to bring me champagne cocktails. Or a troupe of dancers.

Dancers! I loved to go dancing, so I did! Not much chance of that back home, but once I got to England . . . well, that's the thing people forget about the War, isn't it? When you think you're on the fast train to meeting your Maker with the bombs and all, you make the most of it.

Not that I knew that when I landed in Liverpool, all of a quiver. Thank the Lord for my cousin Dolly who met me off the boat and let me share her room in Brick Street till I got myself sorted. Dolly was broad-shouldered and big-boned. Not surprising, when you think of my Da who was her uncle and built just the same. She was a nurse at the Royal Infirmary. A giant of a woman, but all heart. Soft as marshmallow under the layers. Took me under her wing without asking questions.

Dolly and I went dancing on Saturday nights. For all her bulk she was light on her feet like you wouldn't imagine and never short of a partner on the dance floor. The first week or two, we went round the corner to the Parish Hall at the Church of the Holy Name. Then after I'd been in Liverpool a month and saved a few pennies from my skivvying, we took the bus over east to the Grafton with a group of Dolly's friends from the hospital.

She even whipped me up a frock. She was a wonder with a needle, so she was. Said she'd learned it all stitching up wounds at the Royal, but truth to tell I'm sure it was my Aunty Norah as taught her, because she was a beautiful seamstress. My dress for the night was cut down from an old frock of Dolly's: green floral fabric, big splashy flowers with dear little leaves. Nipped in at the waist, with a bow at the back. I loved it all the same.

Oh, the splendour of the Grafton! It was like stepping out of the blackout into a fairy tale. All red and gold, and warm and bright. The glamour of it—like something out of the pictures.

Dolly and I must have made a holy show of ourselves in our home-made clothes, but I thought I'd died and gone to heaven, so help me God. The tables sticky with beer and the air thick with cigarette smoke, to be sure, but everyone dressed like film stars, and dancing as if their lives depended on it. Which maybe they did, because there was plenty of hunger and fear and wretchedness, and bombs dropping willy-nilly. You took your pleasure where you could.

And after seventeen years under my father's roof, it was a wonder to be footloose and fancy-free and carried away by the music. Sheer joy.

—

It's dark again. Night-time, and quiet. I reach for Joseph on his side of the bed, but he's not there. Where is he? Is he out and about where he oughtn't be? And where am I, for that matter? I think I once knew the answer to that. But somehow it's just out of my grasp.

I can hear crying. Someone's heart is breaking. Is one of the little girls hurt? I need to find them, to be sure. I try to get out of bed, but my legs aren't doing what they're told. Neither of them. Not just my old trouble.

Footsteps now. A little light. *Are you all right, Mrs Kelly?* says a voice. She sounds brusque. *Mrs KELLY?*

And that's who I am. Mrs Joseph Kelly. I knew that, for sure I did. I open my mouth to speak and the crying subsides. Was it me, so? *Drink, please*, I say. *Ink, ease.* But the nun understands, bless her heart, and I feel the cup at my lips.

JOY

1951

Mammy is taking Joy and baby Felicity to Liverpool for a week. Father is too busy at work to come, so it will be just the three of them. Mammy is very excited.

"We'll be having ourselves a little holiday," says Mammy. "Seeing Dolly and her brood. It'll do us all no end of good. Oh, I can't wait, I can't wait, I can't wait!"

Aunt Dolly is no more than a name to Joy, although she and Mammy write letters to each other. Joy has learned to spot her writing which is large and looping. Aunt Dolly always ends her letters, "Mind you give a kiss to little Joy from her Aunty Dolly," which Mammy reads aloud. Aunt Dolly knew Joy when she was a baby, because they lived in Liverpool then, long before Felicity was born.

"She was such a help when you were little. I'd have been lost without her," says Mammy. "That was before she'd had Frank, to be sure, but I think she was broody even then. She fairly doted on you. She'll be pleased as punch with Felicity, you wait and see. And I can't wait to see those boys of hers."

Joy is not quite sure why, but she's anxious about the holiday. She knows the rules at home. She knows every creak of the stairs and gurgle in the pipes. What if she can't sleep in a strange bed? Or needs the lav in the night and can't remember the way?

But to voice fear of Aunt Dolly and her boys would upset Mammy. "I don't know if I *like* Liverpool" is the best she can come up with. It's true;

the name makes her queasy because she thinks of liver, which she detests. And she hasn't forgotten about the unexploded bombs.

"Oh, to be sure you'll be loving Liverpool," says Mammy. "Just you wait and see. Besides, we'll be going back to your roots, my lovely. Don't forget you were born there."

Baby Joy's escape from the Luftwaffe in the middle of winter is the stuff of family legend. Everything—from her mild deafness to her inability to sing in tune—is put down to her dramatic start in life. But this doesn't endear Liverpool to her. Why, when Mammy is always singing the praises of St James' End, would you want to go back somewhere so frightening?

"Oh, my lovely, we'll have ourselves a ball, I promise," says Mammy. Joy briefly submits to a hug and then wriggles away. She's a big girl now; she'll be ten in December.

"Don't you worry about a thing. Now, will you watch your little sister for a wee moment while I pack our bags? She always settles for you."

They set out early in the morning on a hot summer's day. It's a long journey, starting with a bus ride to the railway station. Mammy has a powder blue suitcase in one hand, and a bag containing her purse and their tickets, their sandwiches and a flask of tea in the other. Joy carries Felicity and her changing bag. The train is stuffy, and the furry seat fabric is itchy against her bare legs under her flimsy summer dress.

They change trains in Birmingham, which is bewildering because the station is enormous and crammed with people. Joy is petrified of getting separated from Mammy who strides through the station, apparently unconcerned by the crowds. Against her hip Felicity feels hot and heavy, and Joy is very much afraid she needs a clean nappy. Joy keeps her eyes locked on the big red poppies on Mammy's summer dress and follows behind as close as she can.

Once they've settled themselves into their seats on the second train, Mammy says she'll change Felicity's nappy, and then it will be time for some lunch. Joy stares out of the dirty window as the train pulls out of the station. She had no idea the world was so big or so crowded. Wherever she looks there are factories and office blocks and shops and houses. The endless cityscape of Birmingham goes on and on and on, beyond comprehension in its scale. There are building sites wherever she looks: scaffolding and joists and yellow concrete mixers, all competing to fill the gaps.

Very gradually, the city gives way to gentler landscape. Suburbs and towns. Villages and fields. Farmers cutting the first of the corn. The scenery flashes by like pictures in a slide show as the train rattles and shakes its way north west.

And all the time, excitement begins to well up inside her, dispelling the nerves the further they travel from home. It is an adventure. The sunshine makes everything outside seem lit up with promise. Felicity stops fretting and starts smiling at the other passengers in the carriage, and they all compliment Mammy on having such a beautiful baby. A kind man fetches them cups of tea and a piece of fruit cake from the buffet car, and won't even let Mammy pay, for all that she offers.

Eventually, Felicity falls asleep in Mammy's arms, and that leaves her free to read to Joy, and when she tires of that, they sing a few of Mammy's favourite songs, quietly, so as not to disturb the sleeping Felicity. They'd never have dared to sing if Father was with them, because he says Joy's singing gives him a headache. Then suddenly there they are at Lime Street, and there's a tiny man who is Uncle Ron, come to meet them in his very own car, and great big Aunt Dolly waiting at home in Jubilee Terrace with a stew in the oven and a wet kiss for Joy.

—

To her amazement, once she finds her feet, the week with Aunt Dolly and Uncle Ron and the cousins is wonderful, quite beyond expectation. Not that Dolly and Ron are really her aunt and uncle. Dolly is her mother's cousin, but according to Mammy, as close as any sister, if not closer, having left her own family back home in Ireland. That means the cousins are really second cousins.

"Not that it matters," says Mammy. "Family's family."

The boys are Frank, who is eight, and Dennis, who is six. Baby Robbie is only two months older than Felicity. This means that Joy is the oldest.

"This one's my nursemaid and nanny rolled into one!" Mammy tells everyone over tea the first evening. "I'd be lost without her, let me tell you. Felicity made her presence felt coming into the world, shall we say, but this one . . . she practically ran the house till I was properly back on my feet. She's a treasure, Dolly."

"I'm sure she is," says Aunt Dolly, passing round a plate of jam sandwiches. "You mind you do as Cousin Joy tells you this week," she instructs Frank and Dennis with a stern look.

Joy glows. There's not much she's good at, one way and another. Certainly she's the dunce at school. It seemed to take an age for her to learn to read, and she's still slower than most of the others in her class. Somehow her letters get in a muddle. Sums aren't much better. She overheard Father telling Mammy she's thick.

Part of the trouble is that she gets tongue-tied whenever she's put on the spot. She hates everyone looking at her. And when she doesn't have a quick answer, she can feel Father's patience ebbing away. The longer the silence, the more paralysed she becomes. And then Mammy leaps in to fill the gap, and more often than not, takes the conversation off in a new direction altogether just as she's coming up with an answer to the original question.

She likes the idea of being Mammy's treasure.

In practice, this means that when they go out, Mammy and Aunt Dolly pile Robbie and Felicity into Robbie's big pram, and chatter away nineteen to the dozen, hooting with laughter, and Joy finds herself in charge of the older two. Joy isn't used to boys, but Dennis is easy enough. He is happy to let her help him with his shoelaces, and she even cuts up his meat when he gets stuck at tea-time. He loves doing jigsaws and is thrilled to bits when Joy is willing to sort out all the edges and corners of the new puzzle with pictures of trains he had for his sixth birthday.

Frank, on the other hand, isn't quite so co-operative.

"He keeps getting in a strop," she whispers to Mammy at bedtime on the second night. She, Mammy and Felicity are sharing the front room. Joy and Mammy have a settee each. Felicity, in a cot borrowed from a neighbour, is already asleep. "He never wants to do what Dennis and I want to do."

"That's because he's normally top dog," says Mammy. "He's just being a boy, treasure. Find something he's really good at and get him to show you how it's done. Trust me. That'll cheer him up no end."

Mammy chuckles at some secret thought and kisses her goodnight before going off to join Aunt Dolly and Uncle Ron for a nightcap. She'll creep into bed later. *Mammy is happy*, thinks Joy. And it's true: there's a lightness about her mother here. She's fizzing like a glass of Coca-Cola. Joy herself feels . . . what? *Taller*, somehow. Taller than she feels in Northampton.

She snuggles down under the blankets in her makeshift bed. You don't want to be too tall if you're sleeping on a settee, because of the wooden arms. It hurts like anything if you forget they're there and accidentally bump your head in the night. The settees really aren't terribly comfortable: they're covered in knobbly green fabric you can feel through the under-sheet, and the seats slope backwards so that Joy always wakes up with her face jammed into the settee back. Still, it's fun camping out with Mammy and Felicity.

What is Frank good at? she thinks. *Games*. There's a large grassy park just over the road from Jubilee Terrace. She decides she'll ask him to teach her to play French cricket next time they go there. She will be hopeless, but if Mammy's right, that won't really matter.

It works a treat. Frank takes great pleasure in instructing Joy, and she turns out not to be quite as hopeless at French cricket as she thought. Before long, a brother and sister who Frank knows from school join the game, and they all play together until Joy catches the other girl out.

"Great catch!" Frank cheers, and Joy turns pink with pleasure. She knows she's passed an important test. By the evening, when Uncle Ron suggests a game of Snakes and Ladders, Frank insists that he and Joy will play as a team against his father and Dennis.

—

Miraculously, the weather holds. On top of their daily outings to the park, they go further afield. Aunt Dolly sends Frank, Dennis and Joy out for the day with a picnic in a knapsack: sandwiches in waxed paper, hard-boiled eggs, apples and orange squash. They are free to explore swaths of waste ground, to climb trees, to fish for sticklebacks and newts in the stream at the bottom of the park.

Best of all, on their very last full day, they take the train to Formby, Uncle Ron too because it's Saturday, and they run about on the wide sandy beach and play hide-and-seek in the pinewoods behind the dunes. They swim in the sea, shrieking with shock at the cold, and have fish and chips and ices for tea. And that day is especially exciting because Felicity takes her first steps on Formby Beach, and everyone cheers and claps until she sits down with a bump in a wet patch and starts to cry. Mammy, her skirts hitched up into her knickers, sweeps her up into her arms and smothers her in kisses until Felicity stops crying and starts giggling.

"What a clever girl you are, my lovely!" she exclaims. "Oh, but I wish your Daddy had been here to witness the moment! We'll have to tell him all about it when we get home, won't we, Joy? Oh, but you *are* a clever girl, Felicity!" And Joy realizes with a sudden lurching feeling that their holiday is very nearly over, and then it will be back to St James' End and all this will seem like a dream.

When they get home to Aunt Dolly's that night, tired and slightly sunburned, they find their feet are stained black with the mud. By the time all five children have had a bath, the bath is black too, and so are two of Aunt Dolly's best towels.

"Will you look at that?" laughs Aunt Dolly. "You'd think none of us could run to shoes! What a disgrace. That beach is a very devil for its mud."

"It's a blessing my Joseph isn't here, because he'd be having conniptions about those feet, I can tell you!" says Mammy, but she's laughing too, as if she doesn't mind a bit and isn't the slightest bit frightened of Father.

This is the best day of my life, thinks Joy. *I'm never ever going to forget it for as long as I live.*

FELICITY

1956

Felicity has her eyes covered with a blindfold. It's not really a blindfold, just one of Mammy's scarves, but Mammy asked Joy to tie it over her eyes because there's a surprise downstairs.

"Put your other hand on the bannister," says Joy, taking her left hand. "Now, down we go. Carefully, mind. One step at a time."

Felicity absolutely can't wait. She knows Mammy has been busy at her sewing machine, and she knows, too, that she sent Joy into town to collect a special order from Bentham's Drapery. Mammy is making her First Communion dress, and today is the first time she'll see it.

When Joy takes off the blindfold, Felicity gasps with pleasure. The dress is perfect. It has puff sleeves trimmed with lace and a little Peter Pan collar and, best of all, the skirt is full and has layers of stiff petticoats underneath so that it sticks out like a bell.

"It's a skirty dress!" she says. This is the name she invented to describe skirts when she was little. They've always been her favourite. She likes to imagine herself as a dancer, like the one on her music box that performs a special dance called a *pirouette* when you wind the key. Joy gave it to her for Christmas, and it is her favourite present ever.

"To be sure it is, my lovely," says Mammy. "And see, here, there's a little veil to match. All we need now is for you to try it on."

Felicity finds she is still holding Joy's hand, so turns and hugs her sister in delight. Joy grins back at her.

"Joy, my lovely, will you give her a hand? Take off your things, Felicity love, and we'll see how it fits."

Felicity holds up her arms and lets Joy pull off her jersey and blouse, though she could manage perfectly well herself. She likes being babied. She steps out of her skirt and into the dress.

"There are pins, mind, so watch out for those," says Mammy. She has a mouthful of more pins with coloured plastic heads. She fiddles with the back, tugs slightly at the fabric, and then Felicity is all pinned in.

The dress feels as light as a feather. She could almost float away on a cloud of lace. She tries a little spin, and watches with satisfaction as the skirt lifts and swirls round her.

"Oh, but don't you look a perfect angel?" says Mammy. "Joy, my lovely. Would you look at your little sister? Doesn't she look good enough to eat?"

Felicity giggles with pleasure. "Don't eat me, Mammy! Promise you won't eat me!" she says in a babyish voice. "Save me, Joy, save me!"

"Well, I think you'll just about do," says Mammy, just as Daddy walks in through the front door. He's home early. Both Mammy and Joy look startled.

"Joseph!" says Mammy. "I thought you had a sales meeting tonight. We weren't expecting you yet."

"Power cut," says Daddy. "Blessed nuisance. But it looks as if I'm just in time. You never said we were expecting a princess for tea, Mammy. Why wasn't I told? How do you do, your Royal Highness?"

"It's me, Daddy. *Me! Felicity!*" She squirms with delight.

"Felicity? Are you quite sure about that, young lady?" Daddy pretends to be stern. "Then why are you disguised as a princess, I'd like to know?"

"It's my First Communion dress! I'm trying it on so that Mammy can finish the sewing before Sunday."

There's a sudden odd silence.

"Joseph–" says Mammy, just as Daddy says: "Well, well, well! Of *course* it is. And very fetching you look, too, Flissy. Pretty as a picture." Flissy is what she used to call herself when she was little, before she could say her name properly.

"Joy, my lovely, would you take your little sister upstairs to change out of her dress, now?" says Mammy.

"Oh Mammy! Can't I keep it on? I'm a princess! *I'm a princess!*"

"No, my lovely," says Mammy. "We need to keep it all clean and beautiful for Sunday, now don't we? And I need time to finish off that seam, now we know it fits. You go up and change back into your skirt and jersey, now. Your sister will help you, so she will. Off you go, now."

Felicity knows better than to argue, but she stomps her feet noisily as they go up the stairs, because she's annoyed. Joy helps her change, and they hang the almost finished dress on one of Mammy's dress-hangers so that the skirts fall out properly. Felicity can't resist reaching out her hand for one last stroke of the silky fabric.

"Did you have a First Communion dress like this, Joy?" she asks.

Joy gives a little laugh. "Not quite," she says. "It was a lot plainer than yours, Flick. A hand-me-down spruced up a bit by Mammy. We still had rationing when I was little."

They can hear raised voices from downstairs. "Why's Daddy cross? Didn't he like my dress?"

"Of course he did," says Joy, shutting the bedroom door. "He's probably . . . I don't know. Fed up about the power cut. Do you remember when we had one and had to have our tea by candlelight?"

"But that was fun!"

"Fun when it happens at home, maybe. I bet it's an awful nuisance in the factory because everyone has to stop work, whatever they're doing. Then they get behind on orders and that's bad news. It'll blow over, you'll see. Why don't we have a look at those things Father Adrian gave you?"

Felicity climbs onto Joy's bed and sits down next to her, with the large brown envelope all the children were given at the end of their last class. There will be ten of them making their First Communion on Sunday. There's a little book of prayers, an illustrated *Lives of the Saints for Children*, and a booklet called "You and Your First Communion".

By the time Mammy calls the girls for tea, Felicity has almost forgotten Daddy was cross. It's sausages and mash with grilled tomatoes, which is Felicity's absolute favourite.

"Before I fetch the jam roly-poly, I've some news," says Mammy when she's cleared the plates.

"Oh? Another of your little surprises, Bridie?" asks Daddy.

Mammy turns pink but ploughs on. A friend from church has asked Mammy if she knows anyone who might want a piano. "It was her father's pride and joy, but now he's gone, there's no one to play it.

"Imagine that, Joseph!" she says, warming to her theme. "We could have a little bit of a sing-song around the piano on a Saturday night, just like when I was a girl. You know how to play, and the girls and I can sing along. Maybe Felicity could take lessons. Or you could teach her, get her started yourself? What do you say, now?"

Piano lessons! Without quite knowing why, Felicity finds she's desperate for him to agree. But you never know how Daddy will respond to one of Mammy's ideas. *Her hare-brained schemes*, he calls them.

"Oh *please*, Daddy. Please say yes! *Please!*"

"What do they want for it?"

"Not a penny. Valerie just wants it out of the house because it takes up too much room, what with the four kiddies. A bother to dust, she says, and she'll be glad to see the back of it."

"You could say the same for us. We're not exactly overburdened by space, are we? We'll be tripping over it."

"Oh, we'll have a bit of a spring clean and a tidy-up. You'll see. Shall I be telling her you'll arrange collection? You could get some of your factory lads to give you a hand."

Felicity suddenly knows that this is a red-letter day. The beginning of a new chapter. Daddy will say yes because how can he possibly refuse? She'll learn the piano and one day she'll be able to play tunes like Mrs Webster who plays for Prayers at school, only better. There will be singing and dancing, and everyone will watch her and smile and cheer and clap their hands. It will be like wearing her First Communion dress every day of her life.

BRIDIE

2019

There's many a person would say I had no right to become Mrs Joseph Kelly in the first place. You should have seen the letters he got from the Holy Joes of the parish. I can remember all that, clear as the day is long, though it must be decades now. Funny how the past feels nearer than the present.

To be sure, he had a fine name for himself, for his work during the War. Father Joe of the Flying Cassock, who helped with the rescue effort when the bombs rained down night after night, and then slept with his flock in the shelter under the railway arch when their homes were crushed to rubble. Who cut through the red tape that was tying up supplies of blankets and coal; supplies that turned out to be sitting idle in a warehouse down at the docks all along. He even broke into a Government food store to help feed the homeless. A bit of a firebrand, he was in those days. His finest hour, you might say.

His oldest friend, himself as he met at the college in Rome, was sent by the bishop to show him the error of his ways. *You know you'll lose everything*, says he. *The Church will forgive you for sleeping with her, but not for marrying her*. And there's me hiding behind the scullery door, listening to every weasel word.

Well, you can imagine how my Joseph reacted to that. Practically picked up the fellow by the ear and threw him out of the Presbytery into the gutter. What was his name? Baby face, all pink and shiny. Popping eyes. Never spoke to him again.

My Joseph liked to see himself as a bit of a . . . what's the word I'm after? A . . . *whatsit*. Own mind. And that's never going to go down well in the Catholic Church. A big character, who took pleasure in ploughing his own furrow.

Literally, in my case. Ploughed and ploughed it, night after night. Will you listen to me, laughing aloud at my own dirty joke! Let's hope the nuns don't hear.

But I'm telling you, there was no stopping him in his passion, for all that he'd be riddled with guilt afterwards. One minute cradling me in his arms, the next minute down on his knees, begging the Lord God's forgiveness.

He told me he loved me, and I believed him, for all that happened later. I was only twenty-two, for the love of God. What did I know of love? With the end of the War, and a bairn to feed, I was mightily relieved to have a roof over my head when so many others didn't. And I was grateful to find a job I could do while minding the child. Housekeeper to Father Kelly. At the time, it felt heaven sent.

It was no great surprise when he came to my bed for the first time a few months in. I'd seen him sneaking a look at me sideways, when he thought I was too busy with the pots to notice. I was flattered, so I was, that this man—so handsome in his black cassock, so respected in the community—chose me for his little bit of comfort. And if there was a bit of a thrill to it, an edge in the knowledge that we weren't supposed to, so what? Forbidden fruits are often sweet.

I'm not sure he'd accounted for the cost, mind. But when I went to him with my heart in my mouth and told him I was expecting, after the initial shock of it, he was carried along by a tide of righteous indignation against the Church for demanding celibacy of him in the first place. Convinced that it was his duty to marry me. To protect my honour, as the mother of his child. To give a home to little Joy, her being an orphan and all.

Maverick. That's the fellow I'm after. Words are slippery devils, and on a bad day they go sliding all over the place. Just out of reach when you're wanting them. Joseph liked to see himself as a maverick. He was always one for the long words.

I for one didn't realize that by marrying me he'd not only forfeit his job and his livelihood, but even after all of that we still wouldn't be married in the eyes of the Church. Maybe he didn't appreciate what he was giving up. Or how that would feel, years down the line.

And what neither of us knew, heaven help us, was that I'd lose that baby.

Honest to God, it wasn't a trap. Not as some whispered behind their hands. Whatever he told himself later, he witnessed that in person, so he did. Wasn't he the one that sent for the doctor when I started to bleed? We were still in Liverpool then, staying with one-armed Alf, who was an ARP warden with Joseph during the War and took pity on us when we had to leave the Presbytery in a hurry. Alf didn't hold with religion, so he said, but he thought the world of Father Joseph. Reckoned he'd been hard done by.

While I was in the hospital weeping for that wee mite lost in limbo for all eternity, it turns out Alf and Joseph had a man-to-man chat, and when I came home Joseph said we were moving to Northampton where his brother Norman had a job lined up for him in his shoe factory. Imagine the humiliation! Father Joseph Kelly, with his fancy college learning in Liverpool and Rome, becoming a travelling salesman in a town where no one knew who he was in the War.

But that was the point, so it was. No one in Northampton knew us from Adam and Eve. We were plain Mr and Mrs Joseph Kelly of St James' End, where Norman had somehow got hold of a brand-new council house for us, because he knew someone who knew someone, and he pulled some strings. No wonder Joseph could barely meet my eye when he broke the news.

To start with, I was frantic. Honest to God, I'd never heard of Northampton. Couldn't have found it on the map if my life depended on it. It meant waving goodbye to Dolly and the girls I'd gone dancing with who'd become my friends. And the thought that my brothers and sisters were only just across the water, even if I wasn't intending on going home while the old man still lived and breathed. I'd written to Mary-Pat telling her I'd got married, but not that it was a hasty, shameful affair in a Register Office. But she must have heard anyway, because she never wrote back. I'm not sure she ever forgave me. For taking my chance where I could.

Once we got to Northampton, life got a lot better, so it did. Our house in St James' End overlooked a park that stretched as far as the eye could see. It was almost like the countryside, but with shops and a railway and people. The house was a treasure, much nicer than the Presbytery, which was a gloomy old place, let me tell you. The air was cleaner, and Joy soon stopped looking so peaky. Bit of colour in her cheeks. She settled into school and was much less clingy. I wondered then if she'd been more affected by the gossip about me and Father Kelly than I'd imagined. Children have a way of breathing these things in through their skin.

I found it was grand being Mrs Kelly and talking about my husband over the fence to the neighbours as we shared the *craic*. My *husband*. The novelty of it! And that pride gave me a little courage, because he'd kept his distance since the miscarriage. After we moved, I found myself a bit of confidence. I was a married woman and a mother, wasn't I? Even if all of that had come about back-to-front. So I soon persuaded him back into my bed. I knew what he liked. That's no sin when you're married, now is it?

Later, he claimed I seduced him. Right from the start in the Presbytery, and then again when we were Mr and Mrs Kelly of St James' End, Northampton. He said I led him into temptation with my full breasts and curvaceous hips and my wicked female wiles.

But my answer to that is *you were old enough to be my father, Father Kelly*. Old enough to know better. I can't have been the first temptation to cross your path. You were my boss, as well as my priest, and I was just a girl.

Don't tell me you didn't know exactly what you were doing.

JOY

1959

She still can't believe that it took applying for nursing to discover the truth. Was Mammy *never* going to tell her?

Joy hates filling in forms. Reading and writing is an effort, and anything official feels like a test in which she'll be found wanting. But Dolly sits her down one Saturday afternoon with pen and paper. It's raining outside. Uncle Ron has taken the boys to the football. Dolly has a cake in the oven for their return and is now turning her attention to making bread.

"Come on, love," she says with a look that brooks no argument. "You've worked so hard for this. Don't fall at the final fence."

Dolly's been so good to her. More than good, taking her under her wing since Joy arrived in Liverpool not knowing a soul. ("Dolly will be there in your hour of need as she was in mine," sobbed Mammy when she left.)

It was the memory of that golden, never-to-be-repeated holiday that propelled Joy into Dolly's embrace when she knew she had to leave home. Ever since, Aunt Dolly had popped little notes addressed to Joy into her letters to Mammy, and from time to time Joy wrote back: laborious, stiff little letters because writing's a struggle, and there never seemed very much to say. Life at St James' End bore no relation to her memories of the sunshine and seaside and games with the cousins.

In the end, though, when she was fifteen, Joy wrote a long and rambling letter to Aunt Dolly, in which she begged to come and stay, and set out her plans to follow in Dolly's footsteps and train as a nurse.

"Well, you mind you get your School Cert or whatever it's called these days, or there's no chance," wrote Aunt Dolly by return. "Get that under your belt, and then we'll see. But trust me, there's no earthly point in coming up here if you've got no qualifications. It's not exactly Easy Street as they say in the pictures."

Joy responded with a tear-stained letter full of self-pity. Everyone knew that she was thick as tar and wasn't going to get any O-levels. What should she do? To which Dolly replied in the briskest terms. "You may have to work like a dog at those exams, but so be it. If you want to nurse, you'll need to know about hard graft. Come on, Joy. Show a little grit and put your shoulder to the wheel. I have every faith in you."

It was just the shock Joy needed. So what if Father thought she'd never amount to anything? She'd show him. Maybe she wasn't as clever as Perfect Princess Flissy. But whatever anyone said, she knew, just *knew*, she would be a good nurse. She would talk to her form teacher and start paying attention to her studies.

A year later, there she was in Liverpool, shyly knocking on Aunt Dolly's door with a cardboard suitcase in her hand. Terrified, but quietly pleased with herself for having got this far. For having scraped through those beastly exams and plotted her escape, even if she'd broken her mother's heart in the process.

She'd left home to put the past behind her. And Aunt Dolly, Uncle Ron and the boys took her to their hearts, letting her become part of their already crowded family for the two years she needed to fill before starting at the Royal Infirmary. The boys had grown up, of course. When Joy arrived, Frank had just started as an apprentice carpenter down at the docks, with Dennis desperate to follow. Robbie was the clever one, apparently. Precocious. A bit like her sister, though not half as annoying. Only where it was music for Felicity, it was all Airfix models and military history in Robbie's case. "He's a walking encyclopaedia," said Ron in a rare burst of speech.

She got a job as an office junior, earning a pittance, most of which she handed straight over to Dolly for her keep. She spent most of her days sorting post in a windowless basement. But that made her only more determined to make a go of nursing. Now at last she's nearly eighteen and can apply to the Royal. It's the best place to train, says Dolly, though she works at Alder Hey now because she's a specialist children's nurse. There's a month still before the deadline, but Dolly has insisted Joy gets on with the paperwork, pointing out that Joy needs her father's permission because she's under twenty-one.

"You don't want to leave it too late," she said. "In case he's awkward about the signature." Neither of them expanded on this thought; Dolly seemed to know without being told that Father might cause trouble.

"If only it could be Uncle Ron, giving permission," grumbled Joy. "After all, I live with you nowadays."

"If wishes were horses, my love, we'd none of us be working our knuckles to the bone," retorted Dolly. "But if he starts playing up, just you let me know, and I'll have a word."

In the event, Father was as nice as pie. Rolled over and signed the form without a murmur. "Probably thinks the Royal are bound to turn me down," she said when the signed form arrived by return of post. "But what does it matter? I've got the magic mark." She put the paper carefully into the manila folder of documents she was gathering for her application.

"What I don't understand, though, is why Mam hasn't sent my birth certificate," she says now, chewing her pen in the fuggy kitchen. "I've asked her three times. She could have put it in the same envelope as Father and saved a stamp. Doesn't she realize it's important?"

"Really?" says Dolly, sharply. She looks up from her dough. "Not a word? That's odd. Do you . . . I mean, can you remember ever seeing it before?"

"No. I don't think I've ever needed it till now. Why?"

"Nothing," says Dolly, returning to her kneading with renewed vigour. "I didn't realize you were waiting on it. Why don't I write to Bridie? In case she hasn't understood the urgency?"

Even then, the penny doesn't drop. But the following Friday afternoon, Joy's half-day, she gets the shock of her life when she comes home to find her mother sitting at the kitchen table with a cup of tea. Dolly is standing at the stove, stirring vigorously. Brown gravy is spattered on the back of the cooker. They both look like thunder.

"Mammy! What are you doing here?" asks Joy, as her mother gets up to give her a clumsy hug. "Has something happened? Is it Flick?"

"Oh, bless your heart, no!" says Bridie. "Nothing's happened. But you're a sight for sore eyes and no mistake!"

"Your mother has something to tell you," says Dolly. Her expression is pinched. "I'll wet the tea and then she's all yours, Joy. I'll see to it you're not disturbed. And Bridie, you know what we said."

"I know what *you* said," says Bridie tartly. "But this is *my* daughter we're talking about, and *my* business, I'll have you know."

Dolly slams the brown teapot onto the table with such force that a splash of tea spurts out of the spout onto the yellow checked tablecloth. She puts a cup and saucer and the milk jug in front of Joy. "I just hope you know what you're doing, Bridie," she sniffs, and leaves the kitchen without another word.

"Nosy parker, that one, to be sure, butting in where she's not wanted," mutters Bridie to the closed door.

"Mammy! What's going on? What have you said to upset Dolly? And what in heaven's name are you doing turning up on our doorstep unannounced?"

"Upset Dolly! That's a fine thing to say! What about me? And *our* doorstep, is it now?" Bridie's voice is rising dangerously. "When you've a perfectly good home to call your own in Northampton!"

"Oh Mammy! Must you? You know what I mean. It was a slip of the tongue. Now, will you please tell me what this is all about? Whatever's going on?"

Bridie pulls a large brown envelope out of her handbag and slides it across the table towards her, without meeting Joy's eye.

"What's this?"

"You'll see. It's that paperwork you've been tormenting me for."

Joy hesitates for a moment, then slits the flap and pulls out the contents. A birth certificate, dated 2 January 1942, for a child born on 28 December 1941. Her birthday.

"I don't understand. Why does it say JOY BRIDGET MORRIS? And who are VERONICA ANNE and HOWARD JOHN MORRIS?"

"Your parents," says Bridie, and bursts into tears. "Before I was. Look, the other paper."

She jabs her finger at a second document in the envelope. An Adoption Order, made by Liverpool Magistrates' Court, dated 4 June 1942. The Order placed the infant JOY BRIDGET MORRIS into the permanent care of BRIDGET MARY O'LEARY.

"I . . . I don't understand!"

It all comes pouring out, then. Haltingly, tearfully, Bridie explains that Joy is adopted. Her parents were killed in the War, days apart and barely a fortnight after her birth. Bridie hadn't wanted to send her the birth certificate in the post without explanation.

"But . . . the air raid! The hole in the roof? Is none of that true?"

"No, no, no. It's true enough, to be sure," says Bridie, rallying. "The roof came in and nearly did for us both! Crushed my poor old leg to pieces. It was the last of the big raids, not that we knew it, and you just a tiny wee thing. Thirteen people lost their lives that night, including your dear Mammy. And poor Howard a few days before, although we only found that out later."

"And Bridget . . . O'Leary. That's you, presumably? Not Kelly?"

"Joy, my lovely, do you really not remember a time before we lived with your father? For sure, I met him during the War, and he was good enough to take us both on. Do you not remember when I was his housekeeper before we were married?"

Joy's head is spinning. It's as if the world is shifting on its axis, and north is now south. All her old certainties are melting away. *Adopted . . . Mammy not her mother . . . Father not her father.* She struggles to make sense of it. Any of it.

"So I was Joy Morris and Joy O'Leary before I was ever Joy Kelly?" she asks, slowly. "Oh Lord, I'm not sure I know who I am anymore." A thought strikes her. "Why you? Why did you adopt me? Was that normal? Didn't you have to be married?"

"Oh, my lovely! As if I'd have let those Waifs and Strays get their hands on you!" Bridie explains that she was working for Veronica at the time, housekeeper or maid-of-all-work ("not that she ever treated me like a skivvy . . . we were *friends*, so we were"), and after the bombing, when the house was destroyed, she just carried on looking after Joy, with a hand from Dolly on account of her injuries. In war time, all sorts of informal arrangements for orphans came about, because people went missing all the time and families got split up when they lost their homes.

"But we did it properly. All official, it was, I made sure of that. Father Ronald at the Church of the Holy Name talked me into it, and that was sound advice. He gave me a reference and sponsored me for a private adoption, and it was all sorted out through the courts. You see, Howard had no family, and Veronica only had her mother, and she didn't want to know. Father Ronald said it was best to have it all watertight, just in case she changed her mind. There was no one else but me, and I loved you from the day you were born, so I did."

"But . . . "

"And what if I *hadn't* fought for you, tooth and nail, when the good Lord had saved us both and entrusted you to my safekeeping? You'd have been left in an orphanage and shipped off to Australia after the War, likely as not. I wasn't having that, for the love of all that's holy!"

Joy catches the passion in her mother's voice, and, even in the fog of her bewilderment, recognizes that Mammy had a fight on her hands to keep her.

"But . . . what about Flick? I clearly remember her being born. She's your child, surely? And Father's?"

"Joy, *you're* my child, so help me God. I won't have a word said otherwise. Just because you and your sister came into my life by . . . well . . . different routes, it doesn't make a scrap of difference. You were my beloved bairn long before she came along, and there's an end to it."

But there isn't an end to it, thinks Joy. Everything she thought she knew has been blown out of the water. Only one thing remains the same: she is the cuckoo in the nest.

Suddenly, it's as if she's always known. For all the shock, this bombshell simply makes sense of things. Her sense of . . . what would you say? Oddness. Dislocation.

Another thought breaks in: Dolly must have known. All along. Does everyone but her know? How humiliating. She is seized by a tsunami of fury so hot it almost takes her breath away. How *dare* they?

She stands so abruptly that the metal legs of the chair behind her make an ugly scraping sound on the quarry tiles. "There's a lot to take in, Mammy," she says with as much calm as she can muster within the squall of emotion engulfing her. "I think I need to take a walk to clear my head."

"But—"

"But *nothing*, Mammy. *Mother*. Oh, I don't even know what to call you anymore! My whole childhood's turned out to be one enormous lie! I need some air."

Bridie stands then too and tries to put her arms around Joy. But Joy resists the embrace with every fibre of her being. She finds herself repelled by her mother's damp cheeks.

"What I don't understand is . . . why *now*?" she says, breaking free. "Why are you only telling me now, all these years on?"

"Oh, Joy, my lovely. You've no idea what it was like, those days! How tongues wagged! It was you vexing me for the birth certificate and all. You had to know!"

"Are you saying . . . Are you *honestly* saying that if I hadn't needed my birth certificate, you'd have kept quiet about this?" Now she is shouting, hot with indignation. "Don't I have a right to know? Do you have *any* idea what a betrayal this is? Are you ashamed of me or something?"

"Joy! I'm sorry! I only meant—"

But it's too late to hear what Bridie only meant. Joy is out of the kitchen. She pushes past Dolly who is hovering just the other side of the door, grabs her coat, and slams the front door behind her before stumbling into the street.

—

Joy walks the streets mindlessly for several hours, returning only after dark, bone-tired and hungry, a painful blister forming on her right heel. Robbie is already in bed. Frank and Dennis gape at her, open-mouthed, but, clearly under instruction from Dolly, say nothing as she hangs up her coat in the hall. Uncle Ron is out because he's working nights. Of Bridie there's no sign.

An uncharacteristically subdued Dolly warms up a bowl of chicken soup and puts a couple of slices of white bread under the grill for toast. They sit in wary silence while Joy gulps it down, suddenly ravenous. When she's finished, Dolly makes them both a cup of tea.

"You must have known," Joy says at last. "Why didn't you tell me?"

"Not my story to tell," says Dolly.

"I suppose not. It's just . . . just . . . "

"What, love?"

"It explains so much. Now I know why I've always felt second best. Never quite up to scratch. Not good enough. As if I don't belong. Only ever tolerated."

"I'm sure that's not true." Dolly reaches across the table for her hand, but Joy pulls away and sits abruptly back in her chair.

"It is, I promise. You've no idea. Oh Lord, I feel such a fool. So . . . ashamed."

"Ashamed? What on God's earth have you got to be ashamed of, my girl? There's no shame in adoption, you know. Whatever anyone says."

"That's not how it feels! But it's not just that, it's everything. I feel . . . totally thrown. It's like a hall of mirrors. You know, like in a fairground. Everything looks out of shape. Nothing's what I thought it was."

"Now you look here, my girl," says Dolly. "You've had a nasty shock. I'm not defending Bridie, and I'm not saying she's gone about things the best way. But she's always done her best for you. I was there, remember, when it was just the two of you, and I can tell you for nothing, she did everything to keep you safe and well cared for, for all she was barely an adult herself when you came along. What was she? Seventeen, if that? And on her own. It wasn't easy for an unwed girl back then, I can tell you. She fought for you and wouldn't give you up. She loved you. Still does. And love's worth a lot, in my book."

"So you're saying I should be . . . what? *Grateful*? Grateful that she took pity on me? *Rescued* me?" For some reason the suggestion makes Joy feel furious all over again. Her eyes are suddenly full of hot tears.

There's a silence while Dolly pauses to drink her tea. "Just you stop and think for a moment. Who cares what it says on that birth certificate? If you want to make that the story of your life, you go right ahead. The other way of looking at things is that it's just a piece of paper. A bit of history. The past. You need to start looking to the future. Yes, it tells a story about your beginnings. But there's nothing on that bit of paper about what happens next."

Dolly stands up to clear Joy's bowl and plate, and brushes away the toast crumbs with a dishcloth from the sink. "Top up?" she offers, and refills Joy's teacup without waiting for the answer.

"I'll tell you something for nothing, my girl," she says firmly. "We're going to finish those bleeding forms tomorrow and get them off to the Royal if it's the last thing I do. Then you can put all this behind you and get on with your life."

FELICITY

1960

Felicity sits at the piano, stretches out her fingers and starts her scales. She's itching to have a go at the new Bach Minuet, but Miss White has been very clear: scales and arpeggios come first, and every single day. She's working her way through the twelve major scales, and once she's got them well and truly under her belt Miss White says they'll go back to the minor ones and polish them up till they're sparkling. Felicity's looking forward to this; the minor ones have a plaintive feel about them that gives her goosebumps.

Today it's F sharp major. Six sharps! Though, as she's tried to explain to her mother, that means it's almost all the black notes, and probably easier than E major, which is half-and-half and caught her out horribly to begin with.

Not that Mammy really understands what she's talking about. Felicity was trying to explain chromatic scales to her the other day, but she can't seem to get a grip on the fact that a black key can be a sharp *or* a flat. Honestly! Mammy's almost as bad as Joy that way. The only music her big sister likes is the tinny pop that leaks out of her little wireless set. It used to drive poor Daddy up the wall, because it's not proper music at all and it hurts his ears after a long day at the factory.

Thank goodness for Daddy. *He* understands. He learned the piano when he was a boy, although he's very rusty now because he says he's been too busy bringing home the bacon and hasn't played for years. "We musicians must stick together," he says, and winks at her, and she feels ten feet tall.

Without wishing to be unkind, she and Daddy share a love of music that no one else in the family really appreciates. It's a precious gift that gives them a special bond. If only her hands will hurry up and grow! That would make it all so much easier. She knows she's fast, but she wants to be able to leap across the keyboard more easily. Be like the great Franz Liszt who was famous for his musical acrobatics. She mentioned this in her lesson last week, thinking Miss White would be impressed that she's been reading her *Lives of the Great Composers*, but Miss White actually ticked her off. ("It's all about *technique*, Felicity," she said. "Agility and strength, not showing off. Dexterity. You keep up the practice and your fingers will thank you for it.")

Felicity is in awe of Miss White. When she had her first lesson, Felicity thought she looked a bit like a witch, what with her narrow face and greying bun. She even has a black cat, who's called Sooty, and is almost always sitting in the front window when she and Mammy arrive for her lesson. Now, though, Felicity has revised her first impression. She's decided that there's something almost regal about Miss White. She seems to glide across the room as if she has a book on her head. Mammy says this is called *poise*.

During lessons Miss White writes notes in beautiful copperplate writing in Felicity's notebook so that she knows exactly what to practise before next week. She doesn't like chatter, and she is a little bit frightening, but she radiates a sense of calm that Felicity finds reassuring. She's sparing with her praise, but when it comes, her face lights up with pleasure. Felicity is desperate to win her good opinion.

Miss White lives a ten-minute walk away, in a big house called 1 Pemberton Villas. Next to the doorbell, there's a brass plate that says "Miss Edna White, Piano Teacher" and a string of letters which means she's a proper teacher. You can see her grand piano through the large bay window where Sooty sits, although lessons take place on an upright in the back room. Only Miss White plays the grand piano.

Pemberton Villas is much bigger than Felicity's house and seems enormous for just one person. The room where they have lessons has whole walls full of bookshelves, and Miss White has simply masses of records, whereas Felicity's family don't even own a gramophone player. They sometimes listen to concerts on the wireless, but it's not the same as being able to choose a piece of music and playing it whenever you feel like it. Again and again and again if you want.

There's a hall where she has to sit and wait, very quietly, listening to poor Neville Wilkins plod his way through *Frère Jacques* for the umpteenth time before it's her turn. The hall has a tiled floor and is always chilly, even in the summer, but Mammy brings her knitting and doesn't seem to mind. They sit on a sort of bench, facing a glass-fronted cabinet made of shiny dark wood, full of yet more books. On top sits a glass jar of toffees in different coloured shiny paper. If she's played well, Miss White invites Felicity to choose one before she goes home, but never before Felicity has hovered nervously for a few moments, afraid Miss White has forgotten but far too frightened to ask.

Daddy says they're very lucky to have found Miss White and that he can afford the lessons. She trained at the Royal Academy of Music years and years ago and could have been a famous concert pianist if the War hadn't got in the way. There's a framed black-and-white photograph on the upright piano showing Miss White standing beside a grand piano, with a whole orchestra in the background. She's wearing a long dark dress and pearls and holding a bouquet of white flowers, and actually her whole face is smiling, and she looks almost beautiful. "Ah yes, my glory days," she said when she caught Felicity looking at it.

Mammy usually brings Felicity to lessons, even though she's ten and could find her way perfectly well, but last week Daddy came with her, because he said he wanted a chat with Miss White. Felicity wasn't supposed to be listening, but she couldn't help it, really, and she overheard Miss White telling Daddy that she showed real promise.

"You might want to think about a second instrument, Mr Kelly," she said. "It would do Felicity good. Develop her musicianship."

This is a bit of a worry, because Felicity knows that money is always very tight. (*It doesn't grow on trees*, as Mammy likes to say, which is silly really, because whoever thought it did?) They were so lucky to get the piano! It arrived with a great deal of huffing and puffing as the men pushed it up a special ramp, over the doorstep, Mammy flitting around all of a dither about them knocking the paintwork, and rearranging the furniture to squeeze it in. Before long Felicity was sitting on Daddy's lap picking out tunes. The promised sing-songs never happened, because Daddy said he didn't know the songs Mammy liked, and once Felicity started her lessons with Miss White, Daddy was quite insistent that only she played it, because it was a bit ropey and needed to last.

Taking up a second instrument would mean a lot of extra expense. In her secret heart—and she hasn't told *anyone* this, because it seems so impossible—she dreams of learning the harp. Daddy took her to a concert when she was eight where there was a harpist, and Felicity thought it was quite the most beautiful sound she had ever heard. Like running water, a mountain stream perhaps. The harpist was a very elegant lady who wore a sparkly dress like a film star and had long fair hair that flowed over her shoulders. Her fingers travelled over the strings as if she were spinning magic. But the harp is simply enormous and bound to be horribly expensive, probably even more than a piano, and unlike a piano it's not the sort of thing people have cluttering up their houses and want to give away. And there would be lessons, too, and sheet music to buy.

Real promise. What does that mean? Aren't all promises supposed to be real, not pretend? But she knows it's a good thing, because Daddy took her hand on the way home, and called her *Flissy* not Felicity which is his special name for her and so much better than Flick, which is what her bossy big sister calls her.

As they walked along the road, he began to whistle, and swung her arm in a funny way that made her laugh, even though she really had to trot along the pavement to keep up with his long stride. He's so tall and she's so little that they probably made quite a funny pair. But Felicity didn't mind a scrap because she'd made him happy, and it was so lovely to have Daddy all to herself. When they got home, he told Mammy what Miss White had said ("She said she has real promise. How about that?"), and she could hear the pride in his voice.

Does *real promise* mean that she's destined for *glory days*, too? Will the day come when she will be the one in a long dress, bowing on stage to hundreds of people all clapping until their hands are sore? She loves the piano, just *loves* it. She loves the way it's possible to turn a collection of dry old dots on the printed page into something else entirely. It's partly the excitement of bringing a tune to life when she's finding her way around a new piece, because she likes solving puzzles. But it's also because every piece of music seems to contain a secret story, just waiting to be told.

Another reason she's working so hard on her scales today is because Daddy is listening. He can be quite strict about her practice, and because it's a Saturday he's not at work. He's got the newspaper spread out on the kitchen table while Mammy is out collecting the Sunday joint from the butcher and buying vegetables at the market. But Felicity knows he can't really be reading the paper, because if ever she fluffs a note, she hears him sigh. Sometimes he clears his throat, and says, "Again, Felicity. Have another go at that one." One of her parents is supposed to initial her practice book every day and check she's done her boring old theory, and Daddy takes this very seriously.

"Well, your mother doesn't know the difference between a scale and an arpeggio, so it's best I do it," he said.

"I do so!" said Mammy indignantly. "I'll have you know I grew up in a household of singers, even if we didn't have lessons. Aren't those arpeggios the ones that leap about the place like frogs in hot water? But I'd sooner hear one of your tunes, if it's all the same to you."

"But that's the thing, Mother! It's not the same at all, is it Felicity?" Daddy is teasing, but there's an edge to his voice when he calls Mammy *Mother*. "The scales and the arpeggios ... well, they're the building blocks. Absolutely vital to the whole endeavour, if she's going to reach her potential. She can't just skip over them to play *one of her tunes*, because they're more fun, whatever you say. Just goes to show it's best left to me while you do the shopping. The two of us will get on just fine while you're out, won't we now, Flissy?"

With that, Mammy takes her basket and her purse and her umbrella, muttering a little under her breath, and sets off to do the shopping, and Felicity turns her attention back to F sharp major. It's beginning to flow now, which means that in another few minutes she can move on to the arpeggios and then *at last* have a go at the Bach.

—

After lunch, she curls up with a book on her bed. She's almost used to having the room to herself now, though for the first few days after Joy left she couldn't even look at her bed without bursting into tears. Losing her sister felt like losing part of herself. She'd always been there. But that seems a long time ago now.

The house is very quiet. Too quiet. She wouldn't tell Daddy, but Felicity even misses Joy's tinny radio. But at least the shouting's stopped. When Joy lived at home, there were arguments and slammed doors, and towards the end, a chilly sort of silence at mealtimes, which was somehow even worse. Felicity shudders when she remembers how the air in the kitchen seemed to crackle with tension. With Daddy glowering and Joy gazing out of the window, Mammy would look anxiously from one to the other and then try to strike up a conversation about the wet weather or a bargain she'd seen in the shops or the latest scrape the Hooper boys had got into. What Daddy used to call *idle chatter*, in the old days. But now no one would join in.

All you could hear was the scrape of cutlery on the plate, twice as loud as usual. The more Mammy ploughed into the silence with her chatter, the more furious Daddy looked. It was like a pathetic game of catch with only one player. Felicity sat in an agony of indecision, twisting her napkin, asking herself if she should speak and risk Daddy's wrath or leave poor Mammy stranded. In the end, she usually chose silence. She took to concentrating all her energy on cutting her food into tiny, doll-sized mouthfuls and imagining she was feeding them to her very favourite doll who's called Princess Margaret. She still got terrible tummy aches.

She can't forget the night when she woke in the dark to the absolute certainty that the bed next to hers was empty. From downstairs she could hear the sound of raised voices. Not Daddy, this time: it was Joy and Mammy.

"You can't go! You're too young, I tell you!" Mammy was pleading.

"I can and I will." Joy's voice was clear and calm. "It really is the end of the road, Mam. Better for everyone this way."

"No! That's not true!" Felicity failed to catch the rest of her words. And then came Daddy's voice from the little landing at the top of the stairs.

"For goodness sake! Can't a man be allowed to sleep, for the love of God? Some of us have work to do in the morning! Let the wretched girl pack her bags, and there's an end to it. Come back to bed, Bridie!"

Felicity buried her head under her pillow and began practising her scales. Left hand, then right hand; left hand then right. Two hands together, drumming the mattress so that she could feel the vibrations. Picturing the black and white keys. C major: easy-peasy. G major: don't forget the F sharp. D major: add in C sharp too. Now the flats. One-two-three-four-five-six-seven-eight. Seven-six-five-four-three-two-one. One octave, then two. Steady, Flissy, steady. No need to rush.

By the time she woke the next morning, Joy had gone. Her bed was neatly made, as if she hadn't slept in it at all last night. Her hairbrush and comb had disappeared from the windowsill, as had her alarm clock, and when Felicity opened the chest of drawers they shared, she saw that Joy's three were empty. How had she not heard her sister packing? Then again, she was used to Joy creeping in long after she'd gone to sleep. Or had Joy planned it all and packed earlier in the day while Felicity was at school? Surely she would have noticed the gaps on the windowsill when she came to bed? Or were they hidden by the curtains? She began looking for other clues.

Downstairs, she hovered outside the kitchen for a moment, hoping to overhear something useful. But all she could detect was her mother's muffled sobbing. An empty plate yellow with the greasy residue of fried eggs suggested her father had already left for work.

"Mammy?" Felicity was surprised how wobbly her voice sounded. "Where's Joy?"

"Oh, my lovely, come here, won't you?" said Mammy, and pulled her close.

"What happened? I heard shouting. In the night."

"Oh, don't you be worrying yourself," said Mammy. "You come and sit yourself down and I'll see about a nice piece of bacon, why don't I? Then it's school we should be thinking about, or they'll have my guts for garters. Let's see. What day is it today? Will you be needing your plimsolls and Aertex?"

Felicity allowed herself to be swept up in the comfort of her mother's chatter and breakfast-making, so that she could pretend to herself that perhaps what happened in the night had all been a dream. That her mother's eyes were red and puffy, because it was hay-fever season and she suffered awfully with the pollen. That it was a Saturday and Joy had popped out to the shops or was at the pictures with her friend Beryl.

It was ages before Mammy told her the truth: that Joy had gone to Liverpool to stay with Aunt Dolly. It only came out then because the letters started arriving, and Felicity just happened to come downstairs at the very moment the envelope with her sister's writing came through the letterbox.

"Oh, that'll be a letter from Liverpool," said Mammy, with every semblance of calm. "From your sister."

"Liverpool? But why—"

"Ah well, she has her head set on becoming a nurse, so she does. And your Aunt Dolly will see her right. So why don't we sit down and read her letter together over a cup of tea. See how she's getting along. Once we've heard her news, perhaps we might tidy up that bedroom a bit, make the most of the space now you're on your own? I've a mind to wash that old counterpane of Joy's and air those blankets while the sun's out."

Daddy never says her name. It's as if Joy has simply vanished in a puff of smoke. That's hard to imagine because Joy is such a solid person. If Mammy makes any reference to Joy over the meal table, he frowns or looks a bit bored. Sometimes he'll talk across Mammy and ask Felicity about school or her latest lesson with Miss White. Felicity answers his questions and tries to make him laugh with silly stories about something that happened in the playground, because then he stops looking so cross and they start having a nice time again.

It strikes Felicity now that perhaps the house was simply too small for four people, because it feels just right for three. Daddy was right that they barely had room for the piano. How would they possibly make room for a harp even if one arrived at the door on a magic carpet?

Her second instrument needs to be cheap *and* not take up any space. Though there should be more money because Joy no longer *eats them out of house and home*, which is what Daddy used to say about her, and it's true that Joy does have a big appetite. When Felicity grows up, she's going to earn lots of money so that Mammy doesn't have to count the pennies when she goes shopping.

And then she has a *brilliant* idea. She hugs herself with satisfaction. She already has a second instrument, right here, in her own chest. She'll learn to sing.

BRIDIE

2019

I've been asleep again. I seem to drift off at a moment's notice these days, never mind if it's night or day. I don't know what they're giving me, but sometimes I'm away with the pixies. Everything gets blurry.

I was dreaming about our early married life. Mr and Mrs Joseph Kelly of St James' End, Northampton. Respectable, whatever Father Patrick might say. (Father Patrick, that was the fellow sent round to rescue Joseph from disgrace. Himself of the baby face, who parroted the bishop's displeasure.)

I remember happiness in that spanking new house on a spanking new estate. I was proud as punch, keeping the place nice. Meals on the table and laundry on the line. Running up curtains on the old Singer Dolly gave me for a wedding present, her having moved on to a fancy electric one.

Playing houses maybe, like my girls did later, but I was young, for the love of God. If anyone had just cause to enjoy a stroke of good fortune, it was me. Sometimes I had to pinch myself: here's me and Joy, safe and sound, with a nice home and a handsome husband. Happy to turn our backs on the past and face forwards.

Mind you, it wasn't always plain sailing. But then, how could it be? The entire country was reeling from the War. In shock, you might say. Trying to rebuild a life after all that death and horror and suffering. Housing, clothes, food, money: there was never quite enough of anything to go round, and it was still all queues and coupons and make do and mend.

We were lucky, so we were, thanks to Norman. But Joseph had been a priest for almost fifteen years. He was respected in Liverpool. He wasn't afraid of getting his hands dirty, but everyone knew he was a cut above, what with his college learning. Liverpool was almost bombed into oblivion the year I arrived off the boat. The wreckage was shocking. Joseph was in the middle of it and was looked up to for his bravery in picking up the pieces. He'd a certain status. A man people went to for advice. He'd write you a letter or pick a fight with the City Council because he knew the right words to get things done.

Starting all over again in a job he'd never wanted and knew was beneath him was hard, to be sure. Norman wasn't a man for studying, but he'd made a success of himself through his business, and he couldn't help rubbing Joseph's nose in it. There's himself, a bigwig, a proud Alderman of the town, while his brother who went to the Grammar and university was starting at the bottom of the ladder at the age of nearly forty.

Lucky for us, fear that Joseph's fall from grace might damage his own standing kept Norman tight-lipped. He reckoned he'd done his bit and some, coming up with a job and a house for us. We were kept at arm's length, so we couldn't embarrass him and his lah-di-dah wife Marjorie.

Marjorie—now she was a piece of work. The first time we met, she looked so disgusted I thought I must have trodden in dog mess and brought it into her house on my shoes. But no. She thought *I* was the nasty smell, the snotty cow, because I was bog Irish. Made up her mind that I was a floozie and pretended she couldn't understand a word little Joy said because of her Scouse accent. The cheek of it! Lucky for us, Joy was always as good as gold and never answered back, even if I was spitting tacks.

Never did a day's work in her life, our Marjorie, as far as I could see. Lived the life of Riley in that big house in Hardingstone, with her cook and her housemaid. Not to mention the gardener. No children, but all good works and Lady Mayoress this, that and the other. Our paths didn't cross much, to be sure, but when they did, I always made a point of greeting her loudly, having a bit of *craic* about her being the *other* Mrs Kelly and my sister-in-law and all, whether she liked it or not. And I can tell you for nothing, she hated it.

To Joseph's credit, he made a decent fist of being a shoe salesman. No surprises, there. His charm and good looks, not to mention the gift of the gab that made him a fine preacher, helped him along the way. The little bit of commission he earned on top of his salary started small but soon got bigger. We got by, and not too badly at that. We were neither of us prone to running away with the money.

I offered to go out to work myself, but he wouldn't hear of it. Not proper for the new Mrs Joseph Kelly of St James' End who had a house to keep and a child to mind. That suited me just fine at first. I'd had enough of skivvying to last a lifetime. Three cleaning jobs at once I managed when I first came off the boat. Fitzpatrick's offices at dawn, the fish-market when it closed at midday, and three evenings a week mopping floors at Dolly's hospital. I wasn't about to say no to taking the weight off my feet and my wee girl to the park.

You wouldn't recognize St James' End now. The park's still there, or it was last time I checked. But it's a different world. All sorts have moved in. Lots of them coloured like herself. The nun who says she's my favourite. Sister Whatsit. Abigail? You can walk down the street and not hear a single word of English spoken.

Felicity calls it *vibrant*. But maybe that's one of David's fancy words? Like *diversity*, whatever that's supposed to mean. He's all for *celebrating diversity*, is your man David. If Finn is to be believed, he once referred to me in a speech about discrimination in the House of Commons. *No Irish, no blacks, no dogs. You're famous, Grandma*, says Finn, and he's pleased as anything. Well. We didn't have diversity in my day, that's for sure. No walk in the park being a blow-in, I can tell you.

—

It's hard to put things in order. Events, episodes, whatever you call them, are clear as anything, but not how it all fits together. *Face the facts*, says Joy. But even facts aren't as clear cut as she thinks. They get overlaid by memories, by what came later. You can't always remember what you knew and when.

One thing I know now, though I couldn't see it at the time, was that Joseph suffered cruelly when we moved south. While I was busy playing

Happy Families and taking to my fine new life like a duck to water, my new husband had left his heart in Liverpool. He was in mourning.

His first family, the one he'd belonged to all his life and served as a priest for years, wanted nothing more to do with him. He couldn't give or receive the sacraments. While Joy and I toddled off to Mass at St Anthony's on a Sunday morning, he'd dig the garden with the devil's fury. Occasionally, he'd nip into the back of the Cathedral, where the numbers meant he'd not be noticed. But he'd slip out before the end of the service to avoid embarrassing Norman and Marjorie who had a reserved pew in the front row.

His faith remained, or so I've always thought. But he had nowhere to take it. No place to call home. It wasn't long before he'd made up his mind that the Almighty was punishing him for breaking his vow of celibacy. That he deserved everything he was getting. Set adrift in an unforgiving sea. Grief took up residence in his heart and settled in for keeps. A heavy lump, like too much suet. Sometimes he'd look at me as if he couldn't quite remember who I was. As if I was something nasty he'd picked up by mistake in the park.

Perhaps that's when the rot set in. If I'd recognized his sadness for what it was, could I have done something to stop what came later? Or was it always there?

Once you break one boundary, perhaps it's easier to cross the other lines that follow.

But it's easy to be wise in hindsight, so it is.

JOY

1963

Joy aches with tiredness. For some reason, she just can't seem to train her body to cope with night duty. It's all right for the first few days; there's something quite exciting about going to work just as everyone else is packing up for the day, then crawling home while the milkman's still out doing his rounds. A sense of purpose. That she, Joy, has a vital job to do while the rest of the world puts its feet up. But that soon wears off.

A run of nights leaves her feeling that the world is upside-down, topsy-turvy. It's like being on the big dipper, where your head and stomach feel out of step with each other. She assumed it would get easier with practice, but it seems not. Joy and her friend Trisha are as bad as each other. They compare notes on the sheer awfulness of a body-clock out of kilter with daylight. Mind you, Trisha doesn't help herself because she's a party girl and tends to burn the candle at both ends.

Before she started training, Joy honestly hadn't appreciated how physically exhausting nursing would be. Being on your feet all day is gruelling. Then there's the lifting: bed-bound patients need turning over to avoid sores, and others need helping in and out of their beds, their chairs or the bath. It might help if she was taller, but her limbs ache with the effort of it all. For all that Father once said she has the legs of a carthorse, her calves are most definitely feeling the strain. Her feet feel swollen in their black lace-ups.

Being a student nurse has been tough. Not that she really expected anything else. Discipline is strict and everything is inspected, from the starch in their aprons to the neatness of the hospital corners when they make up a bed with fresh linen. Some of the other girls in her intake complain about the regime which they claim is stricter than boarding school.

Not that Joy can comment on that. It's one of the things that she and Trisha have in common, the fact that they both attended secondary moderns, in Toxteth in Trisha's case. Trisha is a freckled redhead with a wicked laugh. By some stroke of luck, they'd been allocated rooms next to each other in the nurses' home, and they are now firm friends.

Their friendship is an unexpected bonus of being required to move into hospital accommodation at the start of her training. At first, Joy was quite bereft at the thought of leaving Jubilee Terrace, but she had no choice. Rules were rules. And it was only fair on Dolly, Ron and the boys.

"Don't you be a stranger, mind," said Dolly. "I'm going to miss having another woman about the house, I can tell you!"

"You know I'll be lost without you, Aunt Dolly," she said. "I'll be round whenever I'm stuck in my studies!"

"Not a bit of it!" Dolly sounded fierce behind her hanky. "You can stand on your own two feet perfectly well these days. You show them, girl! Now, off you go or you'll be missing your bus."

Joy thanks her lucky stars for Dolly on a daily basis. Talking to the other girls, the fact that she'd got a place at the Royal was something of a miracle, considering her barely scraped O-levels. Thank goodness for Dolly helping her prepare for the interview with Matron. That was truly terrifying; Matron has a bearing that makes even the most self-confident boarding-school girls quake in their boots. But Dolly's been a nurse for ever, and they practised and practised the questions, and somehow Joy must have convinced Matron because an agonizing fortnight later, she got the letter confirming her place.

She has no complaints about the strict regime; from her point of view, there are clear rules which are blissfully easy to follow. It's no skin off her nose that they are not allowed out after 10 p.m. Most of the time she just wants to go to bed anyway. She even likes the uniform. It's smart and practical and makes her feel she belongs in a way that her school pinafore never did. She's proud to wear it. Even the wolf-whistles the student nurses attract on their way home are bearable, because their dress is a badge of honour.

And she's held her own. She's good at the practicalities of nursing, she knows that. It's the book learning that's a struggle. She only has to open a book and the words seem to blur on the page. But give her a patient to wash or a dressing to change, and she knows exactly what to do.

She even survived her placement on the general surgical ward under Sister O'Malley. Sister O'Malley is legendary for making student nurses cry. She has eyes in the back of her head and comes down on hapless trainees like a ton of bricks.

"She's a sour-faced old dragon!" complained Trisha after a particularly gruelling shift. They were drinking tea in the nurses' home common room. "She had a right go at me for the way I was cleaning down the sluice room. And then she had the nerve to tell me I'd never make SRN if I didn't turn up to work with properly polished shoes. I ask you!"

Joy laughed. "She's all right really, Trish. Just has high standards. And your shoes could do with a shine, you know."

"It's all right for you, she likes you, Joy. Teacher's pet!"

"Oh, she's a termagant," added Camilla, one of the boarding-school girls, who was rootling in the fridge for milk. "Apparently, she's never been the same since her fiancé went down with his ship in the War."

"But that's years and years ago!" said Trisha. "You'd have thought she'd get over it, wouldn't you?"

Joy tries and fails to picture Sister O'Malley as a giddy girl who once kissed her handsome sailor goodbye at the docks. It's too great a leap. Still, Joy knows what it's like to have the rug pulled from under your feet. One minute, you think you know how the world works, and then the next, everything changes. It's as if you are falling, falling, falling into a bottomless pit. You wonder if you'll ever feel safe again. Sometimes she laughs at herself and her old certainties. Other times, she can't really remember a *before*. Innocence, like virginity, is gone for ever once lost.

Today, she'll find out if it's all been worthwhile. If she's passed her exams and qualified as a State Registered Nurse. There's a noticeboard where they post the results at midday, and she and Trisha are going to go and find out together. The thought of scanning the notice in public makes her feel sick, to tell the truth. The idea of finding her name missing from the list is too much to bear.

———

Two days later, Joy goes round to Dolly and Ron's for a celebration. There's an open invitation to Sunday lunch, and she goes back to Jubilee Terrace whenever her shifts allow. She has three blessed days off now after a run of nights. And this, says Dolly, is a special occasion.

"Come here, you!" Joy finds herself swept into the embrace of Dolly's floury floral apron. "I'm so very proud of you, my girl! Haven't you done well!"

Joy can't keep the smile off her face. "It's still sinking in!" she says. "I've actually done it!"

"You most certainly have! You should be proud of yourself. You've worked your socks off for this."

Dolly marshals her into the house, where Ron and the boys are waiting. Ron grunts something congratulatory and pats her on the back. Frank, Dennis and Robbie offer awkward hugs, and she glows with quiet pleasure. Ron opens bottles of beer, and they all drink to her success before sitting down to one of Dolly's Sunday dinners.

Joy tells them over roast beef and Yorkshire pudding that she plans to train as a midwife.

"More exams?" asks Frank through a mouthful of roast potatoes. "You mental or something?"

"I know! I must be mad. But it's only another six months," says Joy. "I've applied, anyway. Just have to wait and see if they take me."

"What did your Mam and Pa say?" asks Dolly over the washing up. "They must be proud as punch."

"I . . . I haven't told them yet."

"Joy! Why on earth not?"

Joy concentrates on wiping every smear from the glass in her hand. She sighs. "I'll write to Mam, I promise. I just haven't got round to it yet."

"You do that!" says Dolly. "You've got some good news to share, now haven't you? It's a great achievement. She and your Dad will be made up."

"Not sure I'd go that far. But at least it'll show Father I'm not quite as stupid as he thinks, won't it?"

"Stop doing yourself down!" tuts Dolly. "You deserve to be proud of yourself. Look how far you've come. No one can take that away from you."

In truth, Joy does write home from time to time, although the pressures of work and study mean her correspondence has become a little sporadic in recent months. Whatever the past, Bridie's still her mam. On her better days, she even feels a sneaking respect for the young woman who pulled her from the wreckage and refused to let her go. Her mother may not be perfect, but perhaps she did her best with the cards she was dealt.

Mam probably has no idea the effort the letters cost her. The discovery of her adoption makes Joy self-conscious. She sits with a dictionary at her side to get the spellings right, because she can't bear the thought that Father might sneer, and make Mam feel ashamed. Not that he reads them, probably. She can't imagine he's interested.

She's only been back to Northampton once in the last three years, and that wasn't a roaring success. The thing about working shifts is you always have an excuse. But the first Christmas she was nursing, after vacillating until the very last moment, she decided to go. She still doesn't know if her mother believed her when she said that a sudden last-minute change in the rota meant she was unexpectedly free.

Everything felt odd and awkward. It didn't help that she arrived with a heavy cold, her head thick and her eyes streaming. Mother was tearful and clingy in a way that made Joy squirm. Avoiding being alone with her father proved easy; he was vague and distant, as if he couldn't quite remember who she was. Felicity was at first awed into silence by the reappearance of her grown-up sister, and then resentful of her renewed presence in their bedroom. She was self-conscious and awkward with Joy. What had she been told?

Any hole in the family left by her flight had closed over with barely a trace. A wound that healed without a scar. At least Joy now knew the reason why Felicity was the favourite. She had never felt more of an outsider.

After the most cursory inquiry the first night, no one showed any interest in how she was getting on with her nursing course. All the talk was about Felicity's stellar progress on the piano. Her sister had recently started taking singing lessons, too. Piano was one thing; she had only to go round the corner to Miss White's, but the singing involved a complicated journey on two buses that Mother had to do every week, while still ensuring Father's tea was on the table at the required hour.

"It was terrible when we had the snow last week, so it was," said Mother. "The number seven broke down, and we had to tramp all the way home in the dark, didn't we Felicity, my lovely? I was a good hour late with the tea and your father not a bit pleased. But it's worth it, to be sure. She has the voice of an angel, so she has."

Then there was the endless practice. Joy arrived just in time to witness Felicity's star turn at the Christmas concert at St Anthony's. But even though the concert was done and dusted, even though it was Christmas, the practice regime continued. They all sat in silence while Felicity played her scales and sang her exercises under Father's beady eye. A fluffed passage, a single note off key, and Father made her repeat it, until Felicity was dropping with exhaustion. Mam sat in the corner knitting, the occasional trace of agitation betrayed by a quickening of the needles. A dropped stitch.

"He's a slave driver, isn't he?" said Joy one night, just before she and Felicity fell asleep in their side-by-side beds. "How do you put up with it?"

"Daddy only wants what's best for me," came the prim reply.

"If you say so," retorted Joy. She blew her nose and turned over to face the wall.

There was a pause. "Actually, I do say so," Felicity went on. "When I'm playing or singing . . . I go somewhere else in my head. I forget where I am, even. Honestly, Joy, it's the best feeling *ever*."

Joy felt a sudden burst of affection for her sister. If she needed an escape from St James' End, who was Joy to deny her that? If music was her passport out, how could she object? Wasn't escaping exactly what Joy had done? Not that there was any evidence that Felicity was desperate. Yet. Perhaps being her father's favourite was talisman enough.

"You know where I am if you need me, Flick," she said, suddenly forceful. "Ever, I mean. Not necessarily now. Just if."

"What do you mean?" Felicity sounded sleepy. The poor child was exhausted. "Can I come for a visit?"

"Maybe." Joy wanted to backtrack. She needed distance between her new life and the old one. "Perhaps when you're older. We'll see."

—

Thank the Lord all that's behind her, she thinks now, in the safety of Aunt Dolly's kitchen. She has shaken the dust off her feet, built a new life for herself. She and Trisha are off to the pictures tonight. *Cleopatra*, with Elizabeth Taylor and Richard Burton. Yet as she hangs up her tea towel at Aunt Dolly's after their celebratory Sunday dinner, she finds herself wondering what Felicity is doing today.

Presumably Mam will have taken her to Mass at St Anthony's. They still go to Sunday lunch every month with Uncle Norman and Aunt Marjorie in their big house in Hardingstone. Best behaviour for everyone. Though Flick has an easier time of it, not being the changeling. Sit up nicely at table, and then those tedious games of patience while the grown-ups talk, and Aunt Marjorie takes swipes at Mam.

"I don't suppose you've been to the continent, Bridget?" she'll say. (Aunt Marjorie is the only person who doesn't call her mother Bridie.) "Some of our best holidays have been in Paris." Or, "I don't imagine you have time for church flowers, Bridget, given your little job? *So* rewarding. But quite a commitment."

And on a good day, Mam will hold her own, and reply that no, she hasn't been to Paris, but the sights of Dublin are a wonder to behold, or parry the dig about the church flowers by complimenting Marjorie on the clever way her gardener has with the roses. On a bad one, she'll sit there, mute with misery, hoping against hope that Father will leap to her defence.

"Thank you," says Joy, kissing Aunt Dolly goodbye. "For everything, I mean. Not just that lovely Sunday dinner."

Thanks to Dolly's support, she has the job she always longed for and now the coveted letters RCN to prove it. Provided she carries on working hard and passes the next tranche of her exams, her future is secure.

If her nights are occasionally troubled by pangs for the family she has abandoned, days like today remind her that she has a new family in Liverpool who love and accept her for who she is.

She needs to keep her eyes on the horizon.

FELICITY

1964

Felicity is furious. So angry that she's positively trembling. She was so sure she wouldn't get the part that she hadn't told *anyone* at home or at school that she was even going to the audition. She couldn't risk jinxing it. The only person who even had an inkling was Mr Searle who'd told her about the audition in the first place, and she had sworn him to secrecy rather than face the humiliation of anyone finding out they'd turned her down.

Now she's finally got the part (the *main* part in the whole show!) Daddy is kicking up a stink and saying she isn't to do it because it will be a distraction from her piano, that theatre people are seedy, and that she's just a schoolgirl and should be thinking about her studies. *Honestly*. He's actually forbidden her to take the part! But she's got, got, *got* to do it, whether he likes it or not. Nothing on earth is going to stop her. It's a chance in a million. Does he really have no idea what this means to her?

The trouble is that Daddy just won't let go of the idea that Felicity is a child genius who's on the way to becoming a world-famous concert pianist. She's tried to tell him he's wrong on three counts. One, at fourteen, she's hardly a child anymore. Two, she's certainly not a genius. She might be quite good at the piano but she's nothing special. She's known that for years. It's positively *embarrassing* that Daddy clings on to his misplaced ambition for her. And third, even if she could make it, she doesn't *want* to be a pianist. She's going to be a singer or maybe an actress or both.

Why on earth can't he understand? He seems to forget she's practically grown up nowadays and doesn't really want to sit on his lap or cuddle up next to him to play his favourite Mozart duets. Is it because she's still so skinny? When she looks in the mirror, she can see that she's pretty, with her blonde hair and big blue eyes, and she finally seems to be growing taller, but there's no getting away from the fact that her looks are horribly babyish. (If only she had proper breasts. Joy was already *huge* by the time she was fourteen, and so was Mammy by all accounts. Her sister and she are such chalk and cheese it's actually quite funny.)

Not that she wants to look like Joy, who's quite honestly a bit of a lump. And it's probably partly because she looks so much younger than she really is that landed her the role in the first place. When Judy Garland was cast in the film, she had to wear some horrible corset to hide her figure because she was sixteen, and Dorothy is only meant to be twelve. (They won't have that trouble with Felicity, who is what Mammy calls a *late developer*. She supposes she should be grateful, for once.)

But *Dorothy* in *The Wizard of Oz*! Parts don't get much bigger than that. She'll be on stage just about the whole time, singing with a professional company at the Royal. They're touring the country, recruiting a local girl to sing Dorothy wherever they land up. What an opportunity! What if she's spotted by a talent scout and whisked off to London and stardom?

The girls at school will be simply green with envy. Perhaps they'll all buy tickets and throw roses on the stage when she comes on for a bow at the end of the show? And, she reminds herself humbly, this is an opportunity to learn about things like stage presence and ensemble work and the demands of musical theatre. If she's to become a professional performer, she needs to learn her craft. She hasn't a moment to waste.

And Daddy's *wrong* that it's going to be a distraction. If he's really not prepared to let go of the idea that she's going to be a pianist, she'll just have to find a way of persuading him that taking the part will be good for her all-round musical development. There's no way she's going to miss her chance here. If Daddy thinks she's going to turn it down, he's got another think coming. Isn't he always on about her self-discipline and dedication? Well, it's time he saw that determination in action.

And if she's going to be as brilliant as Dorothy as she plans to be, surely he'll recognize that and realize she has talents other than at the piano. It just means working three times as hard, so that she doesn't fall behind in her piano practice or her schoolwork while she rehearses for *Wizard*. (Even calling it *Wizard* makes her feel like a proper actress! *We met doing* Wizard *in Northampton*, she hears herself saying of her friendship with another member of the ensemble. *Of course, I was just a schoolgirl, and it was my first proper role. Before anyone knew who I was!*)

She needs allies. She's fairly certain that Mammy will be on her side; her mother adores musicals, and is also in favour of fun, because she thinks Daddy is far too strict with Felicity, just as he was too hard on Joy. So Felicity just needs to persuade Mammy that *Wizard* will be fun—even if in actual fact it's bound to be jolly hard work. On the other hand, if her mother's in support, that could play either way with Daddy, who always thinks he knows best about anything to do with Felicity. And everything else, actually.

What about Joy? If anyone knows anything about facing down Daddy in one of his moods, it's her sister. And Joy got what she wanted in the end, didn't she? She's got a whole new life in Liverpool and has even been to see the Beatles, can you believe it? Not that it's Felicity's sort of music, but all the girls at school *rave* about the Beatles, and when Felicity let slip that her big sister lived in Liverpool and had actually been to the Cavern Club, she could tell they were seriously impressed. Even Bitchy Betty—who thinks she's the bees' knees and doesn't normally deign to speak to Felicity and her friends—came and asked her if Joy could get her Paul McCartney's autograph. Honestly!

Joy has also found the job of her dreams. Or so she says. Felicity can't think of anything worse than being a midwife. All that pain and screaming and having to handle other women's private parts. Yuk! The very idea makes her shudder. Joy says babies sometimes get stuck or try to come out the wrong way round, and sometimes it's such a struggle that mothers get torn open in the process and have to be stitched together again afterwards. How hideous! Felicity couldn't stomach it; she would pass out at the first sight of all that blood. (Daddy says artistic people are often sensitive.) But she has to admit she's impressed by Joy's guts. You have to be very strong and very calm to manage that sort of thing. If she ever had a baby—not that she thinks she wants to if she's going to be torn in half—she'd want

Joy in charge, no question. When she stops to think about it, Felicity even feels faintly proud of her sister.

While Joy would almost certainly be sympathetic to her battle with Daddy about Dorothy, what can she actually do from a distance of 150 miles? And when did Daddy ever listen to Joy anyway? He behaves almost as if she never existed. Joy says it's because she's adopted and that they've got nothing in common. But that's no reason never to speak her name, is it?

Oh gosh, it's all so difficult! What about Mr Searle? Perhaps he could persuade Daddy? But that could go either way, too. She's aware that Daddy doesn't quite approve of Mr Searle, although he's been the most marvellous singing teacher. Really inspirational. (So much more exciting than her old teacher, even if she was a friend of Miss White's. It's been one of the best things about moving up to the Grammar.) Thanks to him, Felicity has discovered her true calling which she now knows is to sing. Her second instrument has definitely become her first.

It's taken Felicity the last couple of years to work out exactly why Daddy isn't comfortable with Mr Searle. At first, she thought it was his clothes—he never wears a suit and tie, preferring open-necked shirts with long pointed collars in flamboyant colours like mustard or purple and rather garish checked trousers—or because he invited Felicity to call him Bob, which Daddy feels is inappropriate in a teacher. Another possibility was that Daddy simply regarded her singing as of lesser importance than her piano.

Now she realizes it's because Mr Searle is almost certainly homosexual. To begin with this was a bit of a shock to Felicity, too, and she felt very silly, actually, because she had quite a crush on him. He's terribly dishy. (She had a whole scene worked out in her head where she stopped singing one day only to see Mr Searle gazing at her in rapt attention. In her head, Mr Searle told her she had the voice of an angel, and, most thrillingly, confessed that he was madly in love with her and kissed her.)

Her house of cards came crashing down a few weeks ago when Hilary—a brisk girl in the year above—overheard Felicity telling her best friend Lucy at break that she nearly swooned when Mr Searle massaged her shoulders because he said she was tense and it was affecting her voice.

"Grow up, Felicity!" said Hilary kindly. "Surely you know he's a pansy?" It was the kindness which almost undid Felicity because she felt such a fool. Thank goodness the bell rang at that very moment, and she and Lucy had to find their aprons and dash off for Art.

"Do you think she's right?" she asked Lucy on the way over to the art room, feeling slightly sick at the thought.

"Haven't the foggiest," said Lucy. "I don't know how you're supposed to tell. But honestly, Felicity, you'd better get used to it if you're so set on going on the stage. You must realize that the theatre's full of that sort of caper."

Felicity felt herself blush; what a hopeless innocent she was! If she wasn't careful, she would be an absolute laughing stock. She gave herself a good talking to, and since then she has done everything she can to cultivate a more sophisticated persona. She needs to steel herself so that she's not shocked in future. (If her father is less tolerant of Mr Searle's lifestyle, well, that's only to be expected of the older generation and she should probably just feel sorry for him.)

But that doesn't solve her current problem, which is that Daddy doesn't rate Mr Searle all that highly and may not respect his advice. Which only leaves one person she can think of. She will talk to Miss White tomorrow when she has her lesson.

—

She got her way, eventually, but victory came at a price.

Miss White needed some persuading. "Ask yourself, my dear, why this is so important to you," she said when Felicity poured her heart out. "Why are you so desperate to go on stage?"

It felt as if Miss White had just dunked her in a vat of very cold water. She was wearing one of her most impenetrable looks. Felicity gulped. "Because I so love singing," she said. "And it'll be . . . such fun!"

"Well, as long as it's not because you think it's the way to fame and fortune, I can't see any real harm in it," said Miss White. Felicity blushed.

Thank goodness she hadn't said anything about her hopes of being spotted by a talent scout.

Although Miss White put in a good word for her, Daddy sulked and stormed, muttering darkly about the loose morals of theatre types, while Mammy fluttered around trying to pour oil on troubled waters, only infuriating him further with her implication that he was being a little harsh.

"Can you not see what an opportunity this is for her?" said Mammy. "I thought you'd be wanting her to succeed in her music, Joseph. After all the hard work she's put in?"

"Of course I want her to succeed!" said Daddy. "Just not like this. She has a promising future!"

"And surely this will help her?"

"Don't I know what's best for her? Am I not her father, for goodness sake?"

In the end, Felicity won him round the only way she could think of. At bedtime, she meekly bade her parents goodnight and went upstairs to change into her nightclothes. When she was sure her mother had retired for the night, she crept downstairs. Just as she knew she would, she found Daddy sitting in his favourite armchair with a glass of whisky in his hand. He looked up warily.

Without a word, Felicity sat at the piano and began playing Beethoven's *Moonlight Sonata*. At the end, she turned around to see tears streaming down his face and his arms outstretched. "Flissy, come over here and give me a cuddle. You break my heart, you little minx!" And Felicity knew then that the prize was hers for the taking.

—

In the end, it was worth it. *The Wizard of Oz* was—almost—everything she could have hoped for.

What she wouldn't tell her father, wouldn't tell anyone at all, actually, was that to begin with, she thought she'd made the most terrible mistake and perhaps he'd been right all along.

There was just so much to learn. It wasn't just remembering her lines and singing really well, but never putting a foot wrong in terms of the stage directions. Naturally the pros all knew exactly what they were doing, so largely she just had to fit in the gaps they created for her, but for the first few rehearsals she always seemed to be in the wrong place at the wrong time and the other actors didn't hide their annoyance as they kept having to replay scenes. She was constantly apologizing, and frequently in tears.

"Felicity, dear, do at least *try* and get it right," said Rob Williams, the Director, when she'd fluffed things yet again. "You have to remember all eyes will be on Dorothy. We can't afford any blunders."

And if Felicity thought she'd be embraced into the company with open arms she was sadly mistaken. The other performers treated her with bemused tolerance at best, and irritation at worst. By and large they ignored her.

"Darling, there's no chance in hell I'll remember your name," drawled the actor playing the Tin Man when they were introduced at the first rehearsal. "You're Little Miss Northampton to me. Just you make sure you don't tread on my feet. I still bear the scars inflicted by Little Miss Leicester, the brat."

"Animals and children!" threw in the Lion. "You know what they say . . . Never work with either. Have you met your Toto yet, Dorothy?" he added, with a glint in his eye.

That was one of the worst things: dealing with the wretched little dog recruited to play Toto. Felicity had not grown up with dogs and Billy, a lively Yorkshire terrier, appeared oblivious to her attempts to keep him under control. The first couple of rehearsals were disastrous: it was only thanks to the actor playing the Scarecrow, who was a dog lover and showed her how to keep a supply of treats in her pinafore pocket, that she discovered how to stop Billy stealing the show.

As for the singing, though she made sure she knew all the songs backwards even before rehearsals began, it required an extraordinary degree of stamina to ensure she sounded fresh at every performance, when in reality she was absolutely longing to go home to bed. Thank heavens it was only a fortnight's run. Having cried herself to sleep every night during rehearsals she was exhausted before the show opened.

Afterwards, though, she would remember the moment when the doors of the theatre finally opened to the public. There was the amazing sensation of the ensemble finally coming together, as if each performer was a flower opening up under the stage lights. The unforgettable experience of being part of something, of all the different cogs in the wheel slotting together to produce something wonderful.

And above all, the completely glorious feeling of singing her heart out on stage before a live audience who clapped and clapped at the end of every performance. *I must remember this for ever,* she told herself as she came out for the final curtain call on the final night and accepted a bouquet from Rob Williams, who was smiling from ear to ear and even kissed her cheek.

In the end, it wasn't the congratulations of the pros that stayed with her ("Not at all bad, Little Miss Northampton," said the Tin Man). The image burned into her retinas was the sight of her family in the front row as she took her final bow. While Mammy and Joy were up on their feet applauding, she could see her father sitting almost completely still in his seat, with tears coursing down his cheeks, a dreamy expression on his face.

Nothing beats this, she thought. *This is who I am. This is what I want for the rest of my life.*

BRIDIE

2019

I keep hearing music. I think I'm dreaming again. Or wandering. Lost down the rabbit warren of the past. Little Felicity practising the piano in our front room by the gas fire. It wasn't much of an instrument, not that I'd know the difference. It's the sort of thing Joseph knew about, I don't know how. He said it would do to begin with, and we'd see how she got along with her lessons. It didn't do to have an expensive instrument so near a fire anyway.

To be sure she blew us all away with her playing, so she did. Before long she was giving little recitals. At school, at St Anthony's. At the concert for St Vincent de Paul just before Christmas that year when the audience did battle with snow and ice to get there, they were so keen to hear the child play. Wee Felicity, with her blond plaits and little red tartan kilt and a white blouse I made myself.

Oh, she was a picture! Ten-year-old Felicity lifting her hands and beginning her party piece, as if no one else is in the room, and nothing in the world matters but the music. There's Miss White, her teacher, in silent raptures as she witnesses her best pupil shining as bright as a star. There are the Brownies, suddenly quietened by the power of the music, though it's been a long evening already and Felicity's been saved till last. There's Norman and Marjorie, come to support the child prodigy niece, even if it's only St Anthony's Church Hall and not their blessed Cathedral. There's Joseph, sitting in a corner in the gloom, tears of pride streaming down his face. Me, bewildered to have produced this miracle child.

I'm already thinking about the expense of a new piano, and how are we going to find the cash for that, I wonder? Will himself finally sanction me taking that little part-time job at the newsagent on the corner? And then the door opens, sweeping in an unholy blast of cold air and a flurry of snow, and it's our Joy, smart as anything in her nurse's uniform. She must have come straight from work, bless her, and travelled all the way down from Liverpool to hear her sister play.

That was then and what happiness we had of her music. Although Joseph was a hard taskmaster, and never let her off her practice, which for the most part she didn't mind. Her instinct was to be harder on herself than anyone. In the end it was Marjorie, bless her, who came up with the piano. A Broadwood, no less, classy as anything. So she kept telling us. It had belonged to her mother who'd once been a fine pianist, and since neither Marjorie nor her sister played, it was only gathering dust in Hardingstone, and didn't go with the G-plan furniture that was on order for January.

You must be very proud, she says at the end of that concert, and her voice is almost shaking with the effort. It's as if she's seen me properly for the first time. Decided I'm worthy of her notice. And I spot tears in her eyes, too, and I find myself feeling sorry for the poor Lady Mayoress and wonder for the very first time if having no children of her own is the tragedy of our Marjorie's existence. And here am I with two, like chalk and cheese they are, but still mine and the light of my life.

—

But Felicity isn't ten years old anymore, and it isn't the piano I can hear, either. Not quite. The sound of strings, though. A beautiful melody, like water running over stones. Flowers in a spring meadow. (I don't know how music can sound like flowers, but it can so. Sunshine and laughter. Dandelion clocks.) I am smiling. Transported. Bathing in the sheer joy of it.

The *joy* of it! My Joy was eight when Felicity arrived, and I was worried at first she'd take against the baby. She'd been my best beloved for so many years, hadn't she? But even then she was a coper. There was always something so . . . matter-of-fact about Joy. She faced things head on, however unpleasant. Chicken pox. The dentist. Exams.

Joseph called her *stolid*, which I had to look up in the dictionary, because at first I thought he meant *solid* because it's true she was on the chubby side as a child. Which was grand, surely to God, after those years of rationing, if a child had a bit of flesh about her body? But stolid isn't very kind, if you ask me. It means impassive. Bovine, like a cow. Is it really a word you'd use to describe your stepdaughter?

If you ask me, Joy was someone who took things in her stride, and that's a fine quality because in my experience, life has a nasty way of turning up nasty surprises. Maybe it was being a war baby. If you've seen the world fall down around you, a new sister isn't much to get in a lather about.

Even when that sister almost tears her mother in two upon arrival, leaving her helpless in bed with ugly great stitches. While Joseph stood around uselessly, the great lummox, little Joy set about fetching and carrying the baby from her cradle to my bed, and running up and down stairs with the nappy bucket when the wee mite needed changing.

She took to wheeling Felicity round the estate if Joseph was at home to manhandle the baby carriage over the doorstep. It was grand, was that Swan perambulator! Second-hand, to be sure, a welcome hand-me-down from my friend Shelagh Hooper at St Anthony's. With five boys to contend with, the youngest two twins, she informed her husband that she'd finished her family, and that was that, thank you very much.

Poor Veronica bought a brand-new Silver Cross for baby Joy, because she had the money for luxuries, but it disappeared along with everything else she ever owned when Upper Stanhope Street was flattened by the Luftwaffe. I'm not sure Joy ever even slept in it.

While Joy was busy parading her baby sister around the neighbourhood, I took the chance for a kip, and I was mightily grateful. Good practice for Joy, for when she has her own family, I thought then. How else had the O'Leary girls ever learned what they called mothercraft in those days, except by helping with their baby brothers and sisters? My body was a fair way from healing after the birth, which was long and difficult. In all honesty, I wasn't quite the same again, down there, and much less keen on granting Joseph his marital rights. Perhaps that's when the wedge got in between us.

Truth be told, we were both worn out, those first months after Felicity's arrival. She was a colicky baby and a terrible sleeper. I'd forgotten how tiring the broken nights were, and I was still young. Joseph was in his forties, mind, and she was his first, so he'd not had the practice. The demands of an infant were a shock to his constitution.

Is it any surprise he moved out of our bed to the settee? Luckily, he was so besotted with Felicity that one look in the cradle and he forgave her everything. He was less forgiving of me. The meals that didn't appear. The laundry left undone.

So you see, I couldn't have done without Joy, now could I? *Joy to the world, and so you are*, I told her then and I tell her now. When the words will do as they're told.

—

The music has stopped. Somehow I know I have slept. Slept and slept. Floated away on a tide of bliss, dreaming of babies. Oh, I don't want to wake up!

Are you all right, Mrs Kelly? asks a quiet voice. I must have cried aloud.

What time is it? I try to ask. I hear my voice. No words, just a croak. Not that it matters. I remember: I'm in hospital. I have no appointments to keep today or any day. No messages to run. But where is the precious music, for the love of Mary?

Shh, now. Everyone else is asleep, says the nurse. Do I hear a note of reproach in his voice? *Here, let me wipe your face for you*, he says more gently.

I feel my skin being softly dabbed with a towel. St Veronica wiping the face of Christ. I seem to be crying.

That's better. It's all right, Mrs Kelly, he says. *Anthony,* I remember. The night nurse is a man called Anthony, like St Anthony's, where the girls and I found a home, even if their father didn't. I can't remember why. But he was funny like that, my Joseph. Had his principles and couldn't be argued out of them once he'd made up his mind.

It seems so long since I've seen him. I don't think he's visited me once in here. Not *once*. You'd have thought he might have made the effort. I am his wife, after all. His lawful wedded wife. Not just his housekeeper, though I'll admit that's how it started.

But there's nothing to hide now. No need to pretend, now we're married. He's probably trying to protect my reputation, so. He's a good man. For better and for worse.

JOY

1968

When her mother phones, Joy is surrounded by packing chests in her bedsit. The plywood boxes were passed on to her by Frances, a girl who recently arrived from Hong Kong and moved into a room on the ground floor. Joy almost declined the offer: she's surprised she owns enough for packing chests, when she thinks that she arrived in Liverpool with a single cardboard suitcase. But Frances persuaded her, and it seems she was right.

It turns out that Joy has accumulated quite a few possessions in the decade since. Pots and pans, china and crockery, a chopping board, a couple of wooden spoons and her favourite kitchen knife. Bedding and towels. Her clothes. Her precious wireless. None of it is much to write home about, but still. It's all *hers*: chosen by her and bought with her hard-earned cash, a symbol of her life as a fully-fledged adult.

There are few books, which is a relief because they're terrible for gathering dust, and heavy to move. She never had the money for books when she was a student and tended to rely on the library. However, she has quite a pile of back copies of *Nursing Times* and *Midwives Chronicle*. Being a slow reader, she finds the magazine format more digestible, though if she's honest with herself, there are some copies she barely opens before the next issue arrives. She's cancelled her subscription for now.

She loves being a midwife. Her time on the obstetrics ward while nursing sparked her enthusiasm far beyond any expectation she brought to the placement. She was taken by surprise by the whole experience. It was less the babies, oddly, that fired her passion than the sheer courage and endurance of the women as they gave birth. There was something almost elemental about the way nature overtook a mother's body as she went through labour.

And what Joy spotted almost immediately was a niche that seemed tailor-made for her. Alongside highly developed practical skills, the role demands unruffled calm and quiet authority, both of which she has in spades.

So it was with only a slight sigh that she committed herself to another six months' study after she won her stripes as a State Registered Nurse. While the academic side of her training was little easier second time around, at least in midwifery she had a passion for her subject as well as a clear goal in mind.

Five years on, Joy has established herself as a safe pair of hands, even amongst the most mistrustful mothers in her district. If only it wasn't for the patronizing behaviour of some of the male doctors who insist they know best.

Only last week she had a stand-up row with the new Registrar, Dr Keeling, who was of the school of thought that all mothers should give birth strapped to their beds on their backs, preferably with their feet in stirrups. She had left Evelyn Daniels slowly pacing the delivery room while she nipped out to refill her water jug, only to find on her return Dr Keeling hectoring her patient to lie down.

"Hop up on the bed, there's a good girl," he was saying with a trace of impatience. "Better for you and better for baby."

"*Agh!*" groaned Mrs Daniels as a fierce contraction cut in. She turned to Joy in mute appeal.

"Sister . . . Kelly," said the doctor, peering at her name badge. "Give Mum a hand up, won't you? Can't have her dropping her sprog on the floor now, can we?"

"May I have a word please, doctor?" Joy feared for a moment he wasn't going to take the hint, so she walked over to the door, and held it open, leaving the registrar little choice but to follow her into the corridor.

"Well?"

"First of all, my patient has a name. She's called Mrs Daniels," said Joy. "Second, the baby's posterior, so I suggested she walk around for a bit to get things moving. She was in acute discomfort on her back. Third, the last time I checked, the baby's making good progress. Almost turned round. And lastly, this is baby number four. As it happens, I delivered numbers two and three. Mrs Daniels knows what she's doing, and so do I for that matter."

Joy had the satisfaction of watching Dr Keeling's jaw drop before an ugly stain flushed his cheeks. Luckily for them both, another patient at the other end of the ward chose that moment to ring her bell and Joy was able to escape with a quick, "Excuse me, doctor," before he could think of a response.

She gets awful gyp from her colleagues for standing up to doctors, but honestly. Why do they always think they know best? Obviously there are cases when medical intervention is needed—and what a relief that help is on hand in modern-day Britain—but the vast majority of cases are straightforward. She certainly doesn't buy the more extreme ideas of Grantly Dick-Read and others about natural childbirth, but everything she's observed suggests that most of the time women should be simply allowed to get on with the job, with a skilled midwife alongside.

Now, the combined effects of a recently broken heart and an advertisement in *Midwives Chronicle* have propelled her in a new and unexpected direction. The Mercy Clinic in the Eastern Cape of South Africa, founded by Roman Catholic missionaries in the 1890s, is struggling to survive and needs a couple of experienced midwives to take it in hand. She and a colleague from one of the London hospitals she is yet to meet have been employed for an initial three months, after which the agency will review the situation. She is excited and daunted in equal measure.

Will she really need any of her possessions in rural South Africa? She's never travelled abroad and has little idea what to expect. At one level, it seems madness to ship any of her possessions halfway round the world. On the other hand, she doesn't know how long she'll be away, and they are all she has. It might be a comfort to be surrounded by familiar odds and ends from home.

She decides that she'll limit herself to only what will fit in the trunk she bought second-hand on the market. She's just wondering if she can talk Uncle Ron into letting her squeeze a couple of packing cases into his loft when she realizes the telephone is ringing in the lobby downstairs. The mad hope that it will be Richard flares up briefly, but she knows that's ridiculous and swiftly extinguishes the small flicker of hope. (Why on earth would he? He'd been perfectly clear; she'd entirely misread the situation. Pretty embarrassing, actually. She'd been fooling herself all along, imagining that a few drinks and a couple of dances amounted to anything more than kindness. *Pity*, probably, which is even worse.)

The phone rarely rings in the middle of the day, so it's almost certainly a wrong number. But Frances is on nights and won't be pleased to be woken, so Joy reluctantly abandons her sorting and takes the stairs two at a time.

"Liverpool 437," she says. There's a silence on the line, though she can hear someone gasping for breath at the other end.

"Hello?" she adds after a pause. "Is there anyone there?"

She's about to replace the receiver when she hears her mother's voice, sobbing down the line. "Oh Joy! Is that really you? My lovely, can you come? It's your father."

—

An hour later Joy is on the train south, still numb with disbelief. Joseph is dead. A car crash; possibly a heart attack at the wheel. *Joseph is dead. Joseph is dead. Joseph is dead.* The phrase turns in her head in rhythm with the train as it clatters down the line.

Joseph is dead. Joseph is dead. Joseph is dead. She refuses to call him Father these days, just as *Mammy* has been *Mother* ever since Bridie dropped her bombshell about the adoption.

She takes a pen and notebook from her handbag and begins to write a list. *Find F and bring her home. Uncle Norman? Funeral—Father Adrian? Food for wake?*

What else? Will she have to delay her departure for South Africa? Possibly. It all depends on the timing of the funeral and presumably there'll be a post-mortem, so she should probably warn the mission agency. Oh *God . . .* what about her mother? Will Joy need to stay and support her?

She can't. Just *can't*. She's committed to the Mercy Clinic and her new life overseas. It's the chance of a lifetime, both personally and professionally.

Joseph is dead. Joseph is dead. Joseph is dead.

How does she feel? Relieved? Celebratory? *Ding, dong, the witch is dead!* She hated *The Wizard of Oz*, remembers being terrified by it at the cinema as a child, yet the lyrics seem to have stuck fast. *Ding, dong! The witch is dead. Which old witch? The wicked witch.* Then Felicity was in that production at the Royal Theatre, and Joy had to endure it all over again along with all the fawning over her baby sister's brilliance. Dolly made her go, kicking and screaming. And truth be told, Flick had been terribly good. *Wake up, the wicked witch is dead. She's gone where the goblins go, below, below, below.*

Joseph is dead. Joseph is dead. Joseph is dead.

Whether he's gone below or not, all Joy feels right now is resentment. Anger. Long buried rage surges up inside her, a hellishly hot cauldron of fury.

I need to see his body, she thinks. *I need to know he's gone for good and can't do any more harm.* She'll see her stepfather safely buried, do her duty by her mother, and then she's off to Africa. She's not, not, *not* going to let Joseph take this away from her, that's for certain. Mother will cope. Besides, there's Felicity. She'll just have to do her bit.

—

A couple of days later, and Joy has things more or less under control at St James' End. It wasn't easy; when she first arrived with Uncle Norman who kindly met her train, she found her mother in a terrible state. Any gratitude for her older daughter's prompt response to her SOS was entirely overshadowed by Bridie's worry about her younger one, who was apparently in Cornwall on a post A-level holiday with her friend Lucy and a group of other girls from school.

"I can't rest until the poor soul's back home where she should be!" Bridie tells Joy even before she's taken off her coat. "This news will be the end of her! Oh, but they were so close, with the music and all," she says, as Norman carries Joy's suitcase into the hall. "The poor wee fatherless child! My heart's breaking for her!"

"Mother, she's eighteen and will bear it," snaps Joy. The fact that it would be hypocritical to feign grief (*Ding, dong, the witch is dead!*) doesn't stop her feeling put out that Bridie has no such concern for her own feelings. *She's not the only one without a father*, she wants to say. *Nice to see you, too.*

Instead she concentrates on the practicalities that are her forte. A phone call to Lucy's house swiftly establishes that her sister has not gone camping in Cornwall with Lucy and a crowd of girls from the Grammar, as she told her parents, but is actually on holiday alone with a boyfriend. It's the first time that Joy has heard of his existence.

Not that it's a surprise; naturally Flick has a boyfriend. A late growth spurt means that Flick is now taller than her sister by some inches, and slender with it. Willowy is the word. She wears her blonde hair closely cropped, and the gamine style makes her blue eyes bigger than ever. With looks like hers, she can take her pick. (Not so Joy. What a frightful fool she'd made of herself! Why would someone like Richard be interested in her anyway? Far too handsome and charming.)

"Please don't say anything!" begs Lucy. "She'll absolutely *kill* me if you spill the beans. I swore on my life I'd cover for her. You know what your Dad's like."

"As a matter of fact I do," says Joy, suppressing a note of hysteria. *He's as dead as a doornail.* "But that's beside the point. Look, I wouldn't ask if it wasn't really important, Lucy. You tell me exactly where to find her, and I'll keep schtum. But you've probably got a bit of explaining to do to your Mum. She was a bit surprised when I asked for the name of the campsite where you're all supposed to be."

"Oh *no*," groans Lucy. "That's blown it. All right, I've got the address somewhere. Have you got a pen?"

In the end, Uncle Norman offers to drive to St Ives in his Bentley to break the news to Felicity. He will find a guesthouse and stay overnight, but promises to bring Felicity safely home to her mother the next day. Joy phones the mission agency to explain her plight, promising that she will rearrange her passage as soon as she can after the funeral, and then spends the rest of the day making tea for Bridie and trying to sort out arrangements. She speaks to Father Adrian at St Anthony's and he promises to call round during the afternoon.

"Did Joseph leave you any instructions, Mother?" she asks, having found the small walnut desk in what is euphemistically called Joseph's study locked. (The word "study" is laughable, really; the desk sits in a dark corner of the box room, which is otherwise crammed with books. It was his inviolable kingdom nonetheless. For as long as Joy can remember, Joseph had forbidden the girls to touch his precious desk.)

"What do you mean by instructions?" Bridie is sitting in the kitchen, twisting a damp hanky in her hands.

"You know: directions for his funeral, favourite hymns. That sort of thing. And did he have a will? Insurance policies?"

"Oh, I can't be expected to help you there! I've no idea about any of that. That was a husband's business, as far as your father was concerned."

"You mean *Joseph*. *Not* my father." Bridie looks up, bewildered, but somehow Joy can't stop herself. "You mean, as far as *Joseph* was concerned, it was a husband's business." She repeats this with slow emphasis, as if her mother is deaf or doesn't speak English. Bridie blinks at her, uncomprehending.

Joy sighs. "I'll look in his desk. Now, can I have the keys, please?"

"His desk?" says Bridie, alarmed. "Oh, I don't think he'd like that. Not one bit!"

Seeing real fear in her eyes, Joy reminds herself her mother is in shock. She sits at the kitchen table, takes Bridie's hand and forces herself to adopt the tone she would use with a labouring mother at the end of her tether. "Joseph isn't here to object, you know, Mammy," she says. "And we really need to get into that desk, if we're to find out what he wanted. If you can't lay hands on the key, I could probably take a screwdriver to it."

"A screwdriver! Whatever are you thinking? That desk was his father's and precious to him, so it was. Have I not raised you to respect other people's property?" Bridie tuts indignantly, but Joy senses her wavering. "I'll have to see if I can lay hands on the key. A screwdriver, indeed!"

In the end, the key is easily found but the desk yields little more than a neat file of personal papers. Joseph has left his affairs in order, whatever chaos he may have inflicted in life. There is a straightforward will leaving all his worldly goods to his widow, signed and dated soon after Joseph and Bridie's marriage, which according to the attached wedding certificate took place in Liverpool Register Office in 1947.

It strikes Joy for the first time that this certificate is the only evidence that the marriage ever took place. In even the humblest homes in her district in Liverpool, a black-and-white photograph in a cheap gilt frame graces the mantlepiece. Yet she's never seen a wedding picture at St James' End.

"Were there no photographs of your wedding?" she asks Bridie, who hovers at her side.

"Oh no," says her mother with a shake of her head. "Nothing like that."

"Was I there? I don't remember a thing about it."

"Of course you were, my lovely. But it was a very quiet affair, you know."

"But what about . . . I don't know. Bridesmaids. Flowers. A wedding dress. You must surely have had all of that?"

"Ah, no! There was no call for any of that malarkey. It wasn't long after the War, remember. We were still under rationing, so we were!"

"And Liverpool Register Office?" Joy voice betrays her disbelief. Her mother's faith runs deep. Joy can't remember her ever missing Mass. "Did you not want a church wedding, Mother?"

Bridie snatches the certificate from her hand. "It's not always what you want in life that you get, Joy. You know that."

Joy lets it go. Bridie has been a widow for barely twenty-four hours; is it any wonder that she's touchy? She turns her attention back to the desk. There's a pile of bank statements, neatly clipped together with a bulldog clip, and dating back over the last two or three years. And the paperwork associated with Joseph's recent purchase of a two-year-old Ford Cortina.

"Oh, look!" says Joy. "Good news. He had a life insurance policy." This last is a relief, as Bridie's been fretting almost as much about whether Felicity will be able to take up her place at the Royal College of Music as she is about her absence. Finally, underneath everything else, there's a foolscap envelope, sealed and marked STRICTLY PRIVATE AND CONFIDENTIAL. The envelope bears an unfamiliar but impressive coat of arms, a pair of crossed keys.

"What's that you've got there?" asks Bridie.

"I'm not sure. You have a look." Joy passes it to her mother, and slightly to her surprise, given Bridie's earlier squeamishness about Joseph's privacy, her mother slides a finger under the flap and opens the envelope without hesitation.

"Ah yes, I thought it would be that," she says, closing it up again after a quick glance at the contents.

"What is it?"

"A letter from the Holy Father himself, would you believe it. Ancient history now, my lovely."

"From the Holy Father? You're not serious? Why on earth would the Pope write to Joseph?"

"That's between him and our Lord. Nothing to concern you," says Bridie, and tucks the envelope firmly under her arm. Joy opens her mouth to speak and then closes it again, because she can't imagine how to frame the question.

"Now then, what about Father Adrian? Is it not time we were boiling the kettle for his visit?" says Bridie. "The man likes his biscuits, I tell you, so if there are none in the tin, you'll need to be out for a refill of the custard creams."

———

Felicity arrives the next day. Joy happens to be in the street putting the dustbin out, so sees the Bentley turn into St James' End before her mother does. Her sister is slumped in the front seat, fast asleep. She wakes abruptly when Uncle Norman draws up outside Number 12. Joy reads the confusion that crosses her face as she comes to, remembers where she is and why. She opens the car door, pushes past Joy without a word, and launches herself into her mother's arms, crying messily.

"Oh Mammy!" she sobs. "I can't believe it! It's so awful!"

"Come on, my lovely, you're safe home now," says Bridie, taking her in her arms. "I've the kettle on for you. Let's be making ourselves a pot of tea now."

Uncle Norman retrieves Felicity's suitcase from the boot, but declines to come in. "I'm all spent, love," he tells Joy, and it's true, his face is grey with exhaustion. "Time to get myself home to Marjorie. I'll be back in the morning if I can."

"Of course," says Joy. It dawns on her for the first time that Uncle Norman has lost his only brother. For all she knows, he loved Joseph. As for her aunt, she hasn't spared her a thought in all the drama. "You must be exhausted. You've been on the road for ever. How was it? Utterly ghastly?"

"Hah! That niece of mine wasn't best pleased to see me, that much I can tell you," he says. "I suppose I gave her a right old shock. As for that young man! Went as white as a sheet when I turned up on the doorstep. Couldn't see him for dust once he knew the game was up, the little toerag. I've a good mind to take a strap to him! Not that young Felicity would thank me for that. She's a strong-willed miss, isn't she?"

He shuts the boot and goes round to the driver's door. "Still, Bridie will be happier now her lost lamb's home, I suppose," he adds, nodding in the general direction of the house. "No need to tell your mother about the camping trip that never was, eh? I think she's got enough on her plate for now."

"Don't worry. What the eye doesn't see, the heart doesn't grieve over. I'll leave well alone. Thanks, Uncle Norman. I'm so grateful. Mother, too."

"Don't be daft." Norman's voice is brusque. "You're family, aren't you? What else was I going to do?"

Joy stands at the garden gate and watches Uncle Norman drive to the end of St James' End and then left onto the Harlestone Road. She stands there, her hand raised in an awkward half-wave, long after the Bentley is out of sight.

She is suddenly aware that she, too, is bone-tired, even without the drive from Cornwall. She longs for her bed back home in Liverpool. A hot-water bottle under the feather eiderdown she treated herself to when she passed her midder exams. With a sigh, she clips shut the garden gate and heads indoors to see how her mother and sister are faring.

FELICITY

1970

When Felicity wakes, it is with a sinking feeling. It is light, but hideously early; she can hear birdsong outside her window. For a split second, she can't put her finger on what's bothering her. And then she remembers: it is her birthday, and she's told no one. Not a soul in London knows that today is the day she leaves her teens for her twenties.

Twenty today! She feels so old. Old and tired. Twenty is so very much older than eighteen. She's had to grow up fast in the last two years, and that weighs heavily. Thinking back to her eighteenth . . . well, she was a mere child then, surely, for all that she thought then she'd crossed the threshold into adulthood.

Her eighteenth birthday is burned into her memory, a patchwork of ugly scar tissue. Her father's knock on the door with the usual offer of a cup of tea, and his surprise when she refused him entry. She could feel his shock and hurt from the landing. She pulled her dressing gown close around her and put two fingers up in the direction of the door, the childishness of the gesture he couldn't see making her giggle. Her very last A-level paper looming—rotten luck, at one level, to have an exam on your birthday, but wonderful, too, because it provided a double reason to celebrate that night. She'd just have time to nip home and pack between the exam and going round to Lucy's for the leavers' party.

And that night was a big night for a third reason. She was going to sleep with Malcolm. She'd promised him—he'd been nagging for weeks—and they had it all planned, followed by a whole glorious secret week together in St Ives. (As far as her parents were concerned, she was going camping with a gang from school. The poor innocents! It was almost embarrassing, the ease with which she'd pulled the wool over their eyes.) She absolutely couldn't wait. A crossing of the Rubicon that gave her the courage to reject Daddy's knock at the door. *I am an adult. I make my own decisions.*

Pathetic, she thinks now. *What a child I was. Thinking I was in love with Malcolm, that he'd look after me. That we'd be together for ever. Pathetic!* She turns over in bed and sighs deeply. *And that was the last time I ever saw Daddy.*

Now she really *is* an adult, Felicity has decided to dispense with birthdays altogether. Last year—when she was still fumbling about in the fog of shock and confusion that enveloped her after her father's death—she went home out of duty. And it had been utterly awful, for all that Mammy did her best, giving her a hideous mohair cardigan she'd knitted herself, and Uncle Norman insisted on taking them out to the Berni Inn for dinner.

"Well, would you just look at that, girls?" twittered Mam. "Have you ever seen a piece of melon all dressed up like it's going to a party?" Aunt Marjorie glowered from the other side of the table. Joy, home from Africa on furlough and sitting next to her aunt, caught Felicity's glance and rolled her eyes almost imperceptibly.

"What are you thinking, Marjorie? The melon boat or the prawn cocktail? And have you seen the fancy sweet trolley? Isn't this kind of your uncle and aunt, girls?"

Then there was a fuss about the wine, because Bridie asked for Babycham, and Aunt Marjorie shuddered visibly, saying she'd prefer a glass of claret, thank you, if she was eating steak, so Uncle Norman ordered both, and Aunt Marjorie tutted about that, too. Felicity's heart sank because the smell of all that meat made her feel positively sick, but she didn't think now was the time to tell them she'd become a vegetarian.

"Well, aren't I the lucky one, dining in the company of four such lovely ladies!" said Uncle Norman just too heartily when the drinks arrived. "Let me propose a toast to our birthday girl. Many happy returns, Felicity! And here's to the memory of my dear departed brother, who was so very proud of you. May he rest in peace, God bless him." Uncle Norman's voice began to tremble, and then Mammy blew her nose messily.

"*Must* you, Norman?" hissed Marjorie. "Honest to God, you're making a spectacle of us. You, too, Bridget. Pull yourselves together!"

Surprisingly, it was Joy who salvaged the situation by turning to Aunt Marjorie and asking her how the garden was holding up after such a long dry spell of weather and explaining the complicated irrigation measures used by the garden boy at the Mercy Clinic, where the survival of the crops was the difference between eating and going hungry. *Nothing bothers her*, Felicity thought. *And how on earth does she know all that stuff about planting and watering and staving off fruit flies?*

"Well, I don't know how you stand it, all that dirt and poverty," said Aunt Marjorie with a sniff. The claret had stained her lips an unattractive purple. "And the flies! Very insanitary, if you ask me. Each to their own, I suppose."

"But Marjorie, aren't you always the one for good works?" asked Mammy. And that provoked a long monologue from Aunt Marjorie about the various committees on which she served and the patience needed in the face of the shortcomings of her fellow volunteers. Felicity was impressed. When did Joy become so adroit at pouring oil on troubled water? There she sat, as matter-of-fact as anything, but she'd cleverly diverted Aunt Marjorie's fire power away from Mammy and towards another target.

Never again, thought Felicity then. It was bad enough at Christmas. She certainly wasn't spending another birthday with Aunt Marjorie. Better just to forget the date altogether. And it wasn't difficult; it was July and after the end of term and most of the students had packed up and gone home for the long vacation. (Not Felicity: the thought of being marooned at St James' End for any longer than necessary doesn't bear thinking of. She told Mammy she's taking extra classes over the summer and will be going on holiday with friends before the new academic year. She'll need to squeeze in a duty visit to Northampton at some point.)

Thanks to her scholarship, the rent is covered, and she's found herself one job, possibly two, that will keep the wolf from the door once the last few pounds of her grant runs out. Five days a week she's serving coffee at Giovanni's, a tiny Italian espresso bar on the corner of Dean Street. Gio is a frightful queen, but that's no skin off her nose. Par for the course in

Soho, really, and one less thing to worry about as he insists she wears a very short skirt to work ("Good for trade, *cara!*"). At least she knows it's only the customers' hands she needs to keep an eye on.

Fingers crossed, she is hopeful of at least a couple of late-night sessions a week playing jazz piano at O'Donovan's, when her friend Billy Ginger leaves for France. Billy is a brilliant musician, a class act. And destined for greatness: he's landed a top gig at a jazz club in the ninth *arrondissement* in Paris. In all honesty, jazz isn't her forte, but that makes it all the more appealing, because it's something new.

Since the catastrophic loss of her voice, Felicity has felt the need to push the boundaries in every other way possible. There's some sort of logic in experimenting with other musical forms: ever since that wretched psychotherapist suggested her problem was psychosomatic, she's decided to throw herself at every opportunity. To try new things. It is her secret mission to be as spontaneous as her sister is plodding. She clings to the faint hope that if she absorbs herself in anything *but* singing, she'll stop fretting about her voice. And once she stops caring, well, maybe one day she'll wake up and just open her mouth and the music will pour out.

Shall I . . . ? she wonders. *A little warm up? Some vocal exercises? Just to see?* She gets out of bed and stretches. Arms above the head. Loosen the neck. Perhaps today will be the day. A surprise birthday present, maybe? Wriggle the face. Move her mouth around with a chewing motion. Yawn. Breathe. Then . . .

No. Nothing. Absolutely nothing. I can't, I can't, I can't! She throws herself back on the bed and pulls the covers over her head.

———

An hour later and Felicity's alarm wakes her. Time to get dressed and go to work. Birthday or no birthday, she just has to get through the day and out the other side. At least tomorrow she has her first gig at O'Donovan's. Something else to focus on.

She dresses in the short black skirt—the hem is coming undone at the back, but a strip of Sellotape soon fixes that—and a cleanish white blouse that is almost respectable and pulls on her tasselled suede jacket as an outer layer against the wind. It may be July, but summer doesn't seem to have arrived in London. Is it too hot for the boots that Lucy gave her? Lucy is now a dental nurse and has a very rich boyfriend who lives in a mansion flat in Kensington. He's always buying her wildly extravagant presents. The boots—made of stretchy red vinyl with black laces all up the front—are a size five and definitely too small for Lucy who's easily a six. They fit Felicity like a glove.

"Ooh, you lucky so-and-so!" said Lucy when Felicity tried them on. "They're perfect on you! Sexy as hell. How did you end up with such small feet when your legs go on for ever? Now I feel like one of Cinderella's ugly sisters!"

"Won't Patrick mind you giving away his present?" asked Felicity, for politeness' sake.

"He won't even notice," said Lucy. "Honestly, Felicity, he's completely hopeless. He buys things on a whim. It's my fault for admiring them in Biba the other week. They look great on you."

Felicity decides she'll wear the boots. They do show off her long legs to great effect. Gio will be in raptures, and it's worth keeping him on side if she wants to keep her tips. And it is her birthday, after all. Her sexy red boots will be a quiet nod to that. Her secret.

On her way out of her digs, she checks her pigeon-hole where she finds two cards and a third envelope, unstamped. One card (flowers and loopy gold writing) is from Mammy and another (some sort of leaves that are presumably African) from Joy. Joy's arrived three days ago, in fact, because that's how organized she is, but Felicity left it there deliberately. (She already knows without opening it what it will say: *Happy birthday, love from Joy*. No more, no less. You can rely on Joy never to have an original thought.) She tucks them into her bag, comforted, in spite of herself. She shouldn't be snooty about her sister's reliability. To get a card to arrive all the way from Africa at more or less the right date shows thoughtfulness. *Twenty*, she thinks. Twenty years old and two years since Daddy's death. Well, since she last saw him, anyway.

What a simpleton she was! Thinking she was so grown up, and that her adult life was about to begin. Then within days, her father dead, unceremoniously dumped by Malcolm, and her hopes for the future well and truly dashed when she opened her mouth to sing a solo at his funeral and found herself unable to utter a note. ("You're upset," said Mammy. "Understandable," said Uncle Norman. "Histrionics," said Joy.)

No matter how hard she tried, she still couldn't shake off the idea that Daddy's death was her fault. Did he find out what she was up to in Cornwall—that she'd lied to her parents and was away with a boy—and drop dead with shock? Worse still, did he drive into that lamp post deliberately because he was so ashamed of his precious little girl? Or was he distracted, wondering why she refused to open the door on the morning of her birthday? Round in circles the thoughts swirled, tying her in knots of remorse. And *anger*. What a legacy! Was she going to have to carry this burden of guilt for the rest of her life?

As for Malcolm—their great adventure hadn't even been much fun, because their landlady most definitely didn't buy the story about them being newly-weds, in spite of the ring he'd won in a slot machine, that seemed so sweet at the time. She was decidedly sniffy and made no attempt whatsoever to hide her delight at being proved right when Uncle Norman turned up to fetch her home. Talk about embarrassing.

(The weather had been atrocious, and the sex hadn't been much better, because Malcolm was always in such a hurry, so that her main emotion when he abandoned her so unceremoniously was actually relief that it was all over. But there was still a sense of humiliation because Malcolm and she had been going out for six months and thought they were Romeo and Juliet. All that—and then it was over in minutes. Now she wonders if perhaps Malcolm had been as relieved as she was. Perhaps he was just waiting for an excuse to call time. But that was mortifying, too. At least he didn't leave her up the duff. That was the first thing Joy asked, would you believe it! As if they didn't know how to take precautions.)

Excruciating it may have been, but Uncle Norman was a brick, rescuing her like that. She owed him for that. He'd had sharp words with Malcolm at the guesthouse, and then didn't mention his name again all the way home.

All seven hours or whatever it was. Just let her cry until she fell asleep and then bought her lunch at a greasy spoon somewhere near Bristol.

But of course she didn't know, for certain, that he wouldn't tell Mammy. All the way back, she'd worried about what he would do. (And there was Joy at the door, her arms crossed and her lips pursed in disapproval.) She carried on worrying all through the interminable days before the funeral, all through the long weeks afterwards before she went off to college. He'd even driven her down to London to help her settle in.

That was when she finally tackled him, right at the very last minute, when they were actually in the car park at St Agnes Court. "Thank you, Uncle Norman. Thank you for not saying anything. Not telling Mammy. About Cornwall, I mean."

"And why would I do that, eh?" Uncle Norman tucked his big car into a tiny parking space with apparent ease and switched off the engine. "Don't you think your poor Ma had enough to worry about without your shenanigans to distress her?"

"You've been very good to us," said Felicity, suddenly deeply ashamed.

"You're family," said Uncle Norman heavily. "Your father would have looked out for Marjorie if the tables were turned." Felicity wondered if that were true. Uncle Norman was a sweetheart, really; a softer version of her father. A little shorter, plumper, and altogether gentler. She asked herself why on earth she minded so much, anyway, Mammy finding out. It was Daddy she was afraid of.

"The past is the past, anyhow," said Uncle Norman, looking straight ahead. "Just see you study hard and make a success of yourself. Make proper use of your gifts and all that education you had. Make us all proud. Your Dad especially. You know he worshipped the ground you walked on. Couldn't put a foot wrong in his eyes. So don't let us down, eh?"

"I'll do my best," said Felicity, feeling her eyes fill with tears. "If only I could sing," she added in a small voice.

"Oh you'll soon sort yourself out, once you've got yourself straight," he said unlocking his seatbelt. "And you've still got your old Joanna, haven't you? No point moaning, now, is there? Now, shall we go and find these digs of yours?"

There was no medical reason why she couldn't sing, apparently. Nothing technically wrong with her vocal cords. No nodules or polyps or cysts. She didn't smoke, and she didn't have allergies. It wasn't rheumatoid arthritis, thank goodness, or that would have put paid to the piano playing. It was simply that, hard on the heels of her father's heart attack, the Grim Reaper had struck a second time and killed her voice.

Eventually, the Head of Voice (an insufferably smug man called Lorenzo Alessi who made a great deal of his Italian heritage, insisting on being addressed as *Maestro* even though everyone knew he was from Peckham) lost patience and suggested she concentrated on her piano.

"I can't teach you if you won't give me anything to *work* with, *tesoro*," he said with a heavy sigh. "Shame, really. I had some slight hopes when you came to audition. But now's the time to find out if you can't hack it as a singer. Saves heartache all round in the end. Stick to the ivories, I would. Or find a nice rich husband and save yourself the trouble. You're a pretty enough creature."

Ugh! She loathed him, the slimy creep. How dare he imply she wasn't a serious musician? *Bet you don't tell the chaps to find themselves a nice rich wife.* And to insinuate that she had a *choice* about her inability to sing! That it was some kind of feeble mindedness, instead of a . . . a tragedy.

Yes. *Tragedy* wasn't too strong a word for it. It was her personal tragedy—a catastrophic bereavement—and she'd never felt so lonely in her life. No one understood the loss she was experiencing. True, she had the piano to fall back on. But it was little solace when every time she played her father's ghost hovered accusingly over the keys.

—

At the end of her shift at the coffee bar, she wonders if she can face going back to her digs on her own. She feels tired and flat. While she was dead right about the boots—Gio adored them—he'd disappeared off to the cash-and-carry for most of the day, leaving her with his uncommunicative cousin Mario to serve a constant tide of tourists all on her own.

It is only when she is putting her wages in her bag that she remembers the note she found in her pigeon-hole that morning. She slips a finger under the flap and draws out a letter in an unfamiliar hand. *Dear Felicity,* she reads. *It was so good to meet you at Chris's party the other night. I enjoyed our conversation very much. I wonder if you might like dinner one evening? Drop round any time on the off chance—or try the call box on our corridor. Someone usually answers eventually. Very best wishes, David (Hetherington).*

David (Hetherington) . . . which one was he? She remembers the party—a twenty-first, a friend of a friend—but she isn't entirely sure she could place him. Boys do tend to buzz around her. It can be a bit of a nuisance. And she'd had quite a lot to drink, as is her wont. It helps numb things. Daddy would be appalled. He didn't think women should drink at all, bar the odd glass of sweet sherry at Christmas.

Was he the boy with the floppy dark hair who was going to change the world? He was rather charming. A bit earnest, maybe, but sweet. He was staying in London for the summer because he had some kind of holiday job as a researcher in the House of Commons. Or the blond one who was so keen on rowing? On second thoughts, she thinks the rower was called Robin.

Either way she likes this chap's handwriting. Confident, but also elegant. And polite. She hopes it was the dark one. Looking at the address, his hall of residence is practically on the way home. (What would Joy do? Go home and have a bath, probably.) Well, why not? She'll swing by and say hello. He's unlikely to be free at such short notice. But she's meant to be trying new things, isn't she? And better than being on her own and miserable. She'll risk a date with David (Hetherington).

BRIDIE

2019

Mother? I know that voice. Joy. Ever practical, my Joy. Ever since she was a little girl.

Joy comes in the morning, I want to say. *Gah!* comes out instead.

Gah to you, too, says she, and I can hear a bubble of laughter in her voice.

How are you, today, Mother? Flick says she left you fast asleep yesterday. Sleeping like a baby. Her very words, can you believe it? I told her that wasn't how I remember her babyhood. A rotten description, if ever there was one.

I feel her take my hand in hers, and all at once I feel better. Safe. It should be the other way round. A mother should make her daughter feel safe. But I was so young when she came into this world, you might say we grew up together. Ill-equipped at seventeen, perhaps, but all sorts of unlikely things happen in a War.

And when Veronica was killed, what choice did I have? There was no one else. No one but me. I wasn't going to see her sent to an orphanage, for the love of God. A happy twist of fate, some might say. God's good purposes, say I. My own little miracle.

She was always my best beloved, my wee Joy. But she had a way of shrugging off too much affection. Politely, mind, the way you might take off a coat when you come indoors from the cold. A sort of self-defence after all she'd been through? Yet I fought so hard to make sure she felt loved. That she knew she belonged with me. Always had done. Her nursemaid, her rescuer. Her *Mammy* in the end, with the paperwork to prove it.

I never let her out of my sight. She went everywhere with me. With hindsight, you could say we were a happy little unit before Joseph came along. No need to get married. We'd scraped by all right on our own, hadn't we? We'd have found a way through life, somehow or other.

Without Joseph . . . well, without Joseph there'd have been a lot less pain, I'll grant you that. But there'd have been no home. No nice new council house overlooking the park with its green space and fresh air, and St Anthony's just down the road. No Mrs Kelly of St James' End sharing the *craic* with the neighbours over the garden fence.

And above all, no Felicity. And that doesn't bear thinking of. It's all too easy to be wise after the event, so it is. You do your best, don't you? Just sometimes, you have to live with your mistakes.

When he died, it was Joy I wanted. Felicity was away from home, on her holidays in Cornwall, and no telephone. Celebrating the end of A-levels, thank you very much! And that was before she'd even had her results through. A bit of a gamble, if you ask me, though Felicity was always going to do well. There was a boyfriend, if I remember, and Joseph not a bit happy about it. Said she was too young. Whatever was the fellow's name? But then no one was good enough for our Felicity, that's for sure. He might have met his match in that husband of hers, for all they never met. They'd have fought like dogs.

Joy was back in Liverpool then. Gone back to her roots, or some such nonsense. I was proud of her, mind. Proud as anything, though pride's a sin, if you believe the nuns. There's a girl who unlike her sister struggled with her schoolwork since the year dot. Muddled her letters and not much better on the numbers. (There's a fancy name for it, now. Finn told me.) And there's Joseph, for the love of Mary, insisting she's thick as a brick and will never amount to anything, just because she isn't a great one for the exams. Honest to God, he only had to take a look at Norman to know better than that. Norman made his way in the world without letters after his name, didn't he? There were terrible rows between Joseph and Joy. It broke my heart, though I didn't know the half of it then.

So she takes herself off to Liverpool, and makes a life for herself with no help from him. Qualifies as a nurse, no less, and then a midwife, would you believe it? It suits her personality. Miss Sensible, she's always been. Miss Brisk, on occasions too. Just what you need in a hospital. Stand up to those fancy-pants doctors who think they know best. A birthing mother wants a woman at her side, any day. What does a man know about all that's going on down below, I ask you?

At first, she writes that the poverty's terrible. A bit of a shock, after genteel Northampton. Mams and bairns living in tenements not fit for human habitation, so she tells me. I could tell her some stories, so I could.

But by the time Joseph makes me a widow, it's all change in Liverpool. Pop music and dancing and the height of fashion. That last Christmas Joy comes home with her hair swept up and glued in place with lacquer and wearing a mini skirt that's barely decent, so help me God. In my heart of hearts, I'm not sure she has quite the legs for making such a show of herself, but I'm not going to say so, as it's my hunch that she's only wearing it to get a rise out of her father.

It was Norman that called me with the news. We'd only just had the telephone put in, so there was a blessing. Properly shaken up, he sounded. No surprise, it being so sudden, and Joseph barely sixty. It seems he was on his way back to the factory for the monthly sales meeting but never made it. Huge heart attack and died at the wheel of that Ford Cortina he was so proud of. No one else involved, thank the good Lord, the only other victim of the crash being a lamp post.

I had my little job at the newsagent by then, but it was mornings only, and I'd just put a stew of scrag end in the oven for our tea.

And my first thought when Norman tells me is, *Who's going to eat that now, because I'm certainly not going to. What a sinful waste. My Joseph will surely purse his lips and scold me for the extravagance, so he will.*

JOY

1979

Joy stands at the foot of the stairs, listening hard. She thinks the boys have finally settled. Jacob, nearly two, is doubtless curled up in his cot, thumb in his mouth and rear end raised heavenwards, but you can never be entirely sure with Alexander. At four, Alex is an expert in playing for time. He's already tried needing a wee and asking for a drink of water. And he certainly pushed Joy to the far limits of her tolerance with his demand for extra stories.

Of course Joy loves reading to them both. Jacob, in particular, installs himself on her lap and snuggles up with no embarrassment. Alexander is a little warier, but always ends up leaning against her. It's her secret pleasure to feel the warmth of his pyjama-clad body against hers, as he shuffles along the sofa and tucks himself under her arm when he thinks she's not looking. He likes to pretend that he wants better sight of the pictures, but Joy prefers to believe he's not immune to a little human comfort. Nor is she. At least where her nephews are concerned.

The rule is that the boys share the first couple of stories, and when Jacob is tucked up in his cot with the musical mobile to soothe him to sleep Alexander is allowed to choose another book all of his own.

Tonight, he brought her *Where the Wild Things Are*, which Joy hasn't come across before. The illustrations show huge and rather terrifying monsters. But she can see the appeal: the character Max reminds her distinctly of Alexander as a toddler when he was prone to frightening outbursts of fury, especially in the weeks after Jacob's birth. The ending is rather wonderful: Max realizes he is lonely and returns home from his adventures to find his supper still hot and waiting for him.

It's clearly a great favourite with Alexander: he silently mouths the words in time with her reading. Nonetheless, there's a limit to how many times Joy feels it reasonable to read it to him. Whatever his mother's view on bedtime (and Joy suspects Felicity is almost certainly lax) Joy is not prepared to have her whole evening monopolized by a small child. Besides, as she's told her sister on more than one occasion, they will all suffer tomorrow if the children are fractious and tired.

Still, it's been a good ten minutes now and there's no sound of movement upstairs. Joy decides she can clock off. She goes into the kitchen in search of supper: a narrow strip of a room—with tired cupboards and an ancient Aga and every surface heaped with dirty dishes—that offers a fine view through French windows of the overgrown garden and rolling hills in the distance. It's all so green! Even allowing for the fact that it is June, when the countryside always looks its best, she's struck all over again by the verdant surroundings.

Rural Oxfordshire is a world away from the streets of Liverpool. When she's there, she never thinks twice about her surroundings: it's simply home. Her adopted city. But actually, things are going badly in Liverpool. After something of a post-war boom, the city is down on its luck, and it shows. She'd been quite shocked by the change when she came back from South Africa last year. The great port of the British Empire upon which the city's fortunes were built is now a shadow of its former self; in the last few years, factory after factory has closed, casting generations of men and women out of work and onto the dole. She sees the hopelessness in the eyes of her mothers. You can't miss the boarded-up shops, the abandoned vehicles. You can practically smell the despair on the streets.

This, though! The village of Summersby is a glorious green Garden of Eden in Middle England. The air smells sweet and fresh and the birds are singing. She could scarcely believe her eyes when she pulled up outside. She glances outside now, to check on her Mini; it's the first car she's owned, and her pride and joy. Till now, she's always made do with the bus. Now she's done it, Joy can't believe she waited so long. She adores driving: the feel of the engine, the sense of freedom it affords her. Minnie is racing green, and classy. Second-hand, but only two years old and in very good repair. Quite a nip to the engine, too. Not that David is impressed, what with his shiny new Volvo estate.

And really, Felicity and David have fallen on their feet here, even if The White House is scruffy, the paintwork chipped, and the kitchen in need of a refit. ("The White House!" laughed Felicity. "I know you won't believe me, but that's honestly what it was already called. No delusions of grandeur, I promise.")

They've only been in for a couple of months, and there are still some crates to unpack, but it has great possibilities, as David has told her more than once. He has grand plans for an extension, a big open-plan kitchen and a conservatory. They were lucky to find somewhere in the area quite so quickly. Doubtless it helped that David's father gave them a substantial sum of money towards the purchase, and that his grandparents left him a small flat in Chelsea, which is ideal for when Parliament is in session. It's been such a whirlwind since the election. David is one of a clutch of newly elected Conservative MPs in their twenties. The bright young hope of the future, apparently.

And what a brave new world it seems to be, with a massive swing to the Tories ousting a tired Labour Government, and a woman Prime Minister. Not only a first for Britain, but the very first elected female head in Europe. You can't help admiring that.

"Marvellous woman!" David informed her before lunch, starry eyed. "It's that combination of a razor-sharp mind and a housewifely common sense that's so impressive. Amazing charisma. I feel honoured to be part of her team."

"Have you met her?" asked Joy. "Personally, I mean?"

"Well, no." David looked a little deflated. "Far too junior for that, I'm afraid! Though she gave all us new MPs a marvellously rousing speech on our first day in office. And she definitely caught my eye on her way out. Smiled at me. What a day that was! Like the first day at school, but a hundred times better."

"Hmm," said Joy. He really was an overgrown public schoolboy.

"Hmm *what*? Whatever do you mean?" He loomed over her, standing just too close for comfort in the narrow kitchen. "Surely you're not one of those ghastly Trotskyist pinkos?" David's laugh was brash and devoid of humour. His question left little room for contradiction.

"All I'm saying is that I'll wait and see what your shiny new Government does for Liverpool. I don't follow politics, but you only have to open your eyes to see that Merseyside's in poor shape. Not to mention the NHS. Say what you like about Labour, but at least they made a big thing of the NHS in their campaign."

David immediately launched into a spirited defence of his party. With inflation going through the roof and unemployment well over a million, surely she can see that the country needs a firm hand? "And what about the Winter of Discontent?" he demanded, as if it were Joy's personal responsibility. "You of all people must know the damage that did! I mean, what about the gravediggers' strike? Insupportable! Shocking! How can you defend any of that?"

"Darling, *please*," said Felicity, trying to lift a fish pie out of the Aga while balancing Jacob on her hip. "You sound like you've swallowed the party manifesto! Do give us a break. It's Saturday and you're not on a hustings platform. Can't we put the politics on one side just for a moment?"

"But Joy's got to understand—"

"David! Joy hasn't *got* to understand anything! Leave the poor girl in peace!" Felicity's voice was rising. No wonder: Jacob was whimpering, and Alexander had entangled himself in her legs. "Oh no! I think Jacob needs changing. That's all I need! Now the lunch will go cold."

"Let me take him," said Joy. "And Alexander, you come and help me find a clean nappy, and then we can both wash our hands ready for lunch. Let's go and sort ourselves out while Mummy finishes getting the food on the table."

Why David never lifts a finger to help, she thinks now as she opens the fridge, *is beyond me. How can he stand there, lecturing us all about the marvellous new woman PM, while he expects his wife to wait on him hand and foot? What a hypocrite! He's perfectly happy to be snapped with his photogenic young family, but has he ever in his life changed a nappy?* She can't imagine David foraging for his supper if he was the one left behind to babysit. He'd expect a plated meal in the bottom of the Aga.

Mind you, would the circumstances ever arrive? She can't envisage Felicity leaving David unsupervised in charge of the boys. His own sons! Maybe it's her sister's fault? Does she collude in his domestic helplessness? What about all that women's lib that Felicity was so keen on when she was a student? It seems to have gone out of the window. (Not that Felicity is a domestic goddess: Joy is going to have to tackle the kitchen with her Marigolds and a canister of Vim after supper.)

Now I sound horribly judgemental, she thinks. Who's to say Felicity's not perfectly happy running the house while David goes out and makes the world a better place? And David probably grew up with cooks and nannies, so perhaps he can't help being so useless. You can certainly see why he was elected. Young, strikingly good looking—even she will admit this—and highly eloquent, he would surely have made it in politics somehow even if he hadn't been lucky enough to be parachuted into a safe seat. He's a performer to his boots and knows how to take the crowd with him.

She wonders if they are having a good evening. It sounded unbearably tedious to Joy: a summer party arranged by the Chair of the Kings Burton Conservative Association to thank all those in the constituency who had campaigned so tirelessly during the election. Lots of glad-handing and small talk and smiling for photographs in *Oxfordshire Life*. Sprinkling a little fairy-dust on the good people of Kings Burton and its pretty ironstone villages. The man in whose footsteps David is following came from the landed gentry. Well liked and widely mourned when he dropped dead of a heart attack in the House of Commons barely a fortnight before Labour called the election, he nonetheless represents the past. David, with his university education and matinée idol looks, is the future.

Joy makes herself a ham and lettuce sandwich and wonders where to eat it. Although it's mid-June, she fears it will be too cold outside, because there's a chilly wind. She opens the French doors to investigate.

The garden is a jungle, but, like the house, there's potential galore. There's a generous patch of lawn, badly in need of mowing. Plenty of space for the boys to kick a ball about when they're older, although knowing David, he may have his eyes on it for hosting dreary political functions and will be worried about the boys damaging the vista. Someone once took the trouble to plant a pretty herbaceous border on the left, though it's overgrown with weeds. At the far end, there's a well-stocked fruit cage, and a couple of fruit trees—apple and plums, by the look of things.

She thinks of her own neat semi, squeezed onto a corner plot as an afterthought, and robbed of its garden by the neighbours either side. Her little kitchen window box of herbs is the nearest she gets to growing anything. Joy feels momentarily bleak. She wouldn't know where to start with a garden like this, but the spaciousness, the peace and quiet is seductive. It seems to touch a part of her soul that she didn't know was in need of balm.

Yet how can she complain? Her house may lack a garden, but that's one reason it was in her price bracket. She knows she is lucky to have her own home. She's also aware she lives in luxury by the standards of the majority of her patients, let alone the families she worked with in South Africa.

The Mercy Clinic seems a world away now. Such a stunningly beautiful setting, with the undulating hills and the acres of green, green forest. How she misses the light of Africa! Yet such poverty and suffering, too. And an almighty struggle to keep the clinic going. Everything was a battle, from getting hold of medical supplies to ensuring they had adequate hot water. She'd never experienced such peaks of joy and troughs of despair. But it had been good, too. Really satisfying work.

For the first year or so, it was a matter of sorting out the chaos left behind by the former Matron, an elderly nun who had been going slowly blind for years, with the result that the care on offer was haphazard at best. Joy and her British colleague Mary Anne had to start from scratch in terms of restoring order and rebuilding trust in the community. Together they worked their socks off to turn things round, and their temporary contracts were extended. Eventually, a new Matron arrived, a Belgian nun called Sister Emmanuelle, and offered them both permanent positions. Mary Anne declined, homesick for London, but Joy accepted with the proviso she could return home for a month before starting. It was hard to escape the sense of responsibility for her mother.

Joy had been deeply happy at the Mercy. She had a great deal of respect for Sister Emmanuelle, who had trained in one of the best hospitals in Brussels, and they worked well together. If it hadn't been for the dreadful political situation—and thank goodness David didn't start quizzing her about *apartheid*, or she'd have probably been sent packing—she might have stayed for ever. But after years of battling to make do on a wing and a prayer, the Order finally threw in the towel and closed the clinic two years ago. It was a wretched blow when it fell but no great surprise. And slim consolation to know that they left behind a handful of excellent local midwives, trained at the Mercy, who would continue their work in the community.

—

Joy decides it's too cold for supper in the garden. There's a cool breeze; she'll eat inside, probably from a tray in front of the television, two fingers up to Father who forbade the practice. She takes herself indoors, into what she mistakenly called the lounge when she first arrived. It is, David told her in no uncertain terms, the *sitting room*. Which when you think about it, is a pretty daft name. A whole room devoted to *sitting*? True, there's a smart new three-piece suite, but the floor is littered with Jacob's bricks, and Alexander is clearly halfway through building a model railway in the corner by the window. "They need a proper playroom," says David. "I've got the architect on to that."

At the other end of the room, almost obstructed by the sofa, sits Felicity's piano, the famous Broadwood given to her by Aunt Marjorie. (Where will that go in the new order? In the playroom, because you *play* the piano or in the sitting room because you *sit* at the instrument? The rules of the upper-middle class are mysterious. David will know, naturally. Those deeply held convictions of what is socially acceptable are his birth right.)

The current arrangement doesn't exactly invite use of the piano. Is Felicity playing at all these days, or is she too worn down by moving and motherhood? Thank goodness she's well, though. Poor Felicity had the baby blues after Jacob was born. It had been pitiful to see her crumble. The uncontrollable crying, the paralysing anxiety. David was out of his depth; thank heavens that Joy had been back in the country and there to give her a hand.

Poor Flick; she'll freeze to death in that dress if the party is in someone's garden. And it will be, surely; it's so British, to insist on eating outside just because it's summer and not actually raining. Flick's dress is full length but made of some kind of flimsy floral fabric. Almost transparent, in fact. Joy heard her arguing with David earlier because she wanted to wear her favourite trouser suit—which surely would have been warmer on an unseasonal night like this—but David was insistent that only a dress would do. "This isn't London, remember! You need to try and fit in while we're in the country," he insisted. "Can't have you frightening the natives!"

Marriage! thinks Joy. Maybe she got off lightly. Imagine if she had married Richard (she can laugh about that silly crush, now, thank goodness) or anyone else for that matter? The idea that she might consult anybody about what to wear is ridiculous. Not that she cares about clothes, by and large, and unlike her sister, she'd never be anyone's idea of a decorative accessory. Joy's body is stocky and her face homely at best. ("You're no oil painting, but you've a kind face," was the best even her own mother could come up with.) Whereas Felicity has always been pretty, with her fair hair and those little-girl-lost eyes. ("Monday's child is fair of face," as Father was fond of saying, with a soppy grin.) Tall and graceful as a dancer, and barely an ounce gained in spite of two pregnancies.

Being single means Joy can please herself. Decisions are hers and hers alone, not only in matters of dress, but in all the everyday things like what she eats and when and where. How she spends her money. Her time. Children, mind you . . . Children, she would have loved. When her whole life is centred around mothers and babies, it's hard not to wonder what might have been. To admit what she's missing. ("There's still time, you know," says Mother. "You've time yet to meet someone.")

It's true; Joy is thirty-seven, although she'll be thirty-eight by Christmas, so it's theoretically possible. In her heart of hearts, she gave up hope years ago. (Who was she kidding?) Still, she's an honorary mother, hundreds of times over, if you think how many infants she's helped bring into the world. She has a wall full of photos, labelled with the child's name and birthday and birth weight. Something to remember "her" babies by.

A good thing she has these nephews to keep her busy, though it's a fair old way from Liverpool to Oxfordshire. Mind you, that will all be so much easier now she has Minnie the Mini and hasn't got to rely on the trains. And if Felicity's going to be busy being a political wife, perhaps it's good that Joy's not tied as well. It's one reason she felt she couldn't in all conscience seek out another job in Africa when the Mercy Clinic closed, for all that it was a terrible wrench to leave it all behind. Torn in two she may have been, but Joy has a duty as a daughter. Their mother's not exactly old, but she's hopelessly naïve and she's on her own. You never know when she might need help.

—

The next day begins early. The boys wake at the crack of dawn, no doubt exacerbated by the curtains that are not quite big enough to keep out the midsummer morning light. Joy hears Jacob crying, probably in need of a nappy change. There's an ominous thud followed by a cry from Alexander, and the sound of running footsteps as he hurtles out of his bedroom. *No*, thinks Joy. *I will not go and see what's happened. This is my weekend off.* She rolls towards the wall and pulls a pillow over her head.

When Joy comes down to breakfast, it's still only 8 o'clock. Felicity is in her dressing gown, listlessly feeding Jacob a boiled egg and soldiers. Alexander is sitting at the table drawing, surrounded by half-eaten sticky crusts from his toast. Felicity looks pale and tired, and rather cross; there are mascara stains under her eyes, and her hair is dishevelled. Of David, there's no sign.

"Can I make you a cup of tea?" asks Joy, filling the kettle at the kitchen sink.

"Please. Anything to prop my eyelids open."

"Have you eaten? What about some toast?"

Felicity shudders. "No thanks."

"You all right, Flick? You look a bit rough." Joy sweeps Alexander's discarded crusts into the bin and wipes the table around him. "There," she says. "Now you won't get crumbs on your drawing." Alexander looks up briefly, and then returns to his picture. There are four crudely drawn figures standing in front of a square house: Mummy, Daddy, two little boys.

"Just exhausted," says Felicity. "Late night and not enough sleep. Were they all right while we were out?"

"Good as gold," says Joy with a glance at an oblivious Alexander in case he's going to contradict her. "How was the party?"

"Oh . . . *fine*." There's a strained note, half laugh, half sob, in Felicity's voice.

"Fine?" The kettle comes to the boil, and Joy busies herself finding the teapot while her sister collects herself. "Fine as in . . . *not* fine at all?"

"It's just . . . you know, the usual. Pretty little Sloane Rangers in pie-crust collars, fawning all over David. Tory *grandes dames* with whiskers wanting to know if I'll be riding to hounds next season."

"Riding to hounds?"

"It means foxhunting. Do I *ride*, they want to know. Does David *shoot* . . . The implication being, *if not, why not*?"

"Good grief! It's another world! And what does David make of it all?"

"Loves it, of course." Felicity takes a swig of her tea. "It's as if all his Christmases have come at once. Especially the girls in pearls! They're mostly stunning. All perfect white teeth and flicky hair and cut-glass accents."

"Oh, come on, Flick. You can certainly hold your own there. I bet you caused a few ripples of your own in that see-through dress!"

Felicity laughs. "I suppose so. If you count an ancient colonel patting me on the bottom and complimenting David on his lovely wifey, I did all right. It's just not my world."

"*Wasn't* your world, perhaps. But it is now, surely?" Joy makes a sweeping gesture, encompassing the house in the countryside, the Aga, Alexander's little family.

Felicity groans. "Ignore me," she says. "I'm just so tired I could weep. That's motherhood for you."

"Are you sure that's all?"

"What do you mean?"

"Just that . . . you're not expecting again, are you?"

"Oh my stars, no!" says Felicity. "Why on earth do you ask?"

"Just wondered. Call it a hunch." Joy would put good money on it.

Felicity shudders. "Perish the thought! Imagine going through all *that* again . . . "

"You were fine after Alex, don't forget," says Joy. "And I'll help." She changes tack. "By the way, where is David?" She tries to keep her voice as neutral as possible.

"What do you think? Sleeping off the excesses of last night. Everyone's always topping up your glass at that sort of do, whether you want it or not. I was driving, but he drank like a fish. And he has a very demanding job, don't forget, so he needs to catch up on his sleep at weekends. Unlike me." She sighs again.

"Talking of which . . . when did you last play the piano?" asks Joy.

Felicity laughs. "About a hundred years ago. You've no idea what it's like with these two monsters!" She abandons the boiled egg and takes a flannel to Jacob's mouth. "I think we're done here, Jakey, aren't we? Come on out of there."

"Mo-ster!" shouts Jacob.

Joy watches her sister lift Jacob out of his highchair and onto her lap. She nuzzles the top of his head. "And you're a lovely monster, really, aren't you? Even if you are exhausting."

"*I* aren't a monster, Mummy," says Alexander. "Only babies are monsters. And I've drawed you a picture. Can I go and show it to Daddy?"

Felicity coos over the picture and kisses Alexander. "It's lovely, Alex, but let's let Daddy sleep a little bit longer. He's feeling very tired. He'll be up before long, though. He wants to take us all to church."

"Church?" Joy is surprised; much to their mother's distress, Felicity and David got married in a Register Office. After her father's death, Felicity comprehensively turned her back on the Church.

"It's a new thing," says Felicity, avoiding Joy's eye. "He likes us to show our faces at the village church. Important that we're pillars of the community. Good old C of E. It's all 'Onward, Christian Soldiers' and 'All Things Bright and Beautiful'. And there's a crèche, thank God."

"Goodness," says Joy, trying to digest this unlikely picture of her sister's Sunday mornings. "Tell you what, why don't you go back to bed for a bit? Get a bit of shut-eye while you have the chance? What do you think, young man?" she adds to Alex. "Can we manage the baby monster between us?"

FELICITY

1982

Felicity heaves a load of wet washing out of the machine into the laundry basket and carries it out into the garden. The grass is wet with dew and not quite warm enough under her bare feet. Still, it has the promise of a beautiful day.

And what bliss that it's half-term and there's no mad rush to get Alex and Jacob off to school. Alex isn't too bad—he takes his role as the responsible big brother almost too seriously—but Jacob always has to be prised out of bed and is frequently naughty about cleaning his teeth.

All of which would be manageable if it wasn't for Finn who seems to be teething again. Surely he must just about have a full set by now? Of all the boys, he's had the worst time with his teeth. Normally placid, he becomes dribbly and fretful, with flushed cheeks where the tooth is working its way through. Felicity ends up carrying him round the kitchen on her hip—though at almost two and a half he's far too big for that, really—while supervising the big boys one-handed. By the time they all get out of the house the breakfast table is a mess of spilled milk, bowls encrusted with soggy cereal and half-eaten pieces of cold toast which Felicity nibbles at on her return. She rarely has time for a proper breakfast of her own, partly because David hates her to leave the house without a close check of her appearance. Which is all very well, but he's never here to help with the morning chaos. From Monday to Thursday, when Westminster claims him, she might as well be a single mother.

Clothes, hair, make-up. *Camera ready*, he calls it. ("Don't forget— we're in the public eye these days," he says. "You never know when a photographer might be lurking.") Even on the school run Felicity wears smart little jackets and carefully ironed trousers. It's exhausting. Today, in contrast, she's wearing a faded old summer dress from her student days topped with a shapeless navy blue cotton cardigan. Her hair is unbrushed and tied back with an old red-and-white spotted handkerchief. She looks as scruffy as anything. *After running away to the circus*, her mother would say. The boys are still in their pyjamas.

David would be appalled, but he's safely in London, busier than ever now he's a junior minister and all the more so at the moment because of all the late-night sittings as a result of the ghastly situation in the Falklands. Felicity feels sick every time she thinks about it: she can't help but identify with all those mothers of sons on both sides of the conflict, dreading news of maiming, death or disappearance. (David assured her on the phone last night that the end is in sight now, adding, almost in passing, that the opinion polls show a massive swing in favour of the Government. She shudders at the thought of a war being good for anyone.)

Today, then. A beautiful late May day. She has no real plans beyond possibly taking a picnic up to Hangman's Wood. It should be full of bluebells and wild garlic at this time of year, which she will enjoy, and there's a rope-swing in the far corner which the boys adore. Finn's too small for the swing, but he likes running about in the hollows and hiding places. Last time they came across a wigwam of long branches and he took great pleasure in crawling in and out of the tiny entrance. He came home filthy, but happy as Larry. Felicity wonders who built it: it is painstakingly constructed, almost architecturally so, and must have taken hours to find the sticks, cut them to the right length, and then to put it all together. It looks as if it is built to last. She certainly hopes so.

She hangs out the washing, savouring a brief moment of peace. She probably ought to do some tidying today, but even if they stay at home all day, it's a losing battle. There will be spillages and quarrels, and complicated games like yesterday's which involved the contents of the kitchen cupboards being spread all over the floor. By the time she has scrabbled together something for supper and put the boys to bed, the house will still look like a bomb site. Quite honestly, she doesn't mind all that much. She'd rather spend her days having fun, particularly when David isn't here to tut. (Are any of David's precious constituents convinced by the camera-ready face they present to the world, she wonders? Surely anyone who has ever had three small children—not to mention an absent husband—must see through the veneer and know that the reality is much less well ordered?)

She finds herself groaning. Only last night she had to tell Helen Prendergast, the chair of the Conservative Association, that she wouldn't be taking part in the Association's annual tennis tournament. Helen is always nagging her to show her face at constituency events, with no apparent understanding that she has her hands full.

"I'm sorry, Helen, but it's half-term, and I've got the boys at home," Felicity said.

"Surely there's someone who can have them for the afternoon?" said Helen. "It's an important fundraiser, you know. Susan was always a *great* support. You didn't come last year, either, if I recall."

"No, I didn't," replied Felicity, firing off imaginary daggers in the direction of the wife of David's predecessor, and not for the first time. "It was half-term then, too, if I remember. And I'm sure you don't want three little boys getting under everyone's feet. No fun for anyone." *Least of all me, because they'd be bored stiff and start being naughty, and I'd be mortified.*

"I simply don't understand your generation. We always had nannies. I don't know why David doesn't get you an *au pair*, at least."

Felicity closed her eyes and took a couple of calming breaths. She wanted to scream. She wasn't sure if she was more annoyed by the suggestion that she was incapable of making childcare arrangements herself or by the implication that she would choose to squander the rare gift of child-free time on the blue rinse brigade and their precious tennis tournament.

"Well, I'm sorry, Helen," she said as firmly as she could. "But you should probably know I've never played tennis in my life, so I really don't think you're missing much by my staying away."

"Really? How extraordinary. What *do* you play then?"

"The piano, mostly. And I'm terribly sorry—I must dash—the boys are in meltdown. Hope it goes well. Bye!"

Unfair, she thinks now as she hangs out Jacob's precious Scooby Doo pyjama top. The boys were sitting on the sofa in enthralled silence watching *Blue Peter* while she was on the phone to Helen. *I traduced my babies and only further confirmed my failings in Helen's eyes.* She's disappointed Helen and her old biddies, and probably David too.

And told a white lie about playing the piano. She can't remember when she last lifted the lid. At the very least, the *very* least, she should be thinking about teaching Alex.

One reason that Helen has touched a nerve with her talk of *au pairs* is that she and David have been quarrelling about the boys' schooling. Helen's generation probably had all the time in the world for party events because not only did they have nannies, but they also packed their children off to boarding school. David was all for Alex going away to his old prep school in the autumn, but Felicity is dead set against. She can't believe they are even discussing it. Alex is only seven.

The little primary school here in Summersby is perfectly adequate. There are fewer than eighty children, and it's true that it's a little chaotic, with at least as much effort invested in country dancing as times tables because the head's a bit of an old hippie, but it's a happy place. Alex, who is a solemn child and apt to be shy with strangers, has settled in and overcome his initial reserve to make friends. Jacob has followed him with enthusiasm. Their progress is good, too: Alex, particularly, is bright and especially quick at Maths.

School is within walking distance of home, although in all honesty most mornings she ends up taking the car because they're running late. But they always walk home, and when they do it's as part of a cheerful tide of red-sweatshirted children, all of whom know each other, scattering variously to farms and cottages, council semis and detached houses such as their own.

Invitations to play and offers of lift-shares to Cubs and swimming lessons are plentiful, with the result that, three years after moving to Summersby, Felicity finally feels embedded in the community. She has *friends.* (Not necessarily the smart set David would like her to cultivate, but people who take her as they find her, who don't care two hoots that David is their MP. People to muddle through with. To share the load in all the unglamorous but practical tasks entailed in keeping the show on the road.) Why on earth would David want to pluck either of them from the security of their happy little world and banish them to boarding school and all its horrors?

Actually, she thinks she may finally have won the battle, almost by accident. "Oh, for goodness sake, David!" she'd said at the end of a long argument last weekend. "The teaching at Summersby is excellent. Why do you think all the parents are up in arms about the threat of closure?"

"Closure?"

"Yes! Apparently there are mutterings at County Hall that it's too small to be sustainable. I'd have thought you of all people would know!"

David cleared his throat, a sure sign of discomfort. "I'll admit I may have taken my eye off the ball in the constituency. Tell me?" His appeal for help, his sudden humility, as always, undid her. It is part of his charm.

Felicity filled him in on the playground gossip, the proposal to amalgamate some of the smaller village schools in the name of rationalization. "Rolls are shrinking because of Summersby's falling birth-rate, but everyone agrees it's the hub of the community in so many different ways. So there's talk of a protest. A petition at least. Surely we've got a duty to stick with it? Every pupil lost is another nail in the coffin for the life of the village."

She could almost hear the cogs in David's brain whirring. "Fair point," he said. "Presumably if that happened all our Summersby kids would end up being bussed into Kings Burton? Another blow to rural life. I need to look into it. Find out more."

Forty-eight hours later, and the future of Summersby Primary is fast becoming one of David's causes. He had a long conversation with someone at County Hall and is now muttering about asking a question in the House about the future of rural schools. He told Felicity he is wondering about offering himself as a parent governor.

"You were so right, darling," he said on the phone last night. "I'm so glad you've opened my eyes to something of such local importance. See why I need you? You're my eyes and ears in the constituency when I'm stuck in London all week."

The threat, it seems, is over and Alex will stay at Summersby. (Before very long, photos of handsome David Hetherington taking his boys to school or competing in the parents' race on sports day will doubtless appear in the *Kings Burton Gazette*. Summersby Primary will survive and generations of Summersby families will thank their MP for his loyal support of their precious school. A good thing too.) Felicity can't allow herself to think that concern for his children's happiness may have weighed less with her husband than the PR opportunities attached to a strong local cause. The important point, the thing she should hang on to, is that the boys have been spared boarding school. At least for now.

—

Felicity has just finished preparing a picnic and is trying to persuade Finn to use the potty before they set off for Hangman's Wood when the phone rings.

"Mammy! Is everything all right?" Bridie never phones before 6 p.m. when calls are cheaper.

"To be sure it is, bless you my lovely. I'm just back from your sister's and I couldn't wait to tell you all about it. Oh, you won't believe the time we've had! I never thought I'd see the day when I'd be in the presence of the Holy Father!"

Bridie's voice is bubbling over with excitement. Pope John Paul II is visiting the UK—the first a pope has made—and Bridie has been in an absolute lather ever since the plans were announced last year. Torn between joining a coach trip to Coventry with her friends from St Anthony's and seeing the Holy Father in Liverpool in the company of her older daughter, she finally chose the latter.

"Would you believe it—they say more than a million spectators lined the route in from the airport," says Bridie now. "And there were two thousand of us at the Cathedral. Oh, Felicity my lovely, I wish you'd been there with us. Your Aunt Dolly came along, and she loved every moment too. The atmosphere! People crying, people singing. It would have touched your heart, so it would!"

To her astonishment—she hadn't wanted to go in the first place—Felicity feels a stab of jealousy. Her mother and Joy have spent the weekend together, and although she can't begin to imagine how she would have managed the boys in such enormous crowds, Felicity saw the images on TV over the weekend, and was surprisingly moved by the scenes. When Mammy first mentioned it, she really hadn't given it a second thought. No idea what an occasion the visit would be. Now she feels left out.

Why had she been so set against, so sure she didn't want to go? Her Catholicism is part of who she is. David has little sympathy. ("For goodness sake, Felicity, all that adulation for one elderly man. I'm not sure it's healthy. Anyway, I thought you were practically one of us, these days? We don't make that sort of fuss for the Archbishop of Canterbury!")

Felicity can't explain it but she feels a pang of loss. It's all right for Joy—she can drop everything, take a day off work and accompany her mother and Aunt Dolly on the journey of a lifetime—but Felicity has commitments. Complications. It's one thing being single—but try being the dutiful daughter when you are tying yourself in knots trying and failing to be the perfect political wife, let alone bringing up three small boys in the public gaze. She'd like to see Joy juggle all of that.

At that very moment Finn calls her, urgently. "Mammy—I've got Finn on the potty, and we're about to go out," she says. "Will I ring you back tonight?"

———

She's irritated all over again when she eventually calls her mother back that evening. The boys are in bed, finally. They had a wonderful time in the woods, until Alex fell off the swing because he was showing off to the younger two and gave himself a nasty graze on his knee. The shock reduced him to tears, and taunts from Jacob didn't help, and what with having to nurse Alex's hurt pride, reprimand Jacob for teasing, and extract Finn from the wigwam long before he was ready to relinquish it, they were all a bit frazzled by the time they got back home. Supper and baths and an extra story had finally soothed Alex, but it was almost 9 p.m. before she remembered to phone her mother.

"Oh, there you are, Felicity! I thought you'd forgotten your old Mammy!"

"No, Mammy. Just busy," says Felicity. "It's been a long day." *And I'm bone-tired. Tired and starved of adult company.* She has a large glass of white wine in her hand, armour against the inevitable aggravation. "Tell me all about it, why don't you?"

And out it all comes. Bridie pours forth: how wonderful it had been to be there, how they'd queued and queued to get into the Cathedral, and then Dolly needed to spend a penny, so there was an agony of indecision about whether to give up their place in the line, but just when the situation was getting desperate, they finally got through the doors and Dolly was able to use the Ladies in the crypt, so disaster was averted. "And, my, what a building that is! To be sure, there was nothing like it back in my day."

"And did you actually see the Pope, Mammy? Were you close up?"

"Well, just a glimpse of white, really. There were that many people there we were lucky to see past the ends of our noses. And he was surrounded by his official party. You know, the clergy and whatnot. The important thing was that we were there. In the presence of His Holiness. And you can be sure we got closer than anyone did in Coventry. Your Aunt Marjorie will be green with envy. She went with a coach party from Northampton, and it was all outdoors."

Felicity can only imagine. "It was worth all the queuing, then?"

"Oh yes! I'll remember it to my dying day, so I will."

"How's Aunt Dolly? Did she enjoy it, too?"

"Oh, she's a martyr to her bunions, but otherwise well, and yes, to be sure we all agreed it was a day to remember! Thank goodness we had Joy with us, that's all I can say. She was a marvel, getting us seats in the Cathedral and knowing where to find the Ladies and sorting out the tickets for the bus. It's all so much busier than in my day. But our Joy knows her way around the buses like the back of her hand, that girl. She's a wonder!"

"Of course she knows the buses. She lives there, doesn't she?" says Felicity crossly. "And it's bound to be busier. It's years—*decades*—since you lived there, Mammy. That's a lot of water under the bridge."

"Don't be like that! I'm just grateful to your sister for looking after her old Mam. I'm on my knees with exhaustion, as it is. I'm not as young as I was. And Dolly's ten years older, don't forget."

Bully for sainted Joy, she thinks. *Isn't she the perfect daughter?*

"Would Daddy have gone?" she suddenly asks.

"What do you mean, my lovely?"

"If Daddy had still been alive. Would he have gone with you, do you think?"

"What a question! What on earth makes you ask that?"

"I don't know. He'd have wanted to see the new Cathedral, don't you think?"

There's a pause. Felicity listens to her mother breathing. "He had nothing against this pope, for sure," she says eventually. "But I can't see it, really. He left all that behind long ago. Now what about you? How are those wee urchins of yours?"

And Felicity tells Mammy about the picnic and Alex's tears, and how she worries he is too thin-skinned for his own good. She tells her mother about Finn's apparently endless teething, and Mammy reminds her that Alex had been just as bad, but she's probably forgotten. "It will pass, my lovely, you wait and see. You're a wonderful mother, and those boys are a credit to you."

By the end of the conversation, she is calmer, though the odd sense of loss lingers. She can't quite put her finger on the cause of her melancholy. There seems to be an ache somewhere at her core. Something . . . missing. It's probably tiredness. The relentless demands of keeping the show on the road. Three small boys, a house to run and a whole heap of expectations. She adores her children, no question about that, but motherhood is exhausting.

Still, she can't imagine a closer bond. That skin-on-skin experience the moment the midwife presents you with your baby. Something Joy has never had, as a daughter or a mother, so perhaps Felicity should be more generous. Not begrudge her this day of making all Bridie's dreams come true.

Surprised to find her wine glass empty, she takes it into the kitchen for a refill, and then goes into the sitting room. Tentatively, she pulls out the piano stool, adjusts it slightly, and sits at the piano. *Another thing my sister can't do, even if she is a saint and a marvel in every other way.* She stretches her fingers and begins to play, rather cautiously at first and then more fluently as the muscle memory kicks in. She feels the notes begin to flow like water chugging its way through a long-neglected central heating system. The initial juddering of disuse gradually gives way to a swell as the music gushes through her.

Oh, I've missed this! she thinks. *However can I have forgotten how this feels?*

BRIDIE

2019

There are days when I'm entirely lost to myself. All at sea, you might say. A sea of memories I'm floating in, drifting about on the tide. One way, then the other. Flotsam, jetsam.

Ma? I'm going to get a coffee. I want to talk to the Sister, too. I'll be back in a bit. I'd forgotten Joy was here. She's a good girl, is Joy. But I don't know what she wants with talking to the nuns. I thought we'd left all that behind us when . . . when we . . . I don't know when. I can't remember.

You know, I often think of Veronica. *My* Veronica, I mean. Not the one who was a comfort to our Lord on his way to the cross. She had no truck with the nuns, I can tell you for nothing. *Horrible old penguins*, she calls them, when I tell her about my schooldays. I wonder what she would have made of her life, had she lived. She was a force of nature, so she was. She'd an ambition for politics. She'd probably have been Prime Minister.

Call me Vee, darling, she says, but I never could. She had that ease, that confidence that comes with her class, I suppose. And yet no side to her. Not an ounce of snobbery, for all her mother was Lady Arkwright. Lady A disapproved of her daughter's war work, when you'd think any mother would be proud, her being an ambulance driver and all. Veronica grew up in a grand house in Cheshire, so there's me picturing a castle with a moat and a family coat of arms on the wall, but Veronica just laughs it off.

Ghastly place! she tells me, as she takes a drag on her ciggie, and shudders. *Gothic horror. All new money, sweetie, whatever my mother's pretensions. Fearful pile. Utterly hellish. Give me Merseyside any day.*

Such a bright flame of a woman, was Veronica. As glamorous as a film star. I'd never met anyone like her. Everything was a glorious adventure, even the War. Perhaps she had a premonition that she'd die before her time, because I don't believe she wasted a precious moment of her life.

How to describe Veronica? The sort of woman who lights up a room with her dark hair, her huge eyes and her wide mouth. Sex appeal, they call it. *It.* She wore the most exotic clothes I had ever seen. In the early days of my going to work for her, I met her coming down the stairs in a glorious red and gold brocade cape. I'll admit I gasped, in my naivety, she was such a picture. We'd been starved of colour for so long. I couldn't imagine where she found it, what with the coupons and all. She laughed her throaty laugh and told me that when the Prince Regent Theatre was bombed, she'd nipped back at the end of her shift.

Curtains, darling! she says. *I simply scavenged. Aren't we supposed to make do and mend? I couldn't let them go to waste, now could I?*

Lady A disapproved of her daughter's marriage, too. Thought Howard was beneath her, because he grew up in a children's home and hadn't been to private school. Lucky for me, you might say, because she had no interest in any granddaughter. Turned up her nose at the very idea. Howard wasn't *top drawer*, apparently.

To be sure I never met him, but from the photograph in Veronica's bedroom I could see he was as handsome as anything in his RAF uniform. Slicked back hair, as fair as Veronica was dark, and a neat moustache. They'd met at a dance at the start of the War, but now he was stationed near Derby. He hadn't been home in the three months I'd lived in Upper Stanhope Street, though Veronica was able to visit him for a precious two-day leave soon after I arrived. *Spent the whole time in bed, making up for lost time*, she told me afterwards. It's as if they knew what was coming. She broke the news to him then. About the baby, I mean. It blew his socks off, so she said, what with the mumps and all, and him so sure he'd never be a father.

You keep safe, mind! I told his picture as I went round the room with my feather duster. *I'll be lighting a candle for you on Saturday and praying for your safe return, so I will.* Innocent that I was. But you had to have something to cling on to, and if you give up hope, what's the point?

In the end, he was killed in a training exercise, of all stupid things, just three days before the Jerries let loose their fury on us in Upper Stanhope Street. At least Veronica never knew. The telegram was sent to Cheshire by mistake, only turned up the morning after the bombing and there's the poor message boy not knowing how to deliver a telegram to a house with no roof and not much in the way of walls either. So Veronica was spared that pain. And if he loved her as much as she him, he was spared too, now I come to think of it.

But oh, how I loved cleaning that room of hers! She was a terrible slattern, when it came to tidying up after herself, but then that's what I was there for, wasn't I? And she was so good to me, taking me in like that, I'd have walked over hot coals for Veronica, so I would. Clothes draped everywhere. Peacock feathers spilling out of a ruby coloured glass vase. Books and magazines, shoes and shawls all over the place. Lipstick with the lids left off, for all that it was so hard to find in the War.

Her elegant scent. Chantilly, it was called, though you don't say it like that. *French*, she tells me. *Shon-tee-ey*. I can hear her voice now.

JOY

1990

Joy stands on her balcony and takes a deep breath of the sea air. The view is startlingly beautiful. The villa is perched high in the woods, concealed from public view, but its position offers guests a picture-postcard tableau: a clutch of fishing boats and little leisure craft sheltered in the safe embrace of a small harbour. The sea sparkles with pinpricks of silver light.

There's no beach here; to find a stretch of sand you need to clamber over the cliffs, or take a boat round the corner, further down the coastline. A few red-tiled buildings—including a *boulangerie*, an *épicerie* and a small bar, according to Felicity—cling to the sea front, but Saint-Martin-sur-Mer is barely big enough to call itself a village. David likes to tell people it's *un hameau*, in a tone of voice that suggests it's all terribly rustic and undiscovered. On either side of the bay, the cliffs rise steeply upwards, a rocky, scrub-like landscape, peppered with cypress trees, juniper and occasional stunted holm oaks. The colours are almost too rich to believe: azure sky, turquoise sea, terracotta roofs, deep-dark evergreens and magenta bougainvillea, as if painted by an overenthusiastic artist. Joy has to pinch herself to believe she's here and not looking at something in the cinema.

Below her, she can hear that someone—Finn, probably—is already up and splashing about in the swimming pool, which more than compensates for the lack of beach. She stretches—stiff after the long journey followed by an uncharacteristically heavy sleep—and pulls on an old blue and white summer dress.

She pads down the stairs, barefoot and carrying her sandals, enjoying the cool of the tiled floor against the soles of her feet. The villa itself is quiet. Presumably everyone else is still asleep. Unsurprising, really; the plane was delayed, and then there was a long queue to pick up their hire car, made yet more tedious by the need to fill in a series of forms in triplicate. David lost patience in the end, and marched to the front of the line, making Felicity—already snappy—squirm with embarrassment.

"David, please. Just *don't*!" she hissed. "No one knows who you are here, and frankly no one cares! We've just got to wait our turn. We're all in the same boat."

"Yeah, Dad, don't be such an idiot," muttered Alex. "You're so *embarrassing*."

"Oh, for goodness' sake!" David was clearly about to explode. "I just want to see if they can find any more staff. It's *ridiculous*, all this waiting. They're doing it on purpose!"

"Dad!" Alex was scarlet by now. Luckily at that moment, a manager appeared, and it was as if someone had flicked an invisible switch. David snapped into performance mode, and that, combined with his impressively fluent French (thanks, no doubt, to being brought up by a series of French *au pairs*), meant they were soon on their way. Joy was grudgingly impressed by his command of the situation. Whatever else you might say about David, he was a man who knew how to get things done. Even if she spoke French, she couldn't imagine having the confidence to impose her will so forcefully.

I don't know how my sister stands it, thinks Joy as she descends the stairs. *Mind you, here am I enjoying David's hospitality, so that makes me an ungrateful hypocrite.* And there is her sister, flawlessly elegant in a pale-yellow linen shift, a floppy white sunhat and large sunglasses, and carrying a straw basket.

"I'm about to go in search of breakfast," says Felicity. She seems to have recovered from her outburst last night. "Join me?"

"Love to," says Joy. "Let me just fetch my bag, and I'll walk down with you."

They stroll into the village, Felicity pointing out various landmarks as they go, before lapsing into companionable silence. This is the third year Felicity and David have brought the boys to Saint-Martin-sur-Mer, but only the first time that Joy has joined them. It's taken some persuasion; Joy appreciates the offer but has always held back.

There are a number of reasons: much as she loves her sister and nephews, she continues to find David a trial. If his right-wing politics are a sore point, his smug self-satisfaction is worse. She's also reluctant to play the poor relation. She can afford the flight, although she can't help thinking it would have been cheaper to drive down. But not everyone shares her pleasure in driving. She tried and failed to get David to nominate her as a third driver of the hire car. Some excuse about the left-hand drive. But her fear is that there will be restaurant meals and drinks and outings that she can't afford, with a mortgage to pay. Her sister hasn't a clue how most people live.

While she suspects that David and Felicity can easily subsidise her, she hasn't quite found a way to handle this and cling on to her dignity. When the boys were younger, she could always repay the debt by offering to babysit so that David and Felicity could go out. These days, that doesn't wash; at ten, thirteen and fifteen, the boys are considered old enough to join the party, or stay home under Alex's supervision.

In the end, it was her mother who persuaded her. "You know, you'll be hurting your sister's feelings if you turn her down again," she said at Christmas. "She relies on you more than you think, you know."

So Joy has taken the risk, and will join the family for the first half of their two-week break. But it's not been without cost. She may not have upset Felicity this year, but the look on Trisha's face when she said she'd only be free for a single week's walking in Dorset instead of their usual fortnight suggested that she's managed to offend her old nursing friend instead. Which reminds her: she must send a postcard to Trisha. (Or will that rub salt into the wound?) And Linda, come to think of it. Linda, a friend from work, is keeping an eye on Joy's houseplants while she's away. Joy will return the favour and feed the cat when Linda and Geoff go to Corfu in September.

Honestly, why is it so difficult? Joy knows she often misjudges invitations. She never assumes she's anyone's first choice of companion, and then finds herself taken aback if others are hurt when she turns them down.

"Goodness, it's hot already!" she says now, aware that sweat is running down her back. Felicity looks admirably cool. "How on earth do you manage it?"

"Manage what?" Felicity looks up from her reverie.

"To look so cool? Especially with your fair skin. I'd have thought you'd be melting."

Felicity laughs. "Practice!" she says. "I love it here. It's as if I come alive. Oh—stop a moment!" She sniffs the air. "Lavender, sage, rosemary and thyme. Can you smell them?"

"If you say so," says Joy. "Herbs, I'll grant you. But beyond that . . . I'm really not sure."

"Oh, where's the poetry in your soul, Joy?" Felicity is smiling, teasing her.

"I think you know the answer to that! As our revered Father remarked on more than one occasion, there's not an artistic bone in my body."

"Daddy!" Felicity practically snorts. "Since when did he get to pronounce judgement?"

"Since the day I was born," says Joy. "Or, I suppose I should say, since the day he walked into our lives. Married Mother."

"Does it ever bother you?"

"Does what bother me? Father being such a beast?"

"Being adopted. How does that feel?"

"I've absolutely no idea," says Joy, matter-of-factly. "Because I don't know what the alternative would have been."

"I suppose." They've reached the heart of the village now. Felicity greets the baker warmly in French and buys *croissants*, *pains au chocolat* and a couple of *baguette*s. Next door in the *épicerie* they buy jam, fruit, tomatoes, some slices of ham and a couple of smelly cheeses.

"That should do us until supper time at least," she says. "Honestly, Joy, those boys eat us out of house and home, especially Alex. He's a bottomless pit. The only plus is that nowadays I can send him down to the shops to replenish the stocks on the grounds that it's good for his French. He'll grumble terribly, but luckily for me, there's a very pretty girl who helps out in the bakery in the summer holidays."

"Oh?"

"Yes. Marianne. They struck up quite a friendship last year. He goes bright pink at the mention of her name. You can imagine how the others tease him."

Felicity hands a paper carrier bag to Joy, balances her own load in her basket, and continues. "I mean, haven't you ever wanted to do anything about it?"

"About what?"

"Your adoption. I don't know. Retrace your roots or something."

"I can't really see the point," says Joy. "It's not as if there's any mystery. Unlike most people, I know who my parents were, and they're dead and gone. I wasn't abandoned; I was orphaned. End of story."

"But what about counselling?"

"Why on earth would I need counselling?" Joy is beginning to feel quite tetchy. What is her sister on about? "Are you suggesting there's something wrong with me?"

"No, no, no! Of course not! I'm sorry. That's not what I meant at all. It's just . . . "

"What?"

"I suppose I'm trying to make sense of my own life right now. I'm probably offloading that onto you. Sorry."

Joy takes a long deep breath. Felicity has always been melodramatic. Something to do with her artistic temperament.

"Look, I'll admit, when I first found out, it took a bit of getting used to. But that's years ago now," she says. "The truth is, in some ways it was almost a relief. It sort of made sense of things. Helped me understand why I was always the odd one out. Different. A . . . a misfit."

"A misfit? Oh *Joy!*"

"Come on! You know perfectly well how it was!" She dismisses her sister's denial with a wave of her spare hand.

"But do you never wonder about it? How different your life might have been?"

Joy sighs. "Look, if it's taught me anything, it's that I owe it to my birth parents to make the most of my life, because theirs were cut so short. But honestly, I'm fine about it. Why make a fuss about what's done and dusted? You're trying to solve a problem that doesn't exist. Tell me about you, Flick. What do you mean, you're trying to make sense of your life? What's up?"

"Oh, *hell*! I promised myself I wouldn't do this," says Felicity and bursts into noisy tears.

—

Half an hour later, sitting over two small but very strong cups of coffee outside the bar, Joy has a better idea of the source of Felicity's distress. David has got himself into a pickle, according to Felicity. (Those are her precise words: *got himself into a pickle*. As if he's a little boy who's stepped in a puddle and made his trousers muddy.)

More prosaically, he's had an affair. Or a fling, at the very least. Felicity was taking his suit to the dry cleaner when she found a receipt for two nights' dinner, bed and breakfast in a delightful sounding hotel in Devon. The dates on the receipt coincided with a weekend conference on pesticides in Brussels David was due to attend as a junior minister in the Ministry of Agriculture.

"Can you believe it? It was the weekend that both Jake and Finn went down with that horrible vomiting bug!" said Felicity. "They were both wretched, and I was up and down the stairs clearing up sick and changing the sheets and poor old Alex was furious because he had a football tournament and I couldn't go because I couldn't leave the other two. And David was so bloody sympathetic on the phone!"

"So what did you do? When you found the receipt?"

"Double checked the dates and then confronted him."

"And what did he have to say for himself?"

"Oh, Joy, it was *pitiful*. I thought he might try and deny it, but he burst into tears and begged me not to leave him. He said he'd been terribly silly. He'd been under such pressure at work, and it was all a ghastly mistake."

"So who is she? One of the girls in pearls? Pie-crust collar and fluttering eyelashes?"

"Well, this is the really awful thing. It's his researcher, Caroline. *Clever Little Caroline*, he calls her. Awfully attractive, in a very Roedean, jolly-hockey-sticks sort of way. Fresh out of Oxford and terribly eager to please. Silly me, to think I was kind to her because her father's an ambassador and her parents are overseas! I took pity on her, invited her to the house, Sunday lunch and everything. And she was so appreciative, so sweet! She said I was a far better cook than her mother, and asked for my apple crumble recipe. And all the time, she was just waiting to get her claws into my husband. Right under my nose!"

"But Flick . . . it takes two to tango. David's not exactly blameless in this."

"Oh, I know he's been silly. But apparently she practically threw herself at him, simply wouldn't take no for an answer. Very *needy*, he says. I suppose she's looking for a father figure, and he was probably flattered. It turns out she made the booking for the weekend herself and simply sprang it on him. He really thought he was going to Brussels! She was in cahoots with his PA, so that means bloody Moira knew exactly what was going on and did nothing to stop it, and there was I thinking she was my friend. It's all so humiliating!"

"So . . . is it over?"

"Of *course* it's over! I told you—he *begged* me to stay with him. But I still feel so . . . "

Felicity pauses, apparently at a loss for words.

Joy clears her throat. "So *what*, Flick?"

"Mortified. Humiliated. That it's my fault, somehow. That I'm not a good enough wife to him. That I've fallen short. Honestly, I'm always so tired by the time he comes home. He doesn't always get the best from me."

"That's ridiculous!" Joy struggles to keep her temper. "For heaven's sake, Flick, I can't see that you could possibly do more. I'm not surprised you're tired! You're single-handedly bringing up his three children, without him lifting so much as a finger. You go to all those frightful political functions with him and put up with all those stuffed shirts for the sake of his career. Not to mention putting your music on hold so that you can be at his beck and call."

"But you don't understand!" Felicity's voice is rising dangerously. The barman looks up, but Felicity ploughs on, oblivious. "I love being at home with the boys! I don't *have* to go out to work because David's such a good provider. And I'm teaching quite a bit now. So I'm really very, very lucky, you know." The last few words are lost altogether in Felicity's noisy sobs.

Joy meets the barman's eye and mouths "Sorry!", and hopes he understands, but she doesn't speak French. She is horrified; in her right mind, Felicity would be equally appalled by the public scene she's making. She reaches across the table for her sister's hand and squeezes it. "Oh *Flick*," she whispers. "This is terrible. I've a good mind to tell David exactly what I think of him!"

"Oh, please," begs Felicity, a little quieter now. "*Please* don't, Joy. It's really not his fault. She was a little minx, out for what she could get, and I'm blowed if I'm going to let her hurt our family. You know, David's quite upset by all this. In some ways, it's a lucky escape. A warning bell. And it's over now, so it's just a matter of coming to terms with it."

Joy finds herself simultaneously unsurprised and shocked to her core. Unsurprised by David's behaviour, yet shocked that he seems to have convinced Felicity that he's not to blame. How on earth is it possible that he's shifted the responsibility for his infidelity onto his wife? Talk about history repeating itself. Felicity's gone from a bullying father to a bullying husband. (Not that Joseph bullied Felicity, exactly. Quite the opposite. He put his daughter on a pedestal, while holding his wife in contempt and making Felicity complicit in that. Why has Felicity ended up with a man who manages to put her in the wrong?)

She wonders about the boys. Surely children are attuned to their parents' unhappiness, even if they can't articulate it. "Do the boys know what's going on?"

"Nothing's *going on*," snaps Felicity. "I told you; it's over."

"I'm glad to hear it. Did Caroline get the sack?"

"You can't just *sack* someone because you've slept with them, you know. Luckily, he managed to palm her off on someone else in a different department. I insisted. He even made it look like a promotion."

"So she's still lurking somewhere in Whitehall?"

"I suppose so." Felicity looks wary, as if the thought has only just occurred to her. "But he *promised*. Promised me it was over. Besides . . . for all his faults, I love him. I *love* David. I've just got to put what's happened behind me and find a way of living with it. Make a loving home for the boys, and try and be a better wife."

Joy closes her eyes for a moment and tries to marshal her thoughts. How dare David crush the life out of her sister? She badly wants to tell Felicity that she's in cloud cuckoo land if she thinks it's over. Joy doesn't trust David an inch. If it isn't Clever Little Caroline, there will be someone else equally alluring. With their long hours and inflated egos, half the House of Commons is at it, if rumour is to be believed.

She suddenly knows with heart-sinking clarity that Caroline is not the first indiscretion and won't be the last. Yet come election time, David will need his wife and family at his side, posed prettily at the garden gate, the model of Tory respectability. So perhaps he does mean it, when he begs forgiveness. Or at the very least, he thinks he does.

But what does Joy know about what goes on in a marriage? She sighs. "Just tell me what I can do to help, Flick."

Tears well up in Felicity's eyes again. She reaches for a thin paper serviette from the stainless-steel container on their table, wipes her eyes and briskly blows her nose.

"That's a kind offer," she says in a steadier voice. "If you mean it . . . well, I think the best way you can help is to keep an eye on the boys while you're here. Help keep them busy. They know we've been rowing, especially Alex, but no more than that. Anything to give me a chance to lavish a bit of love and attention on David."

She puts a few coins on a saucer and stands up to leave. "Really, I've just got to pull myself together. As long as I can stop wallowing in self-pity, we'll put this behind us. You'll see."

FELICITY

1997

"I thought we had an agreement, Felicity!" David, she notices, has huge bags under his eyes. It's hardly surprising. The run up to a General Election is always punishing, and this time more than most. The Conservatives have been routed. David held on to his seat by the narrowest of margins.

"We did, and I've stuck to it," says Felicity, pouring boiling water into the cafetière. It's 10.30 a.m., late for a weekday breakfast, but they have only just crawled out of bed. She takes a couple of slices of wholemeal toast out of the toaster and puts them on the Emma Bridgewater toast-rack in front of him, noting as she does so that the marmalade is low. She thinks there are a couple more jars in the cellar, but otherwise it's the supermarket. She prefers jam herself, but the habit of providing her husband's breakfast is hardwired into her.

"Look," she says, "I'm not at all surprised you're shaken. It's a massive upset after all these years in power. But it's not exactly a surprise, is it? You know how the polls looked."

David puts his head in his hands. He's plainly exhausted. "God! Even my own wife thinks we got what we had coming to us! With friends like you, who needs enemies? All I'm asking for is a bit of loyalty."

"That's not fair! I came to everything you asked me to. Pressed the flesh and put up with horrible flak on the doorstep from all those people who hate the Tories. I let that slimy reporter from *Oxfordshire World* into the house and smiled through every one of his patronizing questions. I'd say I did my bit."

And some. None of this is my fault. She takes a slug from her mug without thinking, and almost spits out the coffee when she scalds her mouth. "And it's not as bad as it might have been. You hung on to your seat, didn't you?"

"By the skin of my teeth!"

"Maybe. But that's more than heaps of your colleagues. Aren't you just a tiny bit grateful?"

"Grateful? Why on earth should I be *grateful*? When a socialist Government is about to dismantle everything we've achieved in the last two decades? Don't you realize what it means to see the party crashing into oblivion? To be thrown out of the Treasury? Are you seriously asking me to be grateful?"

"I just think you might show a bit of appreciation to everyone who worked so hard on the campaign trail. You may not be a minister anymore, but at least you're still an MP!"

"You haven't got a clue, have you? I'm not sure I *want* to be an MP in opposition. How on earth do you think we're going to get anything done, against a majority like that?"

Felicity manages not to remind him that he has always claimed to believe that Her Majesty's Opposition has a noble calling in holding the Government to account. He's being pretty beastly, but he barely slept last night. Kings Burton declared soon after 2 a.m., and she and David were home within the hour, but he couldn't tear himself away from the TV screen, as seat after seat tumbled like dominoes through the night. By the time he dragged himself to bed it was already getting light.

"And now this! You're swanning off to America without a backward glance?"

Felicity is kicking herself. By some unfortunate twist of fate, the brochure she's been eagerly awaiting arrived in this morning's post. If she hadn't been befuddled by sleeplessness herself, she would have been more circumspect about opening it in front of David.

"Look, nothing's decided," she says. "You know that! We discussed it months ago. You know I've been thinking about it for ages. The deal was not before the election. Not *never.*"

"But I *need* you here. *We* need you," says David, and reaches across the table for her hand. She sees real tears in his eyes. Pitiful. He looks like a little boy, like Alex at his most needy, pleading not to be abandoned at nursery while she and Jake go home. *No; I won't let you bamboozle me again*, she tells herself. *Not after all you've put me through.*

She gets up from the table, under the guise of fetching more milk from the fridge. "Let's take this a step at a time," she says, her voice as soothing as if she is reassuring one of her twitchier piano pupils before an exam. "The course doesn't start until the autumn, and I haven't even been accepted yet. They may not want me."

"Of course they'll want you," counters David. "They'll want your fees, at any rate."

Through her exhaustion, Felicity feels a stiffening of her resolve. She will not let him put her down. She puts the milk on the table with exaggerated care and picks up her mug again. She will take her coffee into the garden before she screams at him.

"Let's park the whole idea for now," she says. "Neither of us is thinking straight after last night. We'll talk more when we've both had some sleep."

—

A week later, David has caught up on his sleep but is still feeling sorry for himself. While the House of Commons—indeed the country—is abuzz with the brave new world of New Labour, the pathetic remnant of the old guard haunt the corridors of the Commons like victims of shellshock. Everyone is stunned, he says. So many Tory grandees have disappeared that the survivors are all at sea. No one knows quite what to do with themselves. From being an up-and-coming minister in the Treasury— with a car and a team of staff—he is now consigned to obscurity on the back benches.

"At least you'll have more time for the constituency," Felicity tells him over supper. It's a beautiful early summer evening, and they are eating in the garden. Everywhere around them the garden is springing to life. Apple blossom, pear blossom. Bright green leaves. Bluebells in the orchard, tulips in the borders.

"Yeah, Dad," says Finn, arriving with a salad. "You're always saying you spend too much time in London. Now you can, like, hang out here a bit. Slow down, even. Good to take it easy at your age."

"Thank you, Finn, but I'm hardly over the hill yet!" says David irritably.

"But it's true, you know," says Felicity. "Not that you're old," she adds hastily, seeing the look on his face. David is forty-nine and twitchy about turning fifty. "I know it's going to take a bit of adjustment, but can't you see it as . . . I don't know. An opportunity. A chance to take stock. You can spend the next few months getting your teeth into local issues. It won't last for ever, this exile."

"I suppose so," says David with poor grace. "It's just so bloody hard. Being thrown on the scrap heap."

"Oh, come on, David! It's scarcely that," says Felicity. "You're still an MP, for heaven's sake! But, you know, now that everything's changed for you, there's an alternative we should consider."

"What? What do you mean? Defect to Labour? Don't be ridiculous!"

"Finn, darling, do you mind fetching the salad dressing, please? I left it on the kitchen side."

As soon as he was out of earshot, she said: "Of *course* that's not what I meant! Now you're being ridiculous! But if you're really fed up about the election . . . why not resign? Better that than sitting on the side-lines sulking! You could always come with me to America."

"And do what, precisely? What might I do while you're doing your . . . your . . . *course*?" He almost spits out the word, as if it leaves a nasty taste on his tongue.

"I don't know. That would be up to you. Think what you're going to do with the rest of your life. Do a Master's too. Set up a business. I just think it's a chance for a . . . a reset. A new enterprise. An adventure, perhaps. We could put it off a year while you line up a successor for your seat, and then go. After all, Alex and Jake are both happily settled at uni, and in a year's time Finn will be off too. He could even look at universities over there. There are some good schools of architecture."

"What's this about me and uni, Mum?" asks Finn. "What are you and Dad plotting?"

"I'm not plotting anything." David takes a slug of red wine. "It's your mother who's doing the plotting. Or should I say, *losing* the plot."

"David! Please. Give me the chance to explain, at least." And Felicity tells Finn that she's considering retraining as a music thanatologist. "Before you ask, that's someone who uses music to help people in their dying."

"That's a bit weird, isn't it, Mum?"

"Weird only because you've never heard of it, perhaps." And she explains that thanatology is a specialist branch of music therapy, hardly known in the UK, but well established in America where there are a number of teaching programmes. There's research to show that the right music played at a deathbed can be highly beneficial to the dying. She's had time to read the brochure now and has been utterly seduced by descriptions of learning to *create sacred space for patients through music*, of discovering how to *anoint people with sound so that they can let go of life*. Something tells her this is for her.

"The thing about thanatology is that it's about medicine and music and spirituality all working in harmony. It isn't just that it's soothing, listening to music. Although of course there's some of that. It's actually been scientifically proven to relieve pain. To make a difference at a cellular level. Something to do with the brain chemistry. Or the soul, depending on your take."

"Sounds a bit tree-huggy to me," says Finn, helping himself to a huge serving of lasagne. "Like giving birth to whale music or something. God— have you talked to Aunty Joy about this? What does she say?"

"Not yet. Why?" says Felicity, more sharply than she meant to. "What business is it of hers?" Joy is relentlessly practical, and there's not a musical bone in her body. She'll probably agree with David that this is sentimental tosh.

"Keep your hair on, Mum. I just wondered. But what's brought this on? And what's it got to do with me?"

Felicity smiles, letting go of her irritation. Finn, at seventeen, is naturally more interested in what it means for him than in her possible new career. "Well, I was just wondering if you might want to look at uni in the States," she says, passing the salad around the table. "But in answer to your question . . . it was partly Grandma dying." Her mother-in-law Marguerite died in February from pancreatic cancer after several long and painful months.

David looks up. "Really? You never mentioned that."

You never asked, thinks Felicity.

"Remember towards the end of her life, when her bed was downstairs?" David had been working long hours at the Treasury and rarely found the time to visit, so Felicity oversaw the reorganization of furniture when it was clear that Marguerite was determined to stay at home until the end. The move downstairs made it easier for the carers and later the hospice team. Fortunately there was already a fully functioning shower room on the ground floor, and plenty of space in the drawing room: a large and sunny room, looking onto the garden, with a dining area one end and a grand piano the other.

In David's absence, Felicity made arrangements for the heavy antique dining table and chairs to be taken into storage, and ordered a hospital bed to be positioned next to the French windows overlooking the garden. It was winter, but Marguerite took pleasure from seeing the birds feeding at the bird table, and, in her last weeks, an emerging carpet of snowdrops.

"I used to play the piano for her when I visited," Felicity tells them. David's parents had a Steinway, not a top-notch instrument by any means, but in reasonable shape, and still regularly tuned despite only ever being played by the occasional visiting grandchild. "She really responded to the music, even right at the end."

"Really? I didn't know that." David is interested at last. "What happened?"

"She became much calmer. I could see her breathing slowed down. The carers noticed too. It was less laboured. As if the pain was easing."

"Go on."

Felicity hesitates, not wanting to admit that she was motivated in part by the limits of her relationship with her mother-in-law. They had never been close; Marguerite was not a woman who encouraged confidences.

In life, she was always exquisitely dressed and coiffured, only adding to Felicity's certainty that she fell short of her mother-in-law's standards. She was also embarrassed, slightly revolted even, by seeing Marguerite in such a weakened state and without her usual armour of make-up. Playing the piano helped fill the time. Better still, it allowed her to lose herself.

"I started taking a selection of music along, to see if some pieces were more soothing than others. It was different on different days, but Chopin seemed the most reliable. I don't really know why."

It was one of the Macmillan nurses who told her about music thanatology. Suki was American and had a sister who was a palliative care nurse back home.

"Apparently there's a hospice in Vermont where they've taken it very seriously and created a Master's programme with the local university," she says. "It's all properly accredited. People come from all around the world to do the training. It's pioneering stuff."

"Cool," says Finn. "But what's the big deal? Can't you just carry on playing the piano to wrinklies, like you did for Grandma?"

"I could, I suppose," says Felicity. "Not that most people happen to have a grand piano at their bedside. But I really want to find out more about it. I mean . . . well, we've always known that there's some kind of link between music and healing, but it was all a bit amorphous. Now there's a body of academic research. Proper patient studies. It's exciting. I want to find out more. Train properly as a practitioner. Apparently it's intense work. You have to tune in to every tiny signal the patient gives you, and then take them on a journey. A lot of it's done using the harp and the voice."

"But Mum . . . I hate to be a spoilsport . . . but you don't, like, *play* the harp. And you don't really sing either. You teach kids the piano, in case you've forgotten. How's that going to work?"

Felicity laughs. "That's why I need to do a bit more homework first. Find out if they'll even take me. But I don't think I'm totally past it, Finn. I've always wanted to learn the harp, as it happens. Since I was little. They teach you from scratch if they accept you on the course, and they only do that if you've got some kind of musical background. It may be ancient history to you, but I do actually have a degree in Music."

She adds, almost as an afterthought: "Besides, I *used* to sing. It was . . . well, something of a passion really."

"Really? I've never heard you."

"Oh, it was a long time ago. When I was about your age. You ask Aunty Joy." Felicity abandons her lasagne, putting down her fork. She picks up her wine glass. It's so long since she tried to sing; she wonders if she can. (She pictures her vocal cords caked in rust. She used to treat her voice like a precious instrument, wrapping her neck in scarves in the winter, keeping an exaggerated distance from any of her schoolmates who had a cold. Her friends used to tease her horribly, calling her a prima donna.) At the very least, all those vocal muscles must be horribly wasted. Withered. Weak. Did she want to go awakening old ghosts? Perhaps it was too late anyway.

She takes a long sip of wine. "At least I got you all playing the piano. I'm not a total failure as a mother. Even if none of you really stuck with it."

"I still play!" objects Finn. "A bit. And Jake wouldn't be doing his course if you hadn't got him playing, would he?" (Jacob is studying music production, funded reluctantly by his father who is not convinced that this constitutes a real degree.)

"Well, I don't see how it could possibly work, if you can only train in the States," says David now. "As you've already pointed out, I've got a job to do right here for my constituents. I can't exactly move lock, stock and barrel to the US when I've only just been re-elected. That would go down like a lead balloon with the party. And you don't want to go jeopardizing Finn's future on a . . . a *whim*."

Felicity sighs. "I'm not suggesting that for a moment. And it's not a whim, any more than politics is a whim for you. It's just as much of a . . . a *calling*."

David snorts. It's an ugly, harsh sound. Felicity drains her glass and refills it without topping up his. *You owe me, you bastard. I could have shopped you to the papers and I didn't. I stayed loyal so that you could hang on to your seat.*

"I will point out that if you're on the back benches, you'll have more time now. You won't be working such long hours, and you certainly won't need to be in London all week. You'll be home a lot more. Maybe it's time for a change for all of us."

BRIDIE

2019

I'm thinking I've forgotten something important, but I can't recall what. Am I late for work? Or is it Joseph, wanting his dinner, and me here asleep in my bed? I can expect short shrift if that's the case, let me tell you. You don't take to your bed by day unless you're on your way out, in Joseph's world. Preferably knocking on St Peter's Gate.

Sloth is one of the seven deadly sins, says he. Best not to remind him of the days when he'd happily take to his bed in the afternoon for the almighty indulgence of one of the other seven. He's not much blessed with a sense of humour.

Such a champion for hard work, you'd have thought he'd be glad of me going for a job. Not to mention the money for the little extras, what with Felicity's music and all. It was one thing, Marjorie giving us the piano—and very grateful I was, too, make no mistake—but there were still the lessons had to be found. Grand gestures are all very well, but week in, week out there are teachers to be paid for, not to mention the bus fares and sheet music. And concert wear, would you believe it! When she reached her teenage years, me running up a bit of velvet on my old Singer wasn't good enough for our Felicity. Nor was anything I did, for that matter. She'd outgrown anything her mother had to offer.

Not that I minded. Not really. For all that I'm handy with a needle, I've never called myself a seamstress. Not like our Dolly or my Aunty Norah. And I was gratified that Felicity was doing so well, so I was. She was singing more now, as well as playing the piano. It didn't take a genius to know she was good. A full, rich voice, like soft velvet or dark chocolate.

Mezzo-soprano, they said, and more tone than anyone her age had any right to. At some point she'd have to make a choice between her voice and the keyboard.

And her father was right: we didn't want our daughter shown up in one of my home-made frocks with a wobbly seam. So that was my bargaining chip with Joseph. I'd go out to work, and that way I could take her into town to choose proper, grown-up concert wear from Beales. He gave in, in the end.

I started off behind the counter at Baker's News. It was part-time, early mornings, and I was in my element. While Mr Baker sorted out the papers for the delivery boys, it was my job to stand behind the counter and serve the customers. Cigarettes, sweets in their tall glass jars, magazines, comics and daily papers. The glass cabinet of pocket-money toys: card games, balsa wood planes, dolls' tea sets, and wooden puzzles, though I didn't often see it open, as the children only came in with their pennies after school.

I picked it up fast enough. Before long, I got to know the customers and their particular likes and dislikes. Don the van driver who bought a twist of humbugs along with his Players. Old Mrs Jenkins who always asked for a tin loaf along with her copy of the *Chron*, then rocked with laughter at her own joke. (*Call yourself a* Baker, *Mr B*?) Our milkman, Fred, who'd been at school with Mr Baker and called in for a chinwag at the end of his round. The sad gentleman in the tweed suit who bought *Jack and Jill* every week for his little boy in hospital, until one day he stopped coming in at all and I couldn't help but fret for them both.

To be sure it was a step up from skivvying. And I was good at it, so I was. I liked the *craic*, but at the same time I made sure not to keep my customers waiting. I kept a sharp eye out for light fingers, and more than once stopped Billy Briggs, who was not the full shilling, poor fellow, from helping himself. I could tot up the bill in my head and count out the change in a matter of seconds. I've always been quick with figures. It makes me wonder what else I could have done with my life, if I'd had the chance of an education. Maybe I could have made something of myself, like my girls.

Either way, Mr Baker could see I was a hard worker, and I won his respect. In truth, I loved it, for the company if nothing else. Joy had left home, and Felicity didn't much need me these days. She and her father were in cahoots, always on about their beloved music, using fancy foreign words I didn't understand. She was all for becoming an opera singer now. She had him wrapped around her little finger, and there was no place for a gooseberry. I was out of my league.

So it gave me a sense of purpose as well as a spot of pin money, that little job. And Mr Baker would have given me more hours, given half the chance, but I didn't dare risk it. Three hours a day, seven till ten, Monday to Saturday, and I could be back running my own home without any complaint from my husband and daughter.

That was my argument, anyway. If it meant Joseph had to get the breakfast and see Felicity off on the bus on schooldays, so be it. It was the 1960s now, and we could try being a modern family, could we not? That's what I told myself. If my daughter didn't need me fussing after her, I'd take a bit of enjoyment where I could.

It was only sometimes that I'd find myself wondering if she minded my absence more than she let on. On Saturday mornings, I'd come home to find her doing her homework at the kitchen table, often still in her dressing gown. Sometimes, there was an air of agitation about her. She wouldn't meet my eye. In the holidays, she took to going out for early morning walks while I was at work.

Sometimes I'd hear her sobbing in her bedroom. But girls are at the mercy of their hormones, when they're growing up, aren't they? Felicity was always emotional. They call it the artistic temperament. In the meantime, if I couldn't understand the details of her musical malarkey, I had at least the comfort of knowing I was a cog in the wheel, helping her on her way.

—

It can't be Joseph wanting his dinner. Joseph's dead. I know that much, even if he visits my dreams more often than you'd credit. He died a long time ago, so he did, leaving me with a stew of scrag end and the need of a proper job.

That first night, safe in the knowledge that Joy was on her way south, I lay awake trying to take it all in. Joseph: dead. Would you credit it? Such a looming great presence, he was, and now no more. Him only sixty, with never a day's sickness in his life, so far as I knew.

And what about the service? Would he be allowed a proper Catholic funeral? He'd mind so, being shunted off to the crematorium with no prayers said. The shame of it! More to the point, what about his immortal soul? Was it in peril after everything? Would the Lord God be merciful? *Hail Mary, Mother of God, pray for us sinners, now and at the hour of our death.*

In the end, I decided I'd take my worries to Father Adrian at St Anthony's in the morning. Tell him everything. But even once I'd calmed down about the eternal fate of himself, there was the fear about us, his family. At least Joy was all right. She'd her new life in Liverpool. Qualifications and a steady job.

What was to become of me and Felicity? A few hours a day at the newsagent wasn't going to pay the rent, if the council even let us stay. It was Joseph's name on the rent book, so help me God. It would be 1941 all over again. Homeless and friendless and having to throw myself upon the mercy of others. Would I have to be going back to Ireland? What sort of future lay for me there, when I'd been a stranger to my own home for nearly thirty years?

And what about Felicity's singing? Her precious place at the Royal College of Music, all there but for the exam results? How in heaven's name would I be able to pay for that? She'd have to stay home and get a job, like so many girls before her.

Besides, the poor child didn't even know her father was dead yet. As far as she knew, he still lived and breathed as he had when she'd set out on her holidays full of the joys of summer. She would take it badly, that was for sure. The two of them were thick as thieves, were they not? Round and round and round the worry went. A treadmill of fear. I was sick to my stomach, so I was.

It was Norman who came to the rescue again, bless his soul. It was the moment I realized that he'd grown quite fond of us over the years. Joy must have telephoned him from a call box at the station, because to be sure we had no car now, not that I ever had a licence. That Cortina was Joseph's pride and joy. He would no more have trusted me behind the wheel than I'd have trusted him to boil an egg. I must have fallen asleep eventually because the next thing I know, I'm woken by the sound of Joy and Norman letting themselves into the house. Joy looks alert, pumped up, somehow, in spite of the hour she must have risen to catch the train. Norman, on the other hand, looks about as bad as I feel.

We've talked about it, Mother, says Joy, once she's detached herself from my arms and put the kettle on the gas. *Uncle Norman's going to drive down to Cornwall and bring Flick home.*

And so he did, returning with a red-eyed Felicity in time for supper the next day. By which time, Joy had booked the funeral at St Anthony's, spoken to the Council about my right to stay put, and started a shopping list for the wake. I tell you, she's always been a coper. Over the next few days, she and Norman sorted out everything else. It turned out there was life insurance that would see Felicity right, music college and all, and Norman had a friend on the Council, a doctor whose receptionist was about to retire, and he was happy to put a good word in for me.

Which only left me the poor child herself to worry about, and that was a full-time occupation in its own right.

JOY

2000

The day of the accident is so prosaic it could be called dull. And yet Joy clings to the memory for dear life. (*Dear life! The irony!*) It's all so ordinary. A Monday in late November, a day off because she has been on call over the weekend. She does some boring but necessary domestic jobs: putting on a load of washing, sorting out her gas bill—it seems the supplier has been overestimating her usage and she is due a cheering refund—and making a phone call to the NHS Pensions Office.

She's still mulling over her retirement plans. She will be fifty-nine next month. Her colleagues are no doubt expecting that she will step down when she reaches her sixtieth birthday. But she is fit and well, and believes she is capable and good at her job. Retirement feels brutal. The lopping off of a limb. At her more positive moments, she knows that life may still hold many adventures: something altogether new, retraining, perhaps, or volunteering. The trouble is that in the normal run of things she lacks the time and energy to explore the possibilities that might lurk around the corner. In the small hours of the night, it feels as if, after so many years cushioned by the purpose of work and its comforting routines, this would be a terrifying fall into the abyss.

A gentler alternative would be to ease the transition by reducing her hours. Now she has no mortgage she could defer her pension for a few years, live on a part-time salary, while dipping her toes in the water of other activities. As long as they'll let her. What if the powers-that-be say no? Put her out to grass? It happens.

The phone call confirms that either course of action is affordable, but that doesn't solve her dilemma. As usual, she consigns the decision into the "too difficult" category. After all, there's no immediate rush. She heats a tin of tomato soup for her lunch and toasts a couple of pieces of sliced bread to go with it. Afterwards she reads the paper with a cup of tea. She washes up her lunch things, and then it's time to find her library books and gather her swimming things.

She is a reluctant swimmer, but knows it does her good. She's overweight, and it shows on her short frame. Her doctor tells her she should lose a stone. There's something rather undignified about divesting yourself of all your clothes in a semi-public place. She tries not to think about the verrucae, the skin cells and other bodily detritus swirling about in the water. She only learned to swim as an adult, and she's not a natural.

Today, she's meeting her former colleague and friend Linda, which is good because it makes it harder to wriggle out of. She also has a pre-paid pass, with seven out of ten swims still left on it, and having paid up front, she can't bear the thought of wasting them. Thinking about it, perhaps she should talk through her retirement options with her friend after their swim. Linda—for many years the indispensable secretary who kept Joy's maternity unit in order—gives every impression of enjoying retirement, although unlike Joy she has a husband and grandchildren to keep her busy.

And that, she explains to the investigating officer, is how she found herself driving along the Queen's Road at a little after 5 p.m., just as it was getting dark and slightly foggy, just as a figure stepped out of nowhere into her path. She's a careful driver, she knows, and is as sure as she possibly can be that she was driving at 28 miles per hour in a 30 zone. She hadn't been drinking (unless you count two cups of tea) and was in full control of her vehicle. All she can remember is a figure looming out of the shadows in front of the car. One minute no one; the next minute, someone. A split second. There was the most awful thud as the person (a man? a woman?) was lifted into the air and then thrown back onto the road. It was so unreal as to be almost comical.

The next hour or two are a foggy blur. Her mouth appears to be full of broken glass, which she spits out onto the pavement, noticing as she does so that it is red with blood. The windscreen must have shattered in the collision. Has she lost a tooth? Someone must have called the emergency services, because she hears the shriek of blue lights; then she finds herself berating a paramedic for not letting her assist the patient. Gently, but resolutely, an overweight policeman with acne scarring escorts her away from the scene.

She's led into a shop where someone puts a cup of tea in her hands. It's a pet shop; she finds herself answering the fat policeman's laborious questions to the incongruous accompaniment of cheeping budgerigars. All of a sudden, the musty smell of small rodents assaults her, bringing with it a burst of nausea so violent that she has to abandon the tea and put her head between her knees to stop herself from vomiting. When she gingerly raises her head again, the policeman asks her to blow into a bag, to give a swab from her cheek, to surrender her phone.

She's assessed by the paramedics, declared not in need of any immediate treatment but warned to look out for whiplash. Before she knows it, she is being driven to the police station to give a statement. "My library books," she hears herself saying. "They're due back today! I'll get a fine if I don't return them."

There's a series of questions. "Why do you think you didn't see him?" she's asked. *Ah*, she thinks, *it was a man*. It seems important that she carefully notes this piece of new information.

"I don't know," she answers. "One minute he wasn't there, and the next he was. It all happened so quickly! Is he all right?"

And yet she knows he isn't. How could he be? While clinging to the faint hope that, miraculously, the man has survived, everything tells her he cannot possibly have. The impact, the sound of skull on tarmac, the shocked faces around her can only mean one thing. Death. *A man is dead, and I killed him.*

They are kind, offering to phone someone. Is there anyone at home they should ring? A family member or neighbour, perhaps? *I want my Mammy*, she finds herself thinking, to her surprise. *I want my Mammy*. But this isn't something Bridie can kiss better. Joy can only imagine her bewilderment, her distress if a policeman turned up at her door. Her sister? But Flick is three thousand miles away chasing rainbows in Vermont. Trisha has her hands full with a disabled husband.

She suddenly feels terribly, horribly alone. In the end, Linda is the only person she can think of: good old Linda, practical and sensible, who will be cheerfully cooking supper for her boring husband Geoff, a retired town planner. And Linda is equally kind. She arrives almost at once, and takes her to her own home, where Geoff hovers, his arms dangling helplessly at his side. Joy finds she can't stop shaking. She is trembling from head to foot and is icily cold.

"It's the shock," says Linda, and wraps her in a tartan blanket. "Why not stay the night?"

Not at all sure she wants to, yet entirely incapable of resisting the offer, Joy accepts a bed for the night and has a bath in an unfamiliar pink bathroom. There's a fluffy pink toilet seat cover and matching pink pedestal mats, and a darker pink floral blind. A blonde-haired doll with a knitted pink dress sits guarding the spare loo roll. (Even the suite itself is pink. It's like being encased in a giant womb, and the overall effect is more alarming than comforting.)

After a bath as hot as she can bear (she resists the rose-scented bubble bath) Joy creeps into the spare bed in a borrowed nightdress. She lies awake most of the night reliving the hideous moment of impact, the sickening thud, which plays on an unstoppable loop in her head. *A man is dead, and I killed him.* The words echo through the night. *I have killed a man.*

When she wakes, there's a blissful split second when she has no idea where she is. But then, in a moment of heart-sinking clarity, she remembers. *I have killed a man.* A man is dead; and the responsibility is hers and hers alone. Why is she alive this morning when he is dead? This is how it will be for the rest of her life, she thinks: every morning she will wake with the terrible knowledge that she has taken someone else's life. How can she possibly live with that? Despair threatens to overwhelm her.

Emotionally, she's wrung out. Physically, she feels stiff but oddly numb, as if she's had a general anaesthetic and the effects are yet to wear off. The effort of getting out of bed feels almost beyond her. She staggers to the horrible pink bathroom, her limbs heavy and uncooperative. She's not sure if it's bruising from the accident but she seems to have aged a decade overnight. *Shock*, she tells herself. *It's just shock. It will pass.*

But will it? *A man is dead and I killed him.* This is a defining moment in her life; there will be a *before* and an *after*, a deep fissure in her life's narrative. Nothing will ever be the same again.

It is several days before Joy goes home. Until then, to her chagrin, she finds she simply cannot cope with the most basic of tasks. No amount of trying to pull herself together seems to overcome the effects of the crash. It is as if she has no control over mind or body.

Although there's no evidence of physical injury, the slightest exertion leaves her exhausted. She can't eat, and she can barely manage the stairs. When Linda finally persuades her to come down to the lounge, she simply sits in front of the television, seeing and hearing nothing. She knows she ought to phone her mother and her sister, but she doesn't have the first idea how to form the words necessary to convey the cataclysm that has befallen her. She spends most of the time in bed, crying. And Joy never cries.

Linda and Geoff are solicitous, to the point where Joy would scream if she had the energy. Linda checks on her hourly, fussing round with offers of tea and toast. "I really ought to ring the doctor," she says more than once. "I think you'd feel a lot better with something to calm your nerves."

But Joy can't bear the thought. Although she is bruised—her seatbelt has left a faint diagonal mark across her chest—she's confident there are no bones broken, and the whiplash is bearable as long as she doesn't try to lift her arms above her head. She is repelled by the idea of being prescribed anything to numb the horror. It is surely right and proper that she suffers; it is only what she deserves.

When it becomes obvious that she won't be going home in a hurry, Linda takes Joy's keys to collect a case of clothes and toiletries from her house. Normally, Joy would be mortified at the thought of her friend-from-work retrieving her tired toothbrush from the bathroom or sifting through her greying underwear. In the circumstances, she struggles to muster the energy to care.

While Linda is out, Geoff—relieved to be given a practical task—chases the police for information about Joy's car and establishes that it has been towed away pending investigation. But even if it isn't a write-off, Joy can't imagine ever wanting to set eyes on her once-beloved VW Polo again. Geoff even rings the library to explain about her overdue books. ("All sorted," he says, in a rather too hearty voice. "Had a bit of a time of it explaining, but we got there in the end. Three-week extension, and nothing to pay.")

On the third morning, a call comes from the police station to say that an officer will call round to update her on developments. Linda, caught up in the drama of the situation, makes the arrangements for 11 a.m. with barely concealed excitement.

Joy washes her hair and dresses with exaggerated care, as if looking neat and tidy will help establish her good character. She desperately wants the police to know that she is a serious, responsible citizen. It takes her twenty minutes, and the effort leaves her drained.

She makes her way slowly downstairs, her heart heavy, and waits in the lounge for the doorbell. For all her dread, there is a certain relief in the moment of reckoning. Eventually, Linda shows in an officer who introduces herself as WPC Carol Thomas. Linda chats inconsequentially as she offers round tea in pretty cups and saucers on a doily-clad tray. Task complete, she plants herself next to Joy on the sofa. Joy finds herself totally unable to speak.

"Well?" Linda asks eagerly. "I suppose you've got some news for us?"

For me. Not us, thinks Joy. *My accident. My news.*

WPC Thomas tells them that Gilbert Maloney (the shadowy figure now has a name) was well known to local police: a homeless man with a record for petty theft and occasional public disorder. He died at the scene, almost instantly. The post-mortem revealed high levels of alcohol in his bloodstream.

"He wouldn't have known what hit him," she says evenly.

Who hit him.

"You see, Joy?" cries Linda. "He was drunk! It wasn't your fault!"

A man is dead. The brutality of the news that Gilbert Maloney died at the scene isn't lessened by the fact that it comes as no surprise.

"I still killed him," she mutters.

"But surely this proves he stepped into the road," says Linda. "He didn't know what he was doing."

"Investigations are ongoing," says WPC Thomas carefully. "Nothing will be certain until the inquest. But there are a number of witnesses who appear to support that theory. Mr Maloney was seen meandering all over the place beforehand."

All Joy can think is *what if.* What if she'd taken the bus that day? Had gone to the library before swimming, rather than afterwards? Had drunk one cup of tea, not two? (She sees herself standing up from the café table, not to ask for extra hot water, but to make her excuses. Imaginary Joy checks the time on her watch, sees the surprise on Imaginary Linda's face, but says firmly, "No time for a top-up today, I'm afraid. Must dash! See you next week!") A few seconds either way and Gilbert Maloney would still be alive.

"Sounds like this Maloney chap only has himself to blame," says Geoff gruffly, having listened to Linda's breathless account of the policewoman's visit over steak-and-kidney pie and peas. Geoff insists on a hot lunch in retirement. "Terrible bad luck, but it could have happened to any of us."

That doesn't help, thinks Joy, as she sits and looks at the congealing gravy on her plate. She lacks the energy to lift the fork to her mouth. *It happened to me. And I wouldn't wish this on my worst enemy.* The tears prickle in her eyes. She feels as vulnerable as a new-born baby. As if she's lost a skin.

"Time I went home," she hears herself say, more abruptly than she intended. "I mean . . . thank you. You've been so good, Linda. So kind. You, too, Geoff. I can't thank you enough for letting me land on you like this. But it's time I sorted myself out. More than time. Could I possibly have a lift home? Or shall I order a taxi?"

It's the longest utterance Joy has spoken since outlining the details of her pension options to Linda over tea in the swimming pool café. A lifetime ago. *Before.* She sees Linda and Geoff exchange a look. Puzzlement? Relief?

"Of course we'll run you home," says Linda, reaching across the table to take Joy's hand. "But are you sure you'll be all right? You still look terribly pale, love, and you haven't eaten a thing for days. I think you're still in shock. Are you certain you're ready?"

"As ready as I'll ever be!" says Joy, retrieving her hand as gently as she can. She sounds rather braver than she feels. All she knows is she needs to get away from Linda's suffocating kindness and start (what—her *life*?) again.

———

It is another three months before the inquest delivers a verdict of accidental death. According to the police, the investigation established that Joy had been driving with due care and attention. For reasons unknown, but almost certainly linked to the quantity of alcohol he had consumed, Gilbert Maloney had stepped off the kerb and into the road, right in front of her. There was nothing she or anyone else could have done to avoid an accident. The coroner was clear that no blame should be attached to the driver.

"Well, thank goodness for that!" says Felicity afterwards. She's back from America for Spring Break and up from Oxfordshire for the day to support her sister, although she arrives late, as usual, just after the proceedings have begun. ("Sorry! Sorry!" she says in a stage whisper, as she wriggles her way through the airless room to join Joy and Linda on the benches. "Terrible traffic, you've no idea!") Joy feels a familiar upsurge of annoyance. *It's not about you*, she thinks.

"You must be so relieved!" Felicity attempts to hug Joy. Joy allows her the briefest embrace before stepping back.

"Of course she's relieved," chips in Linda before Joy has a chance to speak. "Lovely to meet you, Felicity. I must dash now; Geoff's waiting in the car. But I'll ring you soon, Joy. And you just remember—it's all over now!"

But Joy is not sure it will ever be over. The verdict doesn't change anything. *A man is still dead, and I still killed him.* She feels . . . what? Not relieved, but oddly flat. There's no sense of closure.

Outwardly, she is functioning, more or less, in that the disabling paralysis that gripped her immediately after the accident has passed. She's still unreasonably tired, but she can wash and dress and cook a meal and follow a TV programme. She no longer aches. But she's newly terrified of crowds, finding herself claustrophobic and panicky at the drop of a hat. Loud noises make her jump: only last week, when she went out to post a birthday card to her mother, the sound of a police siren saw her cowering behind the pillar box, hands clamped over her ears. She only realized there was anything odd about her behaviour when a complete stranger asked if she was OK. Her doctor has suggested counselling. The leaflet is sitting on the hall table.

For the first time in her long working life, she has been signed off sick, something that makes her feel deeply guilty. As if she's skiving. But the thought of going back to work—of being responsible for the safety of others—absolutely terrifies her.

"You're quiet," says Felicity, as the sisters walk to the car park where Felicity has left her car. "You OK?"

"Not really."

"But surely it's a relief?"

Joy sighs. Felicity has simply no idea. Her sister lives in a parallel universe. "You'd have thought so, wouldn't you?"

"Well, isn't it?" Felicity is fiddling in her purse to find the right coins for the ticket machine.

"Yes. No. Not really. But I suppose it's good to know that someone thinks it wasn't all my fault."

"Of course it wasn't your fault!" Felicity sounds indignant. "You can't be blamed if some old wino throws himself in front of your car! Why do you always assume it's something you did? Honestly, Joy, if anyone's a good driver, you are."

Joy's eyes fill with tears, as they so often do these days. "Was," she mutters, closing her eyes as Felicity navigates the spiral exit from the multi-storey. "*Was* a good driver. Maybe."

"What do you mean, *was*? Oh, come on! You're not giving up driving, are you? Don't tell me you're not replacing the car?"

Joy shakes her head in defeat. "I just can't do it," she says. "I can't bring myself to sit behind a wheel. Even to try. Geoff offered to give me a spin, help me get my nerve back. Even said he'd help me buy a car, as if I couldn't manage that perfectly well on my own. But there's no point."

"No *point*? But you've always loved driving! Just like Daddy! Think how proud he was of his Ford Cortina. And you were just the same with your first car. Remember Minnie? You were always taking her out for a spin, just for the fun of it!"

"Really? Was I really like him?" Joy shivers. She loathes the thought of being likened to Joseph. "I hope you're wrong there. He was only my stepfather, remember."

But it's true she's always enjoyed driving. Or used to, anyway. The physicality of it, as much as the convenience. The feel of the engine responding to the touch of your feet. The sense of adventure, working out routes, exploring new places. The freedom. She could never understand people who complained about long journeys. It took her years to realize that not everyone felt the same way. Is liking cars something that is inherited?

"Do you know, for the first time in my life, ever since it happened . . . I've found myself, well, wondering." Her voice is uncharacteristically tentative.

"Wondering what?"

Joy gives a half-laugh, embarrassed. What will Felicity think? She's always been the down-to-earth one. All she knows is that, since the accident, every single one of her old certainties seems to have been overturned. She feels a desperate need to try and make sense of a new narrative.

"Wondering about *them*. Howard and Veronica. My birth parents."

"Whatever do you mean? You've always said you're not interested."

"I . . . I thought I knew who I was. Now I'm not sure anymore." Her birth mother drove an ambulance in the War, Bridie told her that. Veronica was on duty the night of the bombing, when the roof fell in and nearly did for them both. When did Veronica learn to drive? And who taught her? Did you even have to take a test back then? Was she a good driver? Accidents were prevalent during the blackout: was Veronica ever involved in a fatal collision?

And what about Howard? He was a pilot; did he shoot down many Germans? *I killed a man. A man is dead because I killed him.* Was history doomed to repeat itself? Was there some kind of killing gene?

"Well, did I kill Gilbert Maloney because of some . . . I don't know," she says eventually. "Because of my origins. Some kind of *flaw* in my DNA. Or because of what happened when I was a baby?"

"Joy, that's completely ridiculous, and you know it! It's got nothing to do with any of that. For goodness sake, it was an accident! You heard the coroner. She said quite clearly that no blame should be attached to the driver. *No blame!* Horrible, yes, upsetting, yes. But *not your fault.*"

"Hmm," says Joy. "I suppose." She badly wants to believe the coroner. To believe Felicity. Somehow she can't. Guilt hangs over her head like a storm cloud. She feels so unbalanced. As if she's got vertigo.

She realizes she must phone Bridie, let her know the coroner's verdict. Her mother will be pleased for her. No doubt she'll tell Joy what a relief it is, just as Linda and Felicity have done. Perhaps they can plan a date for Joy to visit Bridie. She'd like to pick her brains about Veronica and Howard. (Can you grieve for people you never knew?) She's not sure why, but for the first time since she knew of their existence, she needs to know more about them. Find out who she is.

They're nearly back at Joy's house. She realizes her sister is asking a question. "How will you get to work if you're not driving?"

"That's another thing," she says, looking straight ahead. "I think I'm going to retire."

"Oh *Joy!*" gushes her sister. "Really? Are you sure that's what you want?"

It's not what she wants in the slightest. But right now, Joy can't see any alternative but to apply for early retirement on health grounds. She hasn't told Felicity, but she has a meeting scheduled with someone from Personnel next Monday. She booked it before the inquest, in the certainty that whatever the outcome, it was time to make a decision. She imagines there will be an Occupational Health assessment. Forms to fill in, finances to sort out.

All in all, it feels like the most crushing defeat. An ignominious end to her long career. And what on earth she's going to do with the rest of her life, she has absolutely no idea.

FELICITY

2002

Felicity is late as usual. How is this still the case now she only has herself to worry about? She had some excuse when the boys were at home but really, you'd have thought she could get her act together now she is in her fifties. This morning, it's her car keys; they've vanished off the face of the earth. Just when she needs to arrive calm and collected and make a good impression.

By the door is her bulging canvas bag, her harp, a carrier of old clothes she wants to drop off at the charity shop, and a box of dry goods for the food bank since she's going into Kings Burton. Honestly! Why on earth doesn't she ever remember to use the key rack that Jacob so lovingly made for her as part of his GCSE woodwork?

Darling Jake, who phoned last night to tell her, very diffidently, that he's Met Someone. He wouldn't say any more for fear of jinxing things, but he wanted Felicity to know. Because if this is the real thing, he knows he's finally going to come out to his father and face the consequences. (Poor Jake! Even at the age of twenty-five, he is absolutely terrified of David's reaction, and hand on heart Felicity can't be sure that David will be supportive. Naturally she suspected for years before Jacob told her, but he always had a wide circle of friends, and since his schooldays brought home a steady flow of attractive girls. David appeared to be under the impression that his handsome middle son was playing the field.)

Unlike Alex, who has been going out with Amélie since they met in a regional debating competition in their last year of school and are now living in a little flat in Putney with baby Henry. David adores Amélie: she is half French, terrifyingly *chic*, and very earnest about her career in the City. ("What on earth does she see in staid old Alex?" said David not so long ago. "Surely she's way out of his league?") As for Finn . . . well, you never know with Finn. He is the most happy-go-lucky of her sons. He's due to graduate this summer and plans to go travelling before settling into a job, completely unfazed by his father's disapproval.

And then she has a flash of inspiration—yes!—her keys are in the pocket of the gorgeous patchwork coat she brought home from Vermont. She always feels good in it, so she'll wear it for luck. She scoops up her belongings and heads out into the chill October air. She'll be fine for time. No need to panic. *Drive carefully*, she tells herself sternly. *Better late than dead on time. Remember what happened to Joy.*

The trouble is, she's nervous. If today goes well, there's a good chance she'll have a permanent job. Maggie, who runs the Daisy Hospice at Kings Burton, heard her speak at a conference in palliative care in Birmingham at the end of last year, and invited her to come in from time to time as a volunteer. She's been a great advocate for her work, fighting Felicity's corner when, at first at least, some of the staff were a bit suspicious of what she had to offer. Now Maggie has asked Felicity to come in to discuss the possibility of joining the team on a more official basis.

Maggie has been mysterious about what's changed, because the hospice is constantly struggling for funding. "Come in and have a chat," she said on the phone. "Let's take it a step at a time."

The job—any job—would be a bit of a lifesaver, and practically on her doorstep, too. Two years in the US where music thanatology was well respected had allowed Felicity to forget that this was far from the case in the UK. Most of her cohort seemed to have found paid employment reasonably quickly after graduation, but not Felicity. Eighteen months on, she is yet to be paid for her work.

Obviously she can still teach the piano, and in an attempt to show willing, she has more-or-less-cheerfully taken on a number of private pupils since her return to the UK, mainly the younger siblings of her former students. But her heart is in music thanatology. She has seen it weave its spell too often to let it go. Now she's discovered it, she feels she's been entrusted with a precious gift that she has a duty to share with the world. Nothing else has brought her such satisfaction. And it's changed her life. It's as if she's finally emerged into the light after a life lived in the shadows. The sense of liberation is profound.

She never wants to charge patients; she doesn't believe the dying, or their loved ones, should have to pay for her services. But she would like to be able to earn a living, not least because David still refuses to take her Master's seriously. He seems to view it as a menopausal flight of fancy. (In front of friends, it has become "Felicity's jaunt across the pond", to be referred to with a light laugh and the hint of a raised eyebrow, the very picture of an indulgent husband who has acquiesced in his wife's pursuit of her latest faddy hobby.)

"You've no idea what hard work it was!" she protested at first. And it's true: as well as the practical element—harp lessons, voice classes, ensemble work, all highly demanding—there was an intense programme of academic lectures in subjects as alien as anatomy, physiology and psychology, along with the history of music in medicine. Then there was the large repertoire of music to memorize. She'd never studied so hard in her life. Felicity felt her mind expanding on a daily basis, as new neural pathways were carving their way into her brain. Terrifying—but exhilarating too. And utterly transformational.

It was hard to convey all that to her family, though she'd tried to share some of her passion on every visit home. Jake—a fledgling music producer, now—was the most interested, though she wasn't sure he really got it. Finn and she had bonded over course work and shared deadlines. But Alex, busy establishing his career in the insurance industry, appeared slightly embarrassed by her apparent desertion of her husband. (As for Joy, she hasn't said much beyond, "Sounds interesting", which could mean anything. But Joy's still not herself. Hasn't been since the accident.)

Yet for all the demands of the course, right from the beginning Felicity knew that this was what she wanted to do, above all else. The sense of vocation only deepened over the months she spent in Vermont. To her surprise, she found herself captivated by the spiritual journey the programme encouraged students to pursue. The Master's was taught in association with a Catholic Hospice, and although there was no requirement for students to profess any kind of faith, merely to nurture their own spiritual practice, Felicity experienced an unexpected homecoming. It's as if the pieces of a jigsaw have all finally fallen into place. She would go as far as to say that at the bedside of the dying she has experienced a taste of the divine.

Never in her life had she felt so free. The place itself was inspiring: a little university town nestling in a valley in the foothills of the Green Mountains where the air was fresh and the views spectacular. She started going for long walks. Eating properly: regular meals, with lots of fruit and salad and vegetables. She gave up alcohol and felt better for it, clear-headed and alert. She made new friends among her fellow students: a young woman who played the harp in an Italian orchestra; a retired French music teacher whose wife had recently died of cancer; a music therapist from California; and a former furniture salesman from Australia. At the start of the course, they had little in common except for their shared dedication to learning how to ease the burden of the dying through music; by the end they were an intimate cohort, fellow initiates into the mysteries of thanatology. Together, they learned an entirely new language.

Best of all—and she hardly dares say this out loud in case she tempts fate—somehow or other she has started to sing again. Before she left for America, she had become increasingly anxious about her voice, lying awake at night wondering what to tell her tutors. In the end, it seemed simplest to say that she hadn't sung since school and was a bit nervous about it as a result, and leave it at that. Her singing teacher, an elderly Buddhist called Taru, seemed to take this statement at face value.

"Then we'll start from the very beginning," he said.

And it had worked. A gentle warm-up to check her range. The basics of posture and breathing. An emphasis on singing softly. "This is music for the bedside, remember," Taru reminded her. "We're not trying to fill the Carnegie Hall. Imagine you're singing a child to sleep."

Slowly, her long-dormant voice emerged from hibernation, blinking uncertainly in the sunshine. At first, it felt like encountering a long-lost relative: dimly familiar but almost unrecognizable. Her new voice was deeper, darker than she remembered, more of a folk sound than opera. Hardly surprising after thirty years. Without forcing it, she felt her vocal cords slowly become stronger. By tiny degrees, the sound became less tentative, more confident.

Her lessons, thank heavens, were private, because more often than not, she wept as she sang. The tears simply flowed. In her early sessions, Taru made no comment. She wasn't sure if he was being polite, or was so focused on his teaching that he hadn't noticed. But a few weeks in, to her discomfort, he raised the subject.

"I wonder if you know why you weep when you sing," he said as the lesson came to an end.

"Oh gosh!" she said, flustered. "How embarrassing! I'm terribly sorry."

Taru smiled. "I don't think there's anything to apologize for. But if we are going to be attuned to our patients, we need to listen to our hearts. Have you asked yourself what your tears might be telling you?"

"Not really. I suppose . . . well, it's a relief to find my voice. I couldn't . . . I mean, I didn't . . . "

Taru's expression gave nothing away. "Go on."

"I didn't think it was possible anymore. To *sing*, I mean. I had some . . . issues with my voice. I thought I'd lost it for good." Saying it aloud sounded foolish.

"It seems not," said Taru. "You're doing well. How do you feel afterwards?"

"Lighter. Freer," said Felicity, suddenly realizing this was true. "As if I've let go of something . . . heavy."

"That's good." Taru nodded. "Just be aware, the shedding of tears is an indication of pressure and pain within. You might want to ask yourself, is there some hidden grief that you are releasing?"

"But I'm so happy here!" she blurted out. "I'm not in pain! I love everything about this course! I feel I've finally found my calling."

Taru opened the door to signal it was time for her to go. "I'm glad you're happy, Felicity," he said. "But you might want to work with a therapist while you are over here. Dig a little deeper. You will be a better thanatologist for it."

Honestly, thought Felicity at the time. *Work with a therapist? How typically American! What on earth would David say?*

Now Felicity finds herself wondering what business of David's it is, whether she sees a therapist or not. Since returning to the UK she is viewing her husband with greater clarity. Achieving her Master's was demanding; it required determination. She had to draw on a deep well of inner strength that she didn't know was there. She is invigorated by her achievement. David's dismissiveness, his lack of understanding of what the last two years have meant to her, suggests she is invisible to him. She thought they would muddle through (after all, weren't they used to living apart?) but the intermittent physical separation of the last two years seems to have widened the gulf between them.

Naturally she felt the tug of home when she was away; she missed everyone horribly. But life in Vermont was so much simpler. Focusing on herself and her music was the most blessed relief. She and David are going to have to work hard to bridge the yawning chasm in their marriage.

She pulls into the Daisy Hospice car park and makes her way into the reception area. She asks the volunteer at the front desk to let Maggie know she's arrived.

"It's the harp lady, Maggie," says the receptionist on the intercom.

Felicity smiles. *The harp lady*. (She loves being the harp lady!) She didn't stop to think whether she needed her harp for this meeting, but it never occurred to her to leave it at home. It's a Celtic harp, so a foot shorter and a third of the weight of a concert harp, but it's still quite a palaver to carry around. Thank goodness she's tall. Yet it's almost part of her these days. Certainly in these surroundings. It's what brings her to the Daisy. It's such a bright and cheerful place; so unlike a hospital. What a shame that some patients are reluctant to accept all that's on offer here. There's an unfounded fear that hospices are where you go to die. It may be a cliché, but the last few years have taught Felicity that the opposite is true. Hospice care is all about helping people to live as fully as they can to the very end of their lives.

"Felicity, you'll remember Stan, I'm sure?" Maggie holds open her office door so that Felicity can wheel in her harp. "You played for Jennifer when she was with us."

"Of course!" says Felicity. Jennifer was in and out of the Daisy a handful of times until her death, always with Stan at her side. They were a slight couple in their eighties who appeared to have grown alike over the years, an impression accentuated by wearing matching glasses and the same closely cropped hairstyles. Even the body language was the same: there was an angular stiffness about their bearing, a suggestion of deep physical pain. They were both hollow-eyed, haunted by fear. The most marked difference between them was the yellowish pallor of Jennifer's skin.

When Felicity first offered to play, Jennifer had refused, politely but clearly.

"Not really our thing, dear," she said. "No offence meant."

"None taken," said Felicity, and went next door to visit one of her favourite patients, a former merchant seaman called Biff who called her *ducks* and swore like a trooper when he was in pain. She had some sea-shanties in mind for him. It always helped to start with something familiar; it was a bit like starting a conversation with a stranger and establishing common ground before going any deeper. Once you'd made a connection, you could vary the tempo and the timbre, and take the listener on a sensory journey. It was all about taking your cues from the patient. Reading the tiniest clues from a twitch of their muscles to the quiver of their pulse. Being fully present in the moment and improvising. Following your intuition.

Biff died that day, alone but for Felicity and her harp. She was just emerging from his room, exhausted from the concentration of the vigil, but with a sense of satisfaction that her music had helped him slip away in peace, when she met Stan in the corridor. There were tears in his eyes.

"That was beautiful, you know," he said. "Jennifer's been asleep, mainly, but I've been listening to every note. Perhaps another time you might play for her?"

"Of course," said Felicity. "But are you sure? She was quite clear earlier."

"That's just Jennifer," said Stan. "She always says no to things she doesn't understand. We're not musical types. But I know she was listening before she drifted off."

Over the next few weeks, Jennifer had a few short stays in the Daisy to allow the palliative care team to manage her pain relief. Felicity gradually got to know them; she never stayed long, playing for a short time to build trust. She needed Jennifer's confidence before the music could work its magic. Stan sat in an armchair a few feet away from the bedside, lost in his own pain. Felicity watched each of them out of the corner of her eye for any tiny sign of an easing of the tension as the music began to work its healing balm.

By the second session, she felt brave enough to suggest Stan pulled up his chair close and held Jennifer's hand. By the third, which she was pretty sure would be the last, she invited him to lie next to his wife and allow the music to caress them. He hesitated for just a moment, before removing his shoes and jacket and climbing stiffly onto the bed. Within half an hour of Stan taking her in his arms, Jennifer drifted into unconsciousness. Very slowly, imperceptibly at first, her breathing slowed and then stopped altogether. Felicity played on until Stan was ready to let go.

"It's lovely to see you again, Stan," she says now. "How are you?"

"I'm well," he says. "Sad. But well." And Felicity notices that he looks a different person: the stiffness has gone, and so has the haunted look behind his eyes.

"Stan has come to us with an exciting proposal," says Maggie. "Do you want to explain or shall I?"

Stan says that he has set up a trust in memory of Jennifer, and the trust will help fund Felicity's work. "What you did for us—well, I can never thank you enough. We were married forty-six years, you know. Forty-six years! Losing her was so terrible. I didn't think I could bear to let her go, but in the end . . . well . . . you have to, don't you?"

He tails off, blows his nose, and then collects himself. "Wonderful place, the Daisy. It made all the difference. Unbearable, but more bearable. We never had children so I've money to spare. And I can't think of a better place for it."

"Stan is generously making a donation to the Daisy's general running costs in Jennifer's memory," says Maggie. "But the Jennifer Trust is something else. It's about supporting some of the therapeutic extras we struggle to fund. Stan and I are hoping you'll agree to join the Daisy's pastoral care team on a permanent basis. Only part-time, but with a proper salary and benefits. What are your thoughts? Do you need time to think about it?"

Of course Felicity doesn't need time to think about it. This is the chance of a lifetime: to work in palliative care in a supportive context. Thank goodness she'd gone to that conference in Birmingham and Maggie had heard her presentation!

She feels a smile break out on her face. "When can I start?" she asks.

BRIDIE

2019

Norman was good to us. For all his lording it over us when we first arrived in Northampton, he loved his brother. He admired him for the way he left his airs and graces at the factory gates, and knuckled down to learn the trade. I'm not sure Norman understood quite what it cost Joseph, but they'd been brought up to respect hard graft, and you couldn't fault Joseph's work ethic. For all that he half-despised selling shoes, Joseph gave it his all.

Norman was badly rattled by his death. That heart attack means he's lost his best salesman, as well as his big brother. Joseph is the older by barely two years, so Norman fears he's next in line. In the weeks that follow, he takes to coming round to St James' End after work, to check up on me, he says. Make sure I'm managing for money. Doing any little jobs I might need done around the house—as if Joseph had ever lifted a finger to mend a window catch or change a lightbulb!

Not that I'm going to stop him. It looks to me more like a chance to chew the fat over a glass of Joseph's precious whisky. To put off for an hour or so the moment of returning to the big house in Hardingstone and that dry old stick Marjorie. She of the good works and the cut-glass accent and the linen napkins at dinner. Another black mark for me, if she knew, to be sure, but she thinks he's still at the factory. And what the eye doesn't see, the heart doesn't grieve over.

But I'm not complaining. Now Felicity's off to college in London, I'm on my own and the house is quiet. I like the company, and Norman's nothing if not kind, for all his bluster. *You'll marry again*, says he, gazing fondly at my breasts as I bend down to top up his glass. His eyes are suddenly full of unspilled tears. *You're a comely woman, Bridie. I can see why a man would give up everything for you.*

Comely, says he. A quaint old word I find I like the feel of on the tongue. I'm young for a widow, to be sure. Not quite forty-three, and I've made sure to keep my figure. I take a good long look at Norman, and I find myself thinking that he's a fine-looking man.

He has that sort of masculinity that often goes with success. Joseph had it, too, when he was younger, especially when he was going into battle with the authorities during the War. But unlike his brother, Norman hasn't shut away his virility in a box marked *Do Not Touch*. And now there's an air of yearning in Norman's eye, and I can see which way the wind is blowing, and to be honest, it's a pleasure to have a man show interest in me, because I'd long become invisible to himself.

So I find myself bending a little further down when I refill his glass, so he can enjoy the view, you might say, and when I'm done with the whisky decanter, I sit on the settee next to him, just a tiny bit closer than I might if we weren't alone, and rest my hand on his knee. He puts his hand on mine and gives it a squeeze. I tell him all about the new job, and make him laugh with stories about some of the funny things you hear at the surgery. And if my hand creeps a way up his thigh and we take a little comfort in each other, where's the harm in that? We're both in need of a bit of kindness. I always made sure to send him home to Marjorie afterwards, for all that he'd rather stay with my breasts for a pillow.

—

I knew Joseph a little in the War. He wouldn't have known me from Eve, of course. I was just one more girl off the boat when I first set eyes on him. It was summer-time, and everyone was holding their breath, hoping against hope the worst of the Blitz was over. The damage was terrible, the city reduced to rubble. People couldn't take much more.

I'm making my way home to Dolly's after my shift at the fish-market. It's a horrible job—the stink is especially terrible, what with the hot weather, and there's blood and guts and fish scales everywhere—but beggars can't be choosers, as they say. I turn the corner into Jamaica Street and I hear an almighty row going on. There's a priest, formidable in his black cassock, tearing a strip off some petty official with a toothbrush moustache and a clipboard.

He was like an avenging angel, I tell Dolly, impressed in spite of myself, not being given to fondness for priests.

Oh, that'll be Father Kelly, says she. *He's something of a legend. A thorn in the flesh of our city fathers.* She tells me about his work during the worst of the air raids, when he became an ad hoc stretcher-bearer. *He's everywhere, all at once,* she says. *No fear for his own safety and not afraid of getting his hands dirty. Sees what's needed and just gets on with it.*

I often used to see him out and about after that. You know how it is once someone's caught your eye, and you keep running into them? One day I pluck up courage, and say, *Hello, Father Kelly,* when our paths cross, and I can't help liking him for the fact he looks surprised to be recognized. He even visited me in hospital when my leg was in pieces after the air raid. So I suppose you could say I was predisposed in his favour.

After the bombing of Upper Stanhope Street, I move back in with Dolly because a room comes spare when her friend Una leaves to get married. Dolly is a godsend: with my leg in plaster, I'm hardly fit to look after a baby to start with. But when the War comes to an end, you've got Dolly and Ron getting married, and I need to find a new home, because three's a crowd, not to mention four if you count wee Joy, and she's growing up fast. Dolly sees the notice at the Church of the Holy Name when she and Ron go to a dance, and she comes home with the postcard in her hand that she filched from the board so that no one else can beat me to it.

Just the thing, she says, *a job with bed and board for you and our Joy.*

At the time, it seems an answer to prayer, so it does. And who's to say it wasn't? It's all very well to be wise in hindsight.

JOY

2003

Joy picks her way along the wintry beach, deep in concentration. Every few moments, she pauses and bends down to examine something at her feet. Her posture is stooped, bent against the blustery wind, and her gaze focused downwards rather than at the grey horizon. Behind her she drags a half-full sack, into which she occasionally adds an item.

As a single woman with a busy job and little inclination for hobbies, Joy has always known that retirement might present challenges. She is someone who thrives on order, even though babies don't always arrive according to plan. But in Joy's experience, a meticulously organized ward and a set of well-oiled procedures provide the best environment for supporting expectant mothers. The calm backdrop for the drama of childbirth. *Be prepared* was one of her professional mantras.

Nonetheless, it has been a shock to find herself so purposeless without the anchor of work. In the immediate aftermath of the accident, she will admit to being quite at sea. As if she had lost her moorings altogether. She knows she has made progress since then, but there are still days when she feels badly adrift.

Today, for example. When there's nothing on her to-do list beyond beachcombing. She tells herself—and anyone else she encounters, not that there are many people out and about on this unprepossessing day—that she is doing this for reasons of good citizenship. For environmental reasons, perhaps; all the rage right now, as Finn keeps telling her.

Neither of these reasons is untrue. She detests the rubbish that spoils the beach. If the plastic that washes up from the oceans infuriates her, the rubbish casually discarded by day trippers enrages her even more. (What do they think is going to happen to it? Do they imagine a fairy is going to clear up after them? Do they not understand the terrible destruction plastic is inflicting on the marine world? Even if the longer-term implications of plastic waste have somehow escaped their notice, can't they see they're marring the natural beauty of the place? The beauty they presumably travelled here to enjoy?) She's not above chasing after them and returning their dropped crisp wrappers and drinks cans. The response varies between mute incomprehension and an angry stream of invective.

There are few visitors at this time of year, thank goodness. While Weymouth draws the crowds all year round, this strip of noisy shingle is much less appealing out of season. Too windswept, too wild. Too rugged and at the mercy of Mother Nature. Joy is at liberty to make her lonely crawl along the beach undisturbed.

As well as tutting over the rubbish (and Joy knows she's developed a worrying habit of muttering her thoughts aloud; she must take herself in hand) she has another motive. She has recently lit upon the absorbing pleasure of sea glass. Hidden in amongst the shingle are small jewels: fragments of broken glass, smoothed into soft-edged pastilles by the buffeting of the waves on the shingle.

The colours are muted, mostly variations upon bottle green, but sometimes including brown, or what was once transparent and is now milk-white. Very occasionally you even find a startling cerulean blue. Joy gathers her finds in a shabby bum-bag she wears around her waist before taking them home to wash and sort. She finds it endlessly fascinating, becoming increasingly discerning in her classification. Nowadays, she keeps only the very best: the smoothest shapes, the most interesting colours. These she arranges in a large glass bowl she chanced upon in a charity shop in Weymouth. The rejected fragments are dutifully put in the recycling bin along with her used jars and bottles.

If she is unanchored, it is in no small part due to the sudden decision to sell up and move south. What she convinced herself at the time was a much-needed fresh start rapidly looked ill thought out, once some of the initial excitement wore off.

When friends—Linda, for example—asked, "Why Dorset?" she was able to answer with some conviction that she had been holidaying there for many years and had long nurtured a dream to move to the south coast, even though the plan was, in truth, a very new one.

"Of course, you'll be nearer your family," said more than one colleague at her hastily assembled retirement party. And that became another argument in favour of the scheme, though careful scrutiny of the map might have corrected this assumption. What mattered to Joy was that the move south represented forward progress of some sort; a bold new venture at a time when she was otherwise feeling so unlike herself.

To begin with, she was occupied with the practicalities of selling her house; as luck would have it, her house in West Derby sold within a week, for a price that made it look as if its purchase had been a clever investment, rather than a decision based on proximity to the Mill Road Maternity Hospital where she got a job on her return from South Africa. (The *Brookside* effect, according to her agent.) The proceeds of the sale, combined with the lump-sum payment from her NHS pension, made it possible to buy a small bungalow with a straggly garden on the edge of Portland. It was affordable—just—because it was desperately in need of modernization, and because the man who had inherited it from his aunt was in urgent need of funds to shore up his business in Hong Kong and wasn't prepared to hang about. When Joy made a cash offer, he almost bit her hand off.

Then there was the business of packing up and moving. She was lucky in her workmen; the most urgent refurbishment—new kitchen, new bathroom, new wiring, paid for out of a legacy from Aunt Dolly—was completed before she moved in. Joy planned to do the painting and decorating herself, consulting videos on YouTube when anything became beyond her rudimentary skills. Carpets could wait; she'd tolerate the swirly patterns until the decorating was finished. (Felicity offered to help, more than once, but Joy kept putting her off. She couldn't bear to see the look on her sister's face when she saw the pebbledash bungalow. Not exactly

Country Living. Felicity, with her period home in leafy Oxfordshire, was bound to turn up her nose.)

In the end, Finn came down on his way to Cornwall for a last-minute surfing holiday before going back to university where he's halfway to becoming an architect. He arrived, suntanned and scruffy in his board shorts, his blond dreadlocks tied behind his neck. (His height takes her by surprise every time; he's always a few inches taller than she remembers. He towers over her. The legacy of having two tall parents, she supposes.) Finn helped her with some of the heavy lifting, moving boxes and furniture without complaint, and best of all, hung her curtains, something that was still prohibitively painful as a result of the whiplash sustained in the accident.

"You OK, Aunty Joy?" he asked over a cup of tea early the next morning.

"I think so, thanks," she said. "Tired from the move, but you've been such a help. We've got loads done. I'm so grateful!"

"I mean . . . *really* OK?" Finn was standing at the kitchen counter, leaning against the new white B&Q units. He shifted his weight awkwardly from one foot to the other.

"Ah . . . " Joy gave her nephew a beady look. "Agent Finn on a mission from HQ? Mum wanting to know that your old Aunt isn't completely doolally?"

"S'not like that," said Finn, shiftily. He took a noisy slurp of tea. "She, like, cares, though. But actually, it was Gran who mentioned it. Says what happened . . . you know . . . left you banjaxed."

Joy laughed, in spite of herself. "I can just hear her saying that!"

"Puts me off learning to drive," added Finn. "Don't think I'll bother. Better for the environment, too."

"Hmm," said Joy. "But I miss it, truth to tell. Desperately. Though I'm doing all right. This move is a fresh start. I'm planning to reinvent myself!"

Finn glanced up, as if he was about to say something, then thought better of it. "Best be off," he said, with a glance at the kitchen clock, and sloped off to the spare bedroom to collect his rucksack. He paused for a moment on the doorstep. "You should let Mum come, you know," he mumbled as he gave her a quick hug. "She misses you!"

He slung his rucksack on his back and loped down the garden path. "And don't feel you have to," he added from the gate.

"Have to what?"

"Reinvent yourself. We like you just the way you are!"

Joy's eyes filled with tears as she waved him off. When did little Finn grow up? She'd ring Felicity and tell her what a help he'd been. Perhaps suggest a visit, in the spring. Maybe Flick could bring Bridie down. Once Joy was all sorted. Properly settled.

—

Sorting took the best part of six months, and, looking back on it, distracted her from the far trickier matter of settling. Whenever she felt at a loose end that first winter, she undertook a practical task: painting the skirting boards; visiting the carpet shop; ordering oddments of furniture.

There was an element of adventure in finding her way about a new area. She took the bus into Weymouth and looked at the shops. Bought a new cream waffle bedspread. Fluffy blue towels. Joined the library and borrowed books on gardening so that she could begin to make plans for the spring. And she walked, endlessly, up and down the beach. Around Portland Bill. Along the coast path. Alone with her gloomy thoughts.

The trouble was, she knew no one. She introduced herself to her neighbours who were polite enough, but it went no further. Now, she wonders how she got through the first winter. Once the novelty of her new project had worn off, she knew she had to take herself in hand. She needed interests, and she needed people.

Joy had never been a great joiner, and she prided herself on her self-sufficiency. Only now did she appreciate the sense of security that came from knowing her community. Of being known, having a place in the landscape. Back home (as she must stop thinking of Liverpool) it sometimes used to irritate her that she rarely left the house without bumping into someone she knew. Mothers, showing off their offspring, the babies morphed into unrecognizable gap-toothed schoolchildren or loutish adolescents. Sometimes she'd run into fellow-midwives or former colleagues from the unit. She knew the shopkeepers. The postman. Here she knew no one. There was no sense of belonging, only isolation and loneliness. Those around her were entirely indifferent to her existence.

The need for people surprised her; she'd always enjoyed her own company. Now, though, without the structure of work, she found she could go all day without exchanging a word with anyone else. Days when all she ever heard was the crash of the waves and the undertow of the shingle, punctuated by the shriek of seagulls. She'd wanted quiet, away from the crowds that still unnerved her, but this was too extreme. Of course, she spoke to her mother on the phone, to her sister, to old friends like Trisha and Linda. But it wasn't the same. She found a new respect for her mother, so long a widow, and retired from her job in the doctor's surgery for years now. Bridie rarely complained of loneliness. Or was it simply that Joy had never asked? Then again, Bridie had her neighbours and her church community, a far-reaching web of friends and acquaintances that she had woven over her sixty years in St James' End.

Joy felt rather less sympathy for Felicity, surrounded by her family and yet remarkably prone to complaining. The first Christmas after Joy's move was a case in point: Joy went to stay with Bridie as usual in Northampton—not an easy journey, crossing London by fuggy underground, laden with Christmas presents—only to discover Felicity chuntering that Joy would not be driving the pair of them over to Summersby on Christmas Day.

"But you *knew* I'd given up the car, Flick!" she protested. "Why don't you all come here to Mother's for once?"

"Don't be ridiculous!" snapped Felicity. "Where would we all sit? And I've done all the shopping and most of the preparation! Do you have *any* idea how much work that involves? Probably not because I always do it! Not to mention the boys and their friends eating us out of house and home. Sometimes I feel I'm running a hotel! David will just have to drive over and pick you up."

"Well, if he doesn't mind . . . "

"How would I bloody know if he minds? And what's the alternative anyway?"

"Ask one of the boys? Or come to us on Boxing Day instead?" ventured Joy, but Felicity was not to be diverted.

"And what would Mammy say to not being with her family on Christmas Day? That wouldn't really be fair on her, would it? Have you thought what *she* wants in all this?"

I'm family, thought Joy. *I'm her daughter, too, in case you have forgotten.*

In the event, David collected them after Mass with moderate grace, although he was uncharacteristically monosyllabic in the car. The atmosphere at The White House seemed unusually tense; Felicity spent most of the day in the kitchen and emerged red-faced and irritable only to eat. She insisted on doing all the washing up herself with an air of martyrdom that could not be contradicted. The day was carried by the boys who were both noisy and attentive to their grandmother and aunt, as they played the usual games of charades after Christmas lunch. David drank heavily, meaning it was Alex who drove them back to St James' End at the end of the day. He was going on to London to join Amélie and her family for the rest of the festive season.

"Well, that was a laugh a minute," said Joy when they'd waved goodbye to Alex.

"Oh, you've just forgotten the rough and tumble of family life," said Bridie. "There are always little quarrels at Christmas. Remember when you two were little? But that's the trouble with being on your own too much. You need to get out of yourself more."

Joy smarted with indignation. However you might describe her childhood, *rough and tumble* didn't come close. Did her mother really have no idea what it was like? The atmosphere so thick you could cut it with a knife. Aunt Marjorie dabbing at non-existent smudges on her cutlery with a hand-embroidered hankie. Picking at the Christmas dinner Bridie had slaved over and turning up her nose because she'd bought Cashel Blue rather than Stilton. Joseph more prickly than ever because drink had been taken. His mockery when Joy failed to understand the rules of Monopoly the year Uncle Norman gave them a set. (How was she supposed to know how you pronounced "Marylebone Station", for goodness sake?) The insistence that Felicity performed a party piece, which she did with aplomb.

"What about Joy?" asked Bridie. "She could give us a poem, surely." But just as Joy was summoning up courage to recite "There was a boy whose name was Jim", Joseph stamped on the idea. "Best not," he said in a tone that allowed no argument. "For all our sakes. Flissy, darling, what about the Haydn next? I'm sure we'd all enjoy that."

Does Mother remember none of this? Or is she harking back to a time when her nephews were small and full of mischief? When David's career was on the up, and Christmas at The White House was an expansive, happy occasion with riotous games of sardines and carol singing around the piano?

"And are you not grateful to your sister for all that cooking?" said her mother. "She goes to a lot of trouble, you know. And it can't be easy, being married to that old yoke."

"I suppose not," conceded Joy, wondering for the first time if there was something seriously amiss with Felicity. (The menopause, perhaps. Perhaps that's what this fandango with the harp had been all about. She'd always been prone to histrionics.) "But surely there's no need to take it out on the rest of us."

"Well, we'll have a bit of peace and quiet now, and you can tell me all about your grand new life by the seaside," said Bridie.

Joy sighed. "That won't take long," she said. "But look, I don't know about you, but I'm done in. I need to go to bed. Can we talk in the morning?"

And that was the moment at which she realized she needed to get a grip on her life. Being on her own was making her maudlin. Her isolation would surely only get worse if she let it. The uncomfortable truth was that you could move to the other end of the country, you could leave the scene of the crime, as it were (*No blame should be attached to the driver*), but you brought yourself with you, whether you wanted to or not. Your damaged, fragile self. She needed some answers about her past, and then she would tackle the future head on. It would be her new year's resolution.

She began the next morning over breakfast. She laid the table with extra care, made porridge for them both (Bridie's favourite) and set out cream in a little jug and a small bowl of soft brown sugar.

"What's all this?" asked Bridie suspiciously. "Is the Holy Father joining us?"

"A Boxing Day treat," said Joy.

"You softening me up for something?"

"Actually Mother," she said, diffidently, as she poured the tea, "I need your help. What can you tell me about . . . about . . . "

"About *what* for the love of all that's holy?"

"About my parents. About Veronica and Howard."

"Well, I don't know what's brought this on all of a sudden!" Bridie was clearly startled. "That's all a long time ago now, take it from me. Why've you suddenly got this fancy into your head? You've never shown the slightest interest."

"I'm not quite sure. Something about the . . . the accident means I'm questioning everything. I just feel I need to *know*."

"Know what, exactly?"

This was impossible! How did Joy know what questions to ask? "I don't know! Something about . . . where I came from. What were they like, my parents? Can you tell me what you remember?"

"As long as you don't try to go chasing after a pot of gold at the foot of the rainbow!" said Bridie tartly. "That way lies heartbreak, for sure it does."

"How can you be so certain? Surely it's my right to find out what I can about my family?"

"Your family? That's a laugh! What have that family ever done for you, I'd like to know!" Bridie was indignant. "Lady Arkwright with her face like a pig's bum. I've told you before, she didn't want to know! And you've a perfectly good family of your own. Aren't I the one that cared for you since the day you were born?"

Joy closed her eyes and silently counted to ten. "Mother, I know. I *know*. And I'm grateful. Trust me, I'm grateful for all you've done for me." *Although that's exhausting in itself, having to be grateful. Why can't I just howl with pain when I need to?*

"It's just there's a . . . a hole. A gap in my history. Look, can you just tell me what you remember about Veronica and Howard? You said she was a friend of yours. What was she like? Do you have any pictures?"

"Well, I'm not sure what I can tell you," said Bridie. "But I do have some snaps, if I can lay my hands on them. I suppose I always knew you might be after asking one day." She lifted herself out of her chair and made her way slowly over to the door. (Her mother had always listed to one side, thanks to her gammy leg, but when did she start to *shuffle*? It was as if Joy hadn't looked at her properly for years. She had shrunk, surely; her clothes were hanging off her.)

"Wait there a minute and I'll fetch you what I have."

Joy sat in agonized silence as she heard Bridie creep slowly up the stairs and then move about in her bedroom. She could hear her mother opening a chest of drawers. Finally, she reappeared with an old brown envelope in her hand. "Here you go, my lovely," she said with moist eyes.

Joy opened the envelope to find two black-and-white photos. A handsome man in uniform, a figure from another era with slicked-back hair and a moustache, smiled out of the picture. "That's Howard, the handsome fellow," said Bridie. "Not that I ever met him. What I do know is that she loved him to pieces."

Joy couldn't think what to say. "Dapper, in his uniform, wasn't he?" she said eventually.

"Not a patch on Veronica! She was a beauty, and no mistake. As dark as he was fair. Here. Have a look at this one. Not that it really does her justice."

The picture of her mother was disappointingly faded, as if it had been left in sunlight too long. What she could see was that Veronica looked very young. Her dark hair was tied back in a chignon at the nape of her neck, and she wore a three-stranded necklace of pearls round her long neck.

"Very much the debutante," said Joy. "She looks as if she's stepped out of *Country Life* or something."

"Well, she did come from money, so I don't suppose there was any expense spared," said Bridie. "It was all formal studio portraits, in those days. None of your digital whatsits."

"I . . . I don't really recognize them," said Joy. For all that the sight of the pictures should have been momentous, she felt surprisingly flat. "They're total strangers."

"To be sure they are, my lovely! You can't remember what you never knew."

"Was she broad shouldered, like me? I can't tell from this." Joy stared at the photograph, willing it to yield its secrets. "Or was that Howard?"

"What are you meaning?"

"Where did I get my looks?" said Joy, her voice shaky. "They could have done me a favour and passed on some of their glamour. I've always felt such a lump compared with Felicity." *No oil painting. Not like fair-of-face Felicity.*

"Now you look here, my lovely," said Bridie with some force. "Didn't I bring you up to know there's more to life than what you see in the mirror? You were always yourself and that's how the good Lord made you." She reached out to reclaim the photographs. "I knew this would lead to trouble. Let's put these away and say no more about it. How about a nice cup of tea?"

"I'll go and put the kettle on," said Joy. She stood up, lifting the photographs out of her mother's reach. "But I think I should keep these, don't you? They're all I've got."

"All you've got? Who do you think pulled you from the wreckage when the bombs were raining down on our roof? Who changed your nappies and wiped your tears and saw you fed and clothed and . . . and . . . *everything*?" Bridie's voice became shrill with distress. "Did I not do everything in my power to keep you safe?"

"Mother, I know, I know. I didn't mean to upset you. I'm sorry. Let me go and make that tea."

—

Despite Joy's efforts to tease out more information during the rest of her stay, Bridie remained tight lipped about Veronica and Howard. "It's a very long time ago," she said repeatedly, however Joy framed the question.

"You've the snaps you wanted. Surely you can leave it be, now? Let them rest in peace, why don't you?"

In the face of her mother's intransigence, Joy had little option but to let it go. There was no one else she could ask. Nonetheless, she returned to Dorset with fresh resolve. She decided she owed it to Veronica and Howard—whose lives had been so cruelly short—not to waste what years she had left to her. Enough of wallowing. She needed to take herself in hand.

As soon as the library reopened after the Christmas holidays, she went in and enquired about voluntary opportunities in the community. In the end she volunteered her services to the Women's Royal Voluntary Service. Aside from a short-lived pang that she couldn't offer to deliver Meals on Wheels—in another life that would have been her first choice—she signed up to help out at the café at the county hospital. Once she'd done so, the relief of stepping into a hospital environment was immediate. This was somewhere where she knew who she was.

By Easter, she had a handful of acquaintances, and, better still, had cultivated the first shoots of friendship with two of her fellow volunteers. Winnie, who must have been almost Bridie's age, was a live wire and prone to funny if occasionally astringent conversation. She'd been a hospital volunteer for more than twenty years and was only too pleased to show Joy the ropes. (She was also in search of a new whist partner because her previous team-mate recently died at the card-table; Joy wasn't convinced but promised to think about it.)

Barbara, meanwhile, was of an age with Joy, and recently widowed. A former primary school teacher, she'd taken early retirement to nurse her husband, and was now at something of a loose end. She introduced herself at a drop-in morning for volunteers.

"It's that 'now what?' feeling, isn't it?" she said over coffee and a biscuit. "I expect you've been too busy with your career for outside interests. I'm just the same. First it was the family, and then it was my teaching. Then poor Keith fell ill. Perhaps we can find our feet together?" Joy warmed to Barbara immediately. There was no side to her, as Bridie would have said.

Barbara told Joy she'd recently joined a walking group and invited her to come along. "It might be more your scene than whist," she said with a hint of mischief. "Winnie's a dear, but she never stops talking. Between ourselves, I'm convinced Reg's dramatic exit was his last desperate attempt to stem the flow. Anyway, the great thing about the walking group is it's pay-as-you-go. No commitment, so you can give it a try without signing your life away."

The group was a revelation; a clutch of other retirees who went out together every Tuesday morning, come rain and shine. They took it in turns to plan a route along the many footpaths around Weymouth, always designed to end up in a pub for lunch.

Most of the members dipped in and out, according to their other commitments, but not Joy; it quickly became the highlight of her week. Shyly at first, she ventured beyond Barbara, and gradually got to know the other members. They welcomed her; it was a relaxed group, open to newcomers. Joy grew bolder and volunteered herself as a named first-aider. She got fitter and stronger; the weekly walking became easier as she lost weight and her muscles hardened. Through the walking group, she found out about the annual Great Dorset Beach Clean and signed up to become a beach-warden with responsibility for her own small stretch of shoreland.

A year after moving, Joy had the tender shoots of a new life and the sense of a possible future beckoning.

FELICITY

2009

Felicity is leafing through the paper on an unusually idle Saturday morning when Jacob phones. In spite of his having lived in Los Angeles for two years now, she's still surprised by how close he sounds. Sometimes, it's true, you get that annoying delay on the line, but more often than not, he could be in the next room. (She has to stop herself commenting on the fact every time they speak, along with fussing about the cost of the call. Apparently Jake has some kind of deal that makes it affordable. A *bundle*, he calls it.) To Felicity, the ease of communication remains astonishing.

"No worries, Mum, it's all covered," says Jake each time, rarely betraying impatience; Felicity always feels a bit of a fool anyway. It's one of the miracles of the modern age, and something that makes Jake's decision to move to California bearable. After a painful break-up, the job offer with a start-up (in Hollywood, too!) couldn't have come at a more serendipitous moment: even though the parting of the ways had been initiated by Jake, the fallout was messy after eight years together. She was glad for him. But that didn't mean she wasn't also heartbroken.

Today he's ringing because he thinks they should celebrate her big birthday next year. "How about it, Mum?" he says. "I could come over for a couple of weeks in the summer. We could all go on holiday. Or have a big bash at yours. I haven't seen the new pad yet. What do you think?"

Felicity is struggling to believe she is about to be sixty. She may be creaking a bit around the knees, but in every other way she still feels so young. (Her father was only sixty when he died. It was a terrible shock, of course, very distressing, but to the teenage Felicity he seemed an old

179

man. Much older than any of her friends' fathers. Embarrassingly so. And much older than Mammy, too.) It strikes her that Mammy has been a widow for more than forty years now. How on earth has she managed? It must have been desperately lonely, especially at the start when they were all in shock. A fortnight after the funeral, Joy flew out to South Africa and a week or two later Felicity set off for London and her new life as a student. Desperate to escape all the unhappiness, the humiliation of her first love affair gone wrong. The tainted memories. Anything to get away from Northampton. Without a backward glance to her grieving mother.

Now she's single herself, she has an inkling of what it must have been like for Bridie, although the circumstances couldn't be more different. Felicity is on her own by choice, not grieving, merely cross about the years she wasted with David. That anger has fuelled her to rebuild a new life. A life that allows her to please herself for once. But she will admit there have been bleak moments. It is undoubtedly odd to be on her own after so many years as part of a couple.

Not that she can complain. Not in the slightest. Felicity knows how lucky she is. Alex and Amélie are only an hour and a half away in Richmond, and now that Henry's got a place at choir school in Oxford, she expects to see a lot more of him. (It is entirely typical of Henry's parents to choose a school based on her presumed availability for grandmotherly duties. There has been no conversation about this, no asking whether she is happy to serve *in loco parentis*. Just the assumption that she has time on her hands while they pursue their busy careers. Not that she minds, really; she loves Henry and will adore going to hear him sing. It's just the thought of boarding school she's struggling with. Henry is not quite eight. He still sucks his thumb.)

Felicity adores her new life in Oxford. After years in the countryside, it's been a revelation to live in the city for a change—and a city of such culture offering whole new horizons. (Nothing like Northampton in the 1960s! Lectures, festivals, concerts and recitals. Like-minded people, who are interested in her for herself, rather than as an accessory of her husband.) She's found herself reclaiming some of the glorious freedom she first discovered in Vermont. For all her initial fears about leaving the familiarity of Summersby, she finds she is in some kind of heaven.

Not that her caution about this house wasn't justified. The whole idea of multi-generational living seemed positively foolhardy when Finn first suggested it, but it has worked out surprisingly smoothly. They seem to be rubbing along remarkably well.

When she and David first separated, she stayed on in The White House on the grounds that he had installed his mistress Jilly in the London flat. Stubborn, perhaps, but she simply changed the locks and sat tight while he huffed and puffed, alternately begging her forgiveness and railing at her for being unreasonable. Unreasonable! When he was clearly incapable of being faithful to her for more than five minutes! She doesn't know how she stood the humiliation for so many years. The inevitable cycle of affair, discovery, confession and abject apology (especially when an election was looming) had finally worn thin. Enough was enough.

Eventually, they reached an *impasse*, tolerably acceptable to both parties provided neither had to be in the same room as each other. (No wonder Alex and Amélie tied the knot in a private ceremony on a beach in the Caribbean.) The arrangement foundered only when Jilly fell pregnant and David became more conciliatory. (Or desperate, depending on your interpretation.) They put The White House on the market, and it was almost immediately snapped up by an American banker who was prepared to pay over the odds to fulfil his wife's yen for a slice of chocolate-box England.

As luck would have it, the sale was completed two months before the financial crisis. Felicity had already decided to rent while she considered her options, and, by the time she was ready to make her move, property prices had taken a nose-dive and that meant Oxford was suddenly a possibility, all the more so when Finn came up with his scheme to buy somewhere together. By pooling their finances, they were able to buy a four-storey Victorian wreck in drastic need of modernization. The house had previously been divided into student flats and had to be entirely remodelled, but Finn oversaw the work, and now they live under a single roof in two separate apartments. Felicity has the basement and the whole of the ground floor, while Finn and Chloe inhabit the top two storeys. The children—Summer and Zac, aged five and three—move happily between the two homes. It works better than Felicity could ever have imagined.

Some kind of family celebration might be good, she decides now. Just the nine of them. Eleven with Joy and her mother. Lunch, a weekend maybe, but not a holiday. That would be too much. Let alone the hassle of trying to co-ordinate diaries, Alex and Amélie have a very different approach to parenting to Finn and Chloe. (Poor Henry is subjected to a programme of educational activities, even on holiday, whereas Summer and Zac are almost feral.) All too exhausting. She'll sound out Finn and Chloe over Sunday lunch, then perhaps give Alex a call and see what he thinks. (Oh, but Jake coming to stay! Not till next year, but *still*. She hugs the happy thought to herself.)

—

The afternoon is spent completing her tax return, something Felicity always leaves until the very last minute. Alex gave her a terrible ticking off when he discovered she had incurred a hefty fine the first year she was on her own and missed the deadline. (Not that it's any of his business. Honestly! How did Alex become so bossy?)

She supposes it was her fault for consulting him about her finances during the divorce. He'd been terribly pained about the whole process, far more than she had anticipated. The moment she made the decision to leave David she had determined not to breathe a word of criticism of him to the boys. (She saved her long list of complaints for Joy.) She thought being studiedly neutral would be enough, but when Alex came over to her rented flat to help her go through her books, he spent a querulous hour finding fault after fault with her chaotic filing system.

"What's wrong, darling?" she asked eventually. "It's not *that* much of a muddle, is it?"

"It's a dog's breakfast, Mother," muttered Alex. And burst into embarrassed tears.

It all came out then. That Alex felt betrayed by his parents' divorce, even though he was in his thirties. That he now believed his entire childhood was built on a lie. That it was all his mother's fault, for abandoning his father after the disastrous election and disappearing off to America.

"And now we're losing our childhood home!" said Alex. "All our precious memories. I wanted Henry to grow up running about in the garden at The White House. Did you ever think for one moment what it would be like for any of us when you took off?"

"Oh Alex, for goodness sake!" protested Felicity. "I've spent my entire life putting everyone else first. Your father . . . his career . . . the three of you. Not that I didn't love looking after you boys. I wouldn't have missed that for all the tea in China. But you'd all left home! It was my turn, to do something for myself at last. And it was a *good* decision, going to America. Transformational for me. Changed my life."

"I can't believe you'd be so selfish! You know Dad needs looking after. He's hopeless on his own, always has been. You practically drove him into Jilly's arms!"

Felicity thought back over the time of her Master's. The transatlantic phone calls, always scheduled to suit David, never mind the time difference. The long flights home at Christmas and Easter when she'd simply picked up the domestic reins and cooked and cleaned for them all as usual. There was never any question about it, no matter how exhausted from her studies or jetlagged from the journey. David's sulks when she talked about her friends in Vermont. His lack of interest in what she was learning, so that it soon became a blessed relief to return to the US and the joyous new world where she was known and understood. Free to be herself.

Did she honestly think their marriage would survive? Naively, it now seems, she thought that with a bit of effort on both sides, they'd be able to slot back into their semi-detached routine upon her return. (Had she known about Jilly? Only that the list of David's conquests was a long one. *Caroline, Fiona, Sophie, Becky, Dominique* . . . at which point she began to lose count.) Why is everything always her fault? Did Alex really have no idea his father was a serial adulterer?

"We did try to make it work, you know," she said, reaching for his hand. Alex snatched it away and blew his nose noisily on a crisp monogrammed handkerchief. "When I came back, I mean. I'm sorry to see you so upset, darling. But you know . . . you never *really* know what goes on in a marriage. You might want to talk to your father before you blame everything on me."

Alex's sobs subsided. "I already have." He looked up at her. "He says . . . he says he wasn't always a very good husband."

Felicity snorted. "Well, that's true at least."

"I suppose what's done is done. Jilly's up the duff—which doesn't bear thinking about, actually—and The White House is a goner." Alex gathered up the pile of papers into a neat stack in front of him. "Looking at this lot, you need to get a grip on your book-keeping, but I think you'll be all right. I assume you'll keep going at the Daisy?"

"Definitely," said Felicity. Kings Burton was eminently commutable from Oxford. "I love the work, and it brings in a steady income. And I've got a few other irons in the fire."

"Oh?" Alex looked warily round the room, as if expecting an unwelcome visitor to emerge.

"Yes. As soon as I'm settled, I'll put the feelers out for some bread-and-butter teaching. But I'm also looking into harp therapy."

"I thought that's what you did." Alex stood up to leave. He was only half listening; he'd warned her earlier he was on a tight schedule. It was date night with Amélie.

"No, not really," said Felicity. *Oh, never mind.* "Thank you for coming, darling. You've been a great help."

Alex raised his eyebrows in amusement. When he smiled, he had his father's boyish charm. "No, I mean it," said Felicity. "I'm glad you think I'll get by, and I promise I'll try and keep my paperwork in order. Now come along, you'd better get going, or you'll be late for Amélie. You don't want to disappoint her."

"Trouble is," said Alex, his hand on the door. "I think I do. Disappoint, I mean. I'm not sure I'm such a good husband either." He turned and left hurriedly before Felicity could say another word.

—

The encounter left her rattled. What did Alex mean? Now as she tackles the wretched tax forms, she wonders whether Alex and Amélie are happy, and if not, if it's her fault. Hers and David's, for setting a bad example. (David never thought it would last: what was it he'd said? That Amélie was out of Alex's league? Bit harsh, surely?) They've survived fifteen years, despite attending universities at opposite ends of the country, and now the pressures of long hours in the office and the demands of parenthood.

The trouble is they always seem so frantic with work, so unbending with rules. Three years in this job, get promoted or move on. Rules about Henry and homework and table manners. Rules about holidays and date nights. When life is organized with such grim purpose, some of the joy seems to get sucked out of it.

It's not her business, really. At least Alex seems to have forgiven her, especially since the arrival of his half-sister Madison, whom he regards as something of an embarrassment. A black mark against David. He treats Felicity with amused tolerance, these days. ("Your dotty old Granny," he tells Henry.) He's made no real attempt to grasp what it is she does. It's all too nebulous for Alex. He likes things you can count.

Thanatology remains her passion. She still pinches herself to have discovered her true calling, even if a little late in life. To be using her musical gifts as they should be used! The fulfilment is beyond imagination. But she's keen to keep expanding her practice, and her tentative experiments with harp therapy have actually been well received. She now has three care homes on her books who between them employ her for six hours a week because they are required to run activities for their residents.

That reminds her: she needs to plan her session for Monday. But first, the dreaded tax return.

BRIDIE

2019

It's that heavenly music I can hear again. The piano-that's-not-a-piano. That stream of notes that starts as a trickle, builds up into a stream, and turns itself into a waterfall. A rainbow of sounds. There's a fancy word our Felicity taught me when she was at her studies at the Grammar school. It means one thing turning into another. But the word's just out of reach, the shifty fellow.

Then the bewitching music pauses and a voice I know speaks. *Excuse the interruption, my darlin', but I need to do my checks*, says the nun I like. The fat black one. I hear the swoosh of curtains being drawn around me. *Time for your girl to take a breather, I'm thinking, while we have a little wash.*

Little wash, little stroke, I think, as I feel her stroking me with the flannel, but oh so gently. She's a kind one, this one. They weren't like this in the old days. No *little strokes* with Sister Bernadette! She had a temper on her, and I'll admit I lived in fear of her. Myself and wee June Murphy, whose sister Aileen had a thing for our John-Joe. We could do nothing right for Sister Bernadette. A big woman, with rosy apple cheeks that belied her character. Trust me, you had to keep a lookout for Sister Bernadette when she turned her gaze on you.

There's poor Junie Murphy with the club foot who can't spell for toffee and barely knows her numbers either. Skin and bone she was, too, and crawling with head-lice, but we were all scrawny back then, weren't we? Half-starved, so we were. My curves only came later. You try telling that to the boys and you get laughed to scorn. With their McDonald's and their

Starbucks and their supermarkets with shelves stacked to the rafters. It's a different world, so it is.

Not that I'm often hungry these days. I lost a fancy for my food a while back. It's the thirst keeps coming upon me, though. My throat's parched and my lips are dry, till someone thinks to bring me the cup. What I wouldn't give for a nice cup of tea! But it's all water you get in here. That and a bit of juice, I think. I'll be asking Joseph next time he comes to bring in a . . . fast? A flag? A thing as you put the tea in for a picnic. Though will he know to keep the milk separate, I wonder? He's never been very handy round a kitchen, my Joseph. But then he always had housekeepers before me. Even married one, to save himself the bother of replacement, so he did.

———

Then I'm asleep again, for sure, because I find myself in that half-waking, half-sleeping state where I'm floating. Not sure where I am, but happy to stay because the angels are starting on their harps again and I'm in a state of bliss. I try feeling to the left side of my bed, because I'm wondering if it's himself as has brought about this happy state in me, but the hand doesn't obey instructions anymore. Besides, I can't hear him breathing.

Then I think, if it's an angel harp I'm hearing, is it at the pearly gates I am? And if that's so, then it's not so bad, truth to tell. I wouldn't mind meeting my Mam again, for one, because it's been years and years. And I can tell Veronica all about Joy, although she might not be there, not being a Catholic, unless I've got that all wrong. Joseph is always telling me my faith is too simple, but as I say, is it any wonder, given I'm a simple woman from the sticks, so I am?

Harp! It's a harp, so help me. Not running water or rainbows but a *harp*, surely to God. Who do I know who plays the harp? None other than my Felicity! Felicity is the one whose long fingers are working their magic, conjuring music from the strings. I'm pleased as punch I've solved that mystery.

I always thought *mystery* should be spelt like *mist*, for isn't it the case that the mist clears, when you solve a problem that's been hidden from sight? Joseph laughs at me when I say things like that. Not always with kindness. Calls me an ignorant *culchie*, which I am so. (I should never have taught him that word.) Maybe that was the charm of me, back in the day. That and my breasts he was so particularly fond of.

But now he's afraid I might embarrass him with my country ways. Or Felicity. They've moved on in the world and left me behind.

JOY

2013

Joy listens to the morning news, feeling suddenly very sick. Her heart sinks to her boots as she tries to take it in. A year after the allegations about Jimmy Savile first hit the media, it's now being reported that Scotland Yard have uncovered 214 separate criminal offences. Three quarters of his victims—*three quarters!*— were children. How is that even possible?

There's something even worse in the thought that much of the abuse took place in children's homes. (The sort of place where she might very well have ended up, had Bridie not rescued her from the authorities.) And in hospitals and hospices, where patients and their families had a right to feel safe. So far, fourteen medical establishments have been named; more will doubtless follow.

Having dedicated her life to the NHS, this is devastating news. Thank God Jimmy Savile never visited Mill Road! She has a dim memory of unpleasant rumours about him back in the 1980s when he visited the secure unit in the old Moss Side Hospital, long since closed now. How many old colleagues and hospital managers are racking their brains now? Trawling through their records? Wondering if he inveigled his way onto the premises with his shiny tracksuit and wandering hands and promise of funds. It doesn't bear thinking about. (The fact that he was a Roman Catholic makes it worse. Not only disgusted by his behaviour, she is shamed by association.)

She is still feeling distressed when she has lunch with Barbara. Barbara is now a good friend; Joy's arrival in Dorset just as Barbara was beginning to emerge from her bereavement turned out to be serendipitous. They have somehow fallen into step with each other. It turns out Barbara's last school was linked to one not fifty miles from the Mercy Clinic, and they have a love for South Africa in common.

Barbara is a life member of the Weymouth Tivoli and has introduced Joy to an entire world of cinema and theatre. She claims that Joy is doing her a favour, because her membership gives her pairs of tickets that she doesn't want to waste. In her turn, Joy has got Barbara involved in the Great Dorset Beach Clean. And then there's the walking group. Barbara has recently taken on the secretaryship. Today the two of them are going to put their heads together on some ideas for the next year.

Barbara lives a fifteen-minute bus ride away, in a double-fronted brick house overlooking the golf course. Her home is as neat as a pin, like its owner. "Keith was a terrible hoarder, bless him!" said Barbara on Joy's first visit. "Never liked to throw anything away, just in case. At long last, after all these years of muddle, I've managed to impose some kind of order."

"You've certainly done that. It all looks very well organized. I bet your classroom was always spick and span when you were teaching."

Barbara laughed. "The family call it minimalist. I'm afraid they were quite affronted at first. But when I offered them the pick of their father's treasures, I think they realized how much of it was old tat."

"Was it hard, sorting everything out?"

"I found the whole thing quite therapeutic, actually. Going through things and enjoying the memories. It was somehow part of letting Keith go."

Barbara is also an excellent cook. Today she has made celeriac soup and homemade wholemeal bread. There's a pretty tablecloth and ironed linen napkins. Joy can never really be bothered.

They chat about the walking group, and the difficulty of planning walks for all abilities. Although the length of each walk is clearly advertised, not all the participants are realistic about their fitness.

"The trouble is, you've got members who forget they're no spring chickens," says Barbara. "Jim, for example. He still thinks he can run a marathon. But did you notice how slow he was last week? I think it's his hip."

"I wonder if we should give walks a grade?" says Joy. "As well as giving the mileage, I mean. Easy or Moderate or Challenging, or something? That might sort the sheep from the goats."

"Worth a thought," says Barbara. She clears the soup bowls and returns with a plate of fruit. "Now, I wanted to ask you something else. What do you think about going a little further afield? A weekend away, for example? Do you think people would enjoy it? I don't think we've ever done anything residential before."

Joy shudders.

"What on earth's the matter? Joy, whatever have I said?"

"It's that word! Residential. It sounds so *safe*, doesn't it?"

Seeing Barbara's bewilderment, Joy tries to explain. "Did you hear the news this morning? About Jimmy Savile? It makes me feel quite ill. He went into residential homes. Children's homes, where kids who were already vulnerable ought to have been *safe*. Instead he inflicted the most appalling damage on them. Damage that they'll never recover from."

Joy realizes she's crying. "It's the scale of it that's so appalling. More than two hundred criminal offences! And there might be more, for all we know. Hundreds of victims who haven't yet summoned up courage to come forward. I just can't get my head around it."

"This isn't like you," says Barbara. "I mean, it's utterly horrible. Don't get me wrong; I entirely agree with you. But I've never seen you like this. You're always so steady . . . So practical. Are you all right?"

"Not really," says Joy, scrabbling about in her handbag for a hanky. "I can't stop crying. It's silly, I know. I'm so sorry! Whatever must you think?"

"I don't think anything except that you're clearly distressed. What is it that's upsetting you? *Please* tell me he didn't come to your hospital . . . "

"No, thank God!" Joy blows her nose. "I suppose it's . . . it's the breach of trust. The thought that he presented himself as such a saint when he was a total hypocrite. Evil and disgusting. He was revered and admired and respected—and yet all the time his so-called *charity* work was just a massive cover for . . . for . . . *that*!"

She feels her hand taken by Barbara, and for once she doesn't withdraw it. They sit in silence for several minutes, while Joy tries to rein in her emotions.

"Joy . . . " Barbara's voice when it comes is very gentle.

Abruptly Joy sits upright. "I'm so sorry! What a show of myself I'm making!"

"Look, it's fine. Stop apologizing. You go ahead and cry. Goodness, you didn't see me when Keith died. I was a weepy mess for months! What are friends for, anyway? But tell me . . . please tell me if I'm butting in, but I can't help feeling there's something more to this. You didn't . . . you didn't meet him, did you? Jimmy Savile, I mean?"

Joy shivers. "Gosh, no! Nothing like that. Thank goodness!"

"Are you . . . sure?"

"Of *course* I'm sure! Don't you think I'd remember?"

And then it happens. A tidal wave of bitterness and misery completely engulfs her. She puts her head in her hands and howls aloud. Sixty years of pent-up grief spills out of Joy in messy, noisy sobs. The fear, the horror, the utter *shame* of it. The utter humiliation at the hands of someone who should have known better. Who stole her childhood. The self-disgust and loathing which has never left her. When she pauses for breath, Barbara puts her arms around her friend, and holds her close for as long as it takes for the storm to pass.

By the time Joy steps off the bus, she is wrung out. Cold, and so tired that she half wonders if she can summon the energy to walk the five minutes from the bus stop to her house. The light is fading, and the street lamps are glowing orange in the gloom. She can't believe what happened this afternoon. Barbara was so kind. But what a performance! Where on earth had that all come from?

In the end, she finds herself at her front door fumbling with the key, without quite knowing how she got there. She can hear the phone ringing inside the house.

"Joy? It's me," says Barbara. "Just wanted to make sure you'd got home safely."

"Oh Barbara! Thank you. That's thoughtful. I'm here, and I'm fine, thanks. I'm sorry about earlier. I've no idea what came over me. I feel an awful fool."

"Look, there's nothing to apologize for. Honestly. But I do wonder . . . "

Joy waits, refusing to fill the silence. Exhaustion sits on her shoulders like a dead weight.

"I wonder if you might want to talk to someone," says Barbara eventually. "You know, get some help."

"Help? What on earth do you mean? I may be old, but I'm not quite past it, thank you!"

"I didn't mean that. Look, you can tell me it's none of my business if you want. You really can. But I do wonder why that news story upset you so much. I wonder if you need . . . some professional support. You know. The doctor. Or the Samaritans?"

"You're quite right, Barbara. It *is* none of your business. Now if you don't mind, I'm tired and cold and I need to get on. Goodbye."

Joy is shaking as she puts down the phone. What does Barbara think she's doing, poking her nose into Joy's business? They may be friends but how *dare* she? She'll have a hot bath, and she might even treat herself to a rare whisky and soda if she still feels wobbly after that. A little stiffener and a bit of time to herself and she'll be right as rain.

Later, Joy sits in her dressing gown in front of the gas stove with a hot-water bottle on her lap, as if she had flu or something. She's made herself a mug of hot chocolate, because she feels in desperate need of the comfort of warm milk and sugar. She's a little ashamed of herself. She can't face ringing Barbara to apologize. Perhaps she'll post her a card in the morning. They are supposed to be going to the cinema the day after tomorrow. *Les Misérables.* She'd been looking forward to it, but it's out of the question now. She's obviously going down with a bug anyway. She can't possibly go.

The Samaritans! How *dare* she? Just because someone got a bit tearful you decide they're suicidal! She would simply pull herself together. The idea that Joy needed to *talk* to someone. How patronizing! She's stood on her own two feet for more than half a century, hasn't she? As if she would talk to a . . . a *stranger* about events that happened in another century.

What on earth would Mother say? Some things were *private*. Ancient history. Stupid, unpleasant memories that she hasn't given a thought for decades. Some things are best left in the past where they belong.

It's only when she wakes in pitch darkness to the sound of a gale blowing that Joy thinks of one person she might talk to. Someone who just might understand. She pulls the duvet closely around her body and hugs her hot-water bottle to her chest.

Felicity, she thinks. *I'll ring Flick in the morning.*

FELICITY

2013

Felicity is not a great listener to the news. She prefers Radio 3, on the whole, and quite often switches off—mentally or literally—when the bulletin comes on. This means that she catches the Jimmy Savile story a day later than Joy, and then only because she accidentally switches on Radio 4 as she rootles in the fridge in search of last night's tuna pasta bake.

She's rattlingly hungry after a morning in the Sunnybank Care Home, an institution that sadly fails to live up to its name. There is nothing sunny about it. The Home is a gloomy, north-facing building that has seen better days, overshadowed by trees that obscure much of the natural light. But there's a new manager called Hilary, who is determined to turn it round. Hilary is relentlessly cheerful and is fond of saying that problems are simply opportunities in disguise. (She offers this insight as if it is an original thought.)

Still, Hilary is very keen on harp therapy, which is good news for Felicity. Today was her second visit. "There!" she had said this morning, beaming round the room at the circle of residents at the end of Felicity's session. "Aren't we all feeling a lot jollier after that? Didn't I say it would do us all good?"

Felicity bridles at Hilary's condescending tone. She can only hope that once the novelty wears off, she will leave her alone to get on with it.

She is utterly convinced of the worth of her sessions. Harp therapy is more interactive than thanatology. It's about inviting patients to play for themselves. One reason it is so therapeutic for dementia sufferers is that it's so sensory. There's pleasure in the touch and feel of the wood and the strings. Anyone can make a beautiful sound simply by playing *glissando*, and the instruments are tuned to the white notes of the piano to make it as easy as possible to pick out melodies.

Even those with quite advanced dementia are capable of surprising the staff with the tunes they remember. You can see the way the patients respond: they hum along, tap their fingers in time, sway to the music. Some simply enjoy the pleasure of stroking the harp. Every now and again you can see tiny sparks of electricity flowing through the tangled maze of a confused brain, as if someone has flicked a switch behind their eyes and the lights have come on.

Felicity is making a name for herself. Sunnybank is a new client, but word is getting out there. She's beginning to be able to pick and choose a bit. She's recently been invited to contribute to a research project measuring the effectiveness of music as a means of pain management for cancer patients. Slightly out of her usual area, but it's a serious academic study, and taking part is tempting. As long as she doesn't have to drop any of her care home sessions.

Felicity puts the pasta bake in the microwave and switches on the radio. She listens in disbelief to the latest revelations about Jimmy Savile. She too is revolted at the thought that this vile man (surely everyone knew he was a creep?) had for so long preyed on vulnerable children and young adults. Children who were disabled or ill or otherwise defenceless. At least one of his victims was as young as five. *Five!*

How on earth did he get away with it? How did nobody challenge his behaviour? Surely they couldn't all have been hoodwinked. Was it simply a matter of the worst sort of groupthink, where nobody dared question what was going on for fear of upsetting the apple cart? The narrative of the loveable eccentric, doing his bit for charity?

In which case, just how many people in authority in the BBC, in the NHS, in the police even, were complicit in this horror? What was it about him that made them turn a blind eye? Were they simply starstruck? Afraid of uncovering something too big to handle?

When she thinks . . . when she *thinks* how much she has had to fight for understanding and recognition for her work, for the value of the therapy she delivers to be accepted by sceptical staff she is even more enraged. She knows her presence in a hospice or care home is only ever by invitation, a privilege that might be withdrawn at any moment. Permission granted simply because she proves her worth, time and again. All she wants is to bring comfort, healing and release. Kindness, not cruelty.

The thought that *that man* was free to release the spores of his wickedness down the corridors of what should have been safe havens appals her. Special schools and children's wards and even—can you believe it?—hospital mortuaries.

She thinks of her sons. Her darling grandchildren. The boys may be safely grown up now and able to fight their corner. But the idea that anyone might damage a single hair on the heads of Henry, Summer, Zac or little Tom makes her want to screech. To draw blood. Claw their eyes out. (Dotty Granny has become Tiger Granny.)

She takes her lunch from the microwave and almost drops the dish, so irate is she. Fury boils up inside her. Blind rage. That this so-called celebrity (just because he presented *Top of the Pops* and *Jim'll Fix it*, programmes of dubious artistic merit anyway) should have been allowed to exploit these helpless youngsters is hideous.

Horrific. Heinous.

That said, she is almost as angry with those who see what is happening and do nothing, *nothing* to stop it. Who walk by on the other side of the road.

The collaborators. The colluders.

Angrier, if anything. That is surely the worst sort of betrayal.

She can listen no more. She has just got up from the kitchen table to switch off the radio when the phone rings.

"Flick? Oh *Flick* . . . " sobs Joy.

"Joy? Are you OK? Has something happened?"

For a few moments, all she can hear are great gulps as Joy tries to bring her emotions under control. "Sorry about that!" she says eventually in a shaky voice. "Everything's fine. Honestly. But are you busy? Can we . . . can we talk?"

—

Forty-five minutes later, Felicity puts the phone down, noticing as she does so that her hand is stiff with the tension of clutching the receiver. She rushes to the bathroom and retches, but brings up nothing. Back in the kitchen, the sight of the tuna bake congealing on the side almost makes her retch again. She watches herself running the cold tap and pouring a long glass of water, adding ice from the freezer and a slice of lemon. Her actions appear very careful and deliberate, as if she is playing a part in a one-woman play. She is aware her knees feel wobbly, as if she might collapse at any moment. She takes her drink and crumples with relief into the old armchair in the corner of the kitchen.

Joy has blindsided her. She cannot imagine why she is so terribly shocked. Her memories of Joy leaving home are blurred. Foggy. She remembers raised voices. An ugly atmosphere. Being *frightened* the whole time, but never sure why. The sensation of . . . what? A bleeding wound at the heart of the family. No more than that.

That Daddy had dealt out the same treatment on her sister should hardly be a surprise, but it is bewildering nonetheless. Because he was always so scathing of Joy, with his cutting remarks and casual cruelty. He gave the impression that she was beneath notice, whereas she, Flissy, was the golden girl. The cherished daughter he adored so much that he *just couldn't help himself*. Didn't they have a *special bond*? A little secret, just between the two of them, that *no one else would understand*.

Especially not Mammy, because she didn't even know the difference between a scale and an arpeggio!

It wasn't so bad, Joy insists. She can't understand why she is so upset all these years later, but something about the Jimmy Savile case has triggered memories she thought were long since buried, like Joseph himself. After all, it only happened a couple of times, and then she made her escape.

Joy fought back. Unlike Felicity.

Little Princess Flissy. Who was told how special she was from the day she was born, and lapped up every little scrap of attention as her birthright. Who adored being so adored. To start with, anyway. Who colluded in the story that she was cleverer than Mammy and Joy put together.

Who'd well and truly made her own bed, so had no choice but to lie in it.

BRIDIE

2019

I missed her singing, to tell the truth, when she stopped. It fairly broke my heart, the house was so quiet. Silent as the grave. It was as if she dropped the singing like a stone down a well. A well so deep that you could scarcely hear the splash when it landed. A brief echo; then silence. Nothing. She lost her voice the day her daddy died, she said. As if it was buried in the coffin with her father.

What do you mean, lost? says I. *How can a voice go missing, in the name of all that's holy? Isn't it there in your throat and your lungs and wherever else a voice sits in a body?*

But no. Her voice has gone AWOL, like our John-Joe who saw terrible things in the War and couldn't get home fast enough and ended up in all sorts of trouble for his pains.

Well, maybe it's just missing in action, says I, *and one day it'll turn up again, safe and sound, like Eunice Parkin's husband who nearly gives her a heart attack when he rings the bell at Number 47 a week after she's had the telegram.*

Well, that's enough to set off the tears again. *You don't understand!* says our Felicity in the familiar cry of her teenage years. And in truth I don't, not appreciating the mechanics of the voice and the delicacy of a singer's relationship to it. There's me thinking it's much like having a sore throat, and nothing some lemon and honey and a good night's rest can't put to rights.

It's not like that, cries Felicity, and maybe she understands something I don't, because from that day onwards, she doesn't sing a note, for all her dreams of the opera.

I suppose it's a good thing she found . . . *himself* . . . my son-in-law whose name I can't recall just now. Slippery fellow, if you ask me, and he led her a merry dance over the years. But he's very handsome, and I think she loved him at first, for all of that, and he put a roof over her head and gave her sons.

Good boys, all. You're not supposed to have favourites, are you? But I'll admit to having a soft spot for Jacob, even if he went and married a man. (Eduardo. Handsome fellow with his American teeth. But oh my good Lord! Imagine what his poor granddaddy would have made of that, God rest his soul! Even Jacob with all his charm would have been hard put to win Joseph around to that wee turn of events. The very idea!)

But she started playing the harp, my Felicity, which filled some of the vacuum left by that chocolatey voice. Though I think that came later, because for so many years there was marriage and babies and what's-his-name's career. Electioneering. Hobnobbing. Photos with the children by the garden gate. Floral frocks and summer parties in the country, smart suits and dinner parties in town.

It's as if I've conjured her out of the air. *Just taking a little break, Mammy*, she says in her sweet, soft voice by my ear. *I'm off to the canteen for a coffee. I'll be back again soon.*

She's holding my hand, my good one, and I try to give it a little squeeze to show I've heard. I don't want to let go, to let her leave me. But that's selfish. You must let your children go.

—

It's dark now, and quiet. I can hear snoring, but it's not Joseph, that's for sure. Too lady-like. I'm just beginning to wonder if it's one of my girls when I remember, clear as daylight. I'm in hospital, so it'll be one of the other women in the ward. That's why I can hear footsteps, too. Soft footsteps, crepe soles.

And my girls aren't really girls, I suppose, though they're always your babies, aren't they? Not so long ago there was an old, old lady on the wireless, and it's her hundredth birthday. She's asked about her children, and she says she can finally stop worrying, now her youngest is in a really good care home. The interviewer roars with laughter, but I find myself thinking, what do you know? She's spot on, Mrs a-century-old-today. You never stop worrying for them.

My beautiful, beautiful babies. All I wanted was to love them and keep them safe. Honest to God, that was my true intention. But there's a kind of blindness in us all, sometimes. We see, but we don't see.

All my attention was on seeing my girls housed and fed, and brought up in the fold of the Church, never mind that their father was in exile. (Not that they ever knew. Would they have believed that Joseph was once a priest? *The past is the past*, says he. *Besides, I promised Norman*.) That was more than enough to keep me occupied.

Exhausting, what with Joseph not being the easiest man to live with. He was eaten up by his disappointment, so he was. His grief got worse, not better, with age. It spread like canker through his heart.

And what will I tell my Maker, when we're eye to eye? That I did my best, I suppose. Even if it wasn't enough, I did my best, so help me God.

JOY

2019

The moment the automatic doors swoosh open to admit her to the General Hospital, Joy finds herself quickening her step. Her brain switches into on-duty mode and propels her forward on autopilot. Sister Kelly in her lace-up shoes, brisk and purposeful, no time to waste.

Except the memory muscle is out of step with reality, which is that, infuriatingly, she's still recovering from her knee replacement six weeks earlier. To her annoyance, in spite of the rigorous self-discipline she's applied to the exercises her physio gave her, she's still not right, and should in all likelihood be less stubborn about using a stick. She knows that her expectations of herself are absurd; all the signs are that she's on the road to an excellent recovery. Nevertheless.

Nor, of course, does she know her way around this particular hospital where her mother is almost certainly dying. Still, old habits die hard, and everything about the place (the antiseptic smell, the drab pastel colours, the reassuring sense of purpose within the hustle and bustle) is familiar. It's as if she's hearing her mother tongue spoken all around her after a long time in exile overseas. Like coming home.

She smiles—well, more of a grimace, really, given the pain—and reminds herself to steady her pace. Bridie is stable, according to the staff nurse from the stroke ward she spoke to just as the train pulled out of Euston, and if it takes a few minutes longer to reach her bedside than Joy would ideally like, well, never mind. Joy needs to be in a fit state to manage whatever lies ahead. She'll need her wits about her.

The trouble is that it's already taken her the best part of six hours to get here, what with the train, the Tube, the train and the wretched bus again, all the time lugging her old suitcase with the wonky wheels, and her patience is frayed thin. Ridiculous; if only she still had her car, she'd have been here in half the time. (Although come to think of it, the knee surgery might have prevented her driving this soon after the op anyway.) Thank heavens for Barbara who dropped everything and ran her to the station.

Joy gives herself a brisk mental shake. Whatever the rigours of the last few hours, she's here now, and Bridie awaits on the ward. She will find out exactly what the tests have shown and ask for a prognosis. Once she knows what's what, she can speak to her sister who currently remains in blissful ignorance that their mother isn't at home happily dozing the afternoon away in front of the TV.

Later, she does just that. Felicity is predictably shrill. "Why am I only hearing about this *now*?" she cries. "I could have been there in a fraction of the time it took you."

And a fat lot of use that would have been, thinks Joy. Then reproaches herself. (Why didn't she ring Felicity from the train? She can come up with all manner of excuses. She can't abide people who make phone calls on trains, especially personal ones. She didn't want to worry her until she had a clearer picture. Force of habit, in that case; big sister knows best.) *Because I knew you'd flap*, she manages not to say.

"Sorry, Flick. But you know, there's nothing much either of us could have done, before they'd made the full assessment. With a stroke, there's a whole raft of tests to do. Blood tests, a brain scan and so on, to see what's going on."

"Oh, *Joy*," says her sister. "Is she going to . . . to be *all right*?" Joy can hear a sob in her voice, a sliver of fear, and feels a stab of remorse. It simply hadn't crossed her mind to ring her sister when Bridie's neighbour phoned, her voice brimming with self-importance.

Elizabeth and Bridie always go to Senior Screen at the Empire on a Wednesday morning. Joy suspects her mother sleeps through the films, these days, as she can never remember very much about what she's supposed to have seen. Occasionally she can muster the title, when pressed (she was very vocal after *Philomena*, for instance), but Joy's given up asking anything about the plot.

On the other hand, Bridie's very keen on the tea and biscuits served beforehand. The fact that refreshments are offered free of charge, courtesy of the council, gives Bridie a sense of personal triumph. It's as if she's pulled one over on the authorities, especially on custard cream days. (Digestives she views as second rate; Rich Tea an insult. The one occasion when Elizabeth was away visiting her sister and Joy took her mother to Senior Screen, Bridie went into a flat spin at the sight of a plate of Nice biscuits. "They're skimping on us wrinklies again!" she shouted, with a venomous glare at the volunteer in a tabard pouring the tea. "Greedy bastards! Probably keeping the Bourbons for themselves and palming off this pile of shite on us.")

It was when Bridie let her custard cream slip to the floor that Elizabeth knew something was amiss and raised the alarm. Bridie was slumped forward in her chair and couldn't be roused. The Empire staff had been quite magnificent, and the ambulance was there in minutes.

"They're on their mettle, this being Senior Screen," said Elizabeth with relish. "They have extra training, specially. Ever so good, the staff. Especially that Dean with the nose ring, for all he looks a fright with his acne. Held your mother's hand till the paramedics arrived and made me a nice sweet tea to settle my nerves."

Joy lets out a long breath. Flick is hopeless with illness, always has been. Practically allergic to hospitals. How on earth she managed to give birth three times, let alone bring up a clutch of free-range boys, with their stitched knees and broken collarbones, without having a nervous breakdown is a mystery. But she's still her sister.

"Well, she's ninety-four, don't forget," she says now. "But it seems to have been quite a small stroke, and she's stable for now. She was incredibly lucky it happened when it did, you know."

"Lucky? To be taken ill at the Empire in front of the world and his wife? How on earth was that lucky?"

"Lucky for the simple reason that she was in hospital twenty minutes later." Joy can hear her tone is brisk, but can't stop herself. "If it'd happened in the middle of the night, it would all be looking much less hopeful. This way, there are options. Thrombolysis. Clot busting treatment. All depending how she does. But we're just going to have to take it a few hours at a time."

She pauses, to let her sister absorb the fact that Joy knows what she's talking about. She thinks she can hear muffled sobbing the other end of the line. "Look, Flick, come now, if you can. Please come. There's not much we can do, but come and hold her hand, at least. My hand, too, for that matter."

We're in this together, she wants to say, but can't quite. It never feels like a partnership of equals. She will always be the older sister, the responsible one. The one who does the heavy lifting, both literally—Felicity has always been slight—and metaphorically. Her job is to make sensible decisions about her mother's care, while simultaneously managing her sister's hysterics.

Suddenly, tiredness washes over Joy, sufficiently overwhelming to blot out her irritation. Her head spins, and her knees tremble. She feels every one of her seventy-seven years. She remembers she hasn't eaten since breakfast. A half-drunk cup of coffee is sitting in the sink at home alongside her porridge bowl, abandoned as she swiftly packed her suitcase. Clean underwear, a nightdress, a couple of spare blouses. Toothbrush, toothpaste and supermarket own-brand face cream; her glasses and needlework so that her hands are not idle as she keeps watch at Bridie's bedside. She tried to be practical, but she honestly doesn't know how long she'll be away from home.

She gives Felicity directions to the ward, and then, little as the prospect appeals, she takes herself off to the hospital café in search of a cup of tea and a sandwich. She needs fortification against the trajectory of what may well be Bridie's last days. Illness followed by crisis and death, as exhausting as it is inevitable. By the time Felicity arrives, she needs to be herself again, strong and in control of her emotions. Fully in charge.

—

An hour later, Felicity appears in a flurry, her dreadful patchwork coat flapping about her ankles, her untidy hair escaping from its chignon. Catching sight of Joy, she breaks off her conversation with the nurse at the desk and falls upon her sister with a cry of relief.

"You've no idea what a dreadful journey I've had! The traffic was *terrible*. And then the horrid little man in the car park said the space I was in was reserved for doctors. I told him about Mammy, but he was so unsympathetic! Said everyone had their sob story and I could damn well park in the public car park like everyone else. What an absolute *beast*."

"Well, you're here now," says Joy and gives her an awkward hug. Felicity is extravagantly tactile, but Joy has never been big on touching. "Come on, Flick. Chin up, old thing. Pull yourself together. Mother needs us."

She steers her towards the bed where a frail-looking Bridie lies motionless. Her face is visibly lopsided, drooping down on the right. She's on a drip and wired up to a monitor.

"Oh!" gasps Felicity. "Doesn't she look . . . "

"What?"

"*Small*, I suppose. She's a shadow of herself these days, isn't she? A wisp."

Joy wonders when Felicity last looked at their mother properly. Certainly, Bridie has shrunk by some inches over the last few years, and she's shed several pounds. Joy is not convinced that Bridie bothers to eat when she's not there to supervise, for all her protestations. Elizabeth helps with her shopping, but every time Joy visits, she finds mouldy food in the fridge.

"Don't you go throwing away my food!" Bridie objects when Joy points this out. "I'm a pensioner, remember? Not made of money. When you've lived through rationing you don't go wasting a bit of cheese just because it's got a wee bit of mould on it." Joy has taken to clearing out the fridge when Bridie's asleep, and restocking with fresh supplies before she leaves. But there's only so much you can do at a distance.

"People always say that," she says now. "I think it's something to do with the bed. The monitors and everything. They tend to dwarf a person. It's seeing her out of her familiar surroundings."

Felicity pulls up one of the plastic chairs by the bed. "Mammy, darling, it's me," she says, taking her mother's hand in hers. "I'm here, now. You don't need to worry about a thing. Joy and I are both here." She turns to her sister. "I don't know what to say!"

"Just talk to her the way you always do. What did you talk about last time you saw her?"

"Are you suggesting—?"

"I'm not suggesting anything," says Joy. And she really isn't. If Felicity chooses not to visit Bridie very often, when she's only an hour away, practically on the doorstep, that's up to her.

"I just mean . . . chat. About normal things. Tell her what you've been up to. How are the boys?" (Boys! Joy can't help herself: her three nephews will always be boys, although Finn, the youngest, will be forty next year, and Joy is a great-aunt four times over.)

Felicity's face lights up. "Oh, Mammy!" she says. "The boys are all well. I'll ring them later and they'll all send their love, I know." Once prompted, she starts chattering happily about the family, allowing Joy to take a back seat for a minute. She notices how animated Felicity becomes talking about the grandchildren. There's a story about Summer who is working on an eco-project for school, and Felicity's frustrated efforts to teach Zac the piano when he won't sit still for more than five minutes. Tom is learning to talk and coming out with the usual funny nonsense.

Her sister's family, their crises and their triumphs, are her life. The shared living arrangement with Finn and Chloe means that the three little ones are in and out every day. She sees plenty of Henry, too, who even at fourteen seems to prefer staying with Granny to shuttling between his divorced parents. One way and another, Felicity's life continues to be a round of babysitting and school pick-ups and glue and glitter on the kitchen table.

How is it possible to have travelled from the narrowness of St James' End to the abundance of her sister's world? Where Joy has fled intimacy, Felicity has surrounded herself with people. Did she consciously set out to create something as different as possible from their childhood? Or did it just happen? For Felicity, three sons in five years meant chaos and noise, a permanently whirring washing machine, and a regular sea of friends drifting in and out of the house. Football. Fights and fallings out between the three siblings. Rowdy games. Raucous arguments. Mealtimes at a long refectory table, characterized by noisy conversation between whoever happened to be in the house at the time.

Joy can't remember a single occasion when she invited a schoolfriend home, or Felicity doing so either. Not once. The Formica kitchen table round which they ate was big enough for the four of them, but no more. Even then, their Father's long legs made the space feel cramped. She remembers little conversation, and less laughter. Their father didn't tolerate noise, unless it was classical music. Somehow his ears—though sensitive to the sound of Radio Luxembourg played at the lowest possible volume behind the closed kitchen door—could tolerate the discordant sounds of Felicity's music practice in the living room. *Not fair. Not fair at all. Just because I wasn't musical. And I wasn't his.*

—

The afternoon wears on. The sisters sit at their mother's bedside, taking it in turns to hold her hand, chatting in a desultory way. Bridie is stable but unresponsive. The machines bleep into the silence. From time to time, the nurses come and make their checks. Eventually, since there's no change in her condition, they decide to leave. Joy will go to their mother's house, Felicity back to Oxford.

"They will ring us, won't they?" Felicity asks anxiously, for the third time. "I mean, if anything . . . happens."

"You mean if she dies?" Why does Flick have to pussyfoot?

"Or wakes up!" says Felicity, her eyes welling. "You said . . . they said . . . she might wake up, didn't they?"

"I'm sure they'll let us know if there's any change," says Joy, silently chiding herself. Felicity has always been emotional. "They've got our mobile numbers. Are you sure you're all right to drive home?"

"Of *course* I am. I'm not *that* useless!" snaps Felicity. Her hand flies up to her mouth. "Oh God . . . I'm sorry . . . I didn't mean—"

"I know you didn't," says Joy. "I just meant . . . it's been a long old day. I'm shattered."

"I can't bear the thought of it." Felicity shudders. "I mean, going back to Number 12. All cold and empty, no Mammy. *You're a braver man than I am, Gunga Din!*"

"Better. A *better* man than I am. I looked it up!"

"Goodness! You mean to say that Daddy was actually *wrong* about something? After all those years he quoted it at us?"

"That's exactly what I mean. Who'd have thought it?"

And suddenly, there's an unexpected moment of complicity. Felicity makes a choking noise; a sob that turns into improbable laughter. Out of the blue, the sisters find themselves convulsed with honking bursts of laughter, inappropriately loud in the quiet of the stroke ward. Like guilty schoolgirls, they make a dash for the corridor, clutching each other by the arm, tears streaming down their faces. The moment of sisterhood carries them all the way to the car park, and the ten-minute taxi ride Joy takes to the house that was once their childhood home.

Joy lets herself into Number 12, but hesitates a moment before switching on all the lights. She knows this will alert Elizabeth, who has no doubt been eagerly anticipating her arrival. Can she face dealing with her? Garrulous Elizabeth, who never uses one word where ten might do instead. Who drops by for a quick cup of tea and stays all afternoon.

But this is the same Elizabeth who keeps a close eye on Bridie, takes her shopping and may even have saved her life today. If there's fresh food in the fridge, it will be because Elizabeth has carried it in from the supermarket. How dare Joy avoid her? She puts on the lights and takes out her phone. She'll forestall a visit by ringing her at once with a quick update, and plead tiredness if Elizabeth offers to come round. And then she really must forage for supper, search for fresh sheets and run herself a long hot bath.

FELICITY

2019

Felicity feels distinctly shaky after Joy's phone call. She struggles to take it in. Mammy has had a stroke and is seriously ill in hospital. She can't believe it happened this morning, and Joy's only just thought to let her know. Why did Elizabeth ring Joy in the first place? Felicity's her daughter too.

Oh *God*. She's going to cry. Mammy—who she thought was indestructible—may actually be about to die. May even die before Felicity has the chance to say goodbye. It's all very well knowing she's ninety-four, but somehow she can't process the thought of losing her.

It is pressingly urgent that Felicity is at her bedside. She rings Chloe, at work upstairs in her studio under the eaves, and explains she can't pick up the children from school and nursery. She cancels her evening lesson (a relief, actually) with Berthe, whose musical talents unfortunately fail to match her enthusiasm for taking up the piano late in life. She retrieves the car keys, which are miraculously where they should be, and sets off into the traffic.

Felicity hates hospitals. They scare her rigid. Something about the purposeful activity and the smell of antiseptic seems designed to raise levels of anxiety. That's partly why she so much prefers the Daisy and hospices in general. It's one of the great failures of modern western society to insist that births and deaths should take place in hospital.

She fought like billy-o to have her own babies at home, but David wouldn't let her. Thought it looked bad for his image, that it implied a lack of faith in the NHS. It was one in the eye for him when Finn was born on the bathroom floor. (Even then, David managed to make Finn's birth all about him. Before she knew it, there was a headline in the *Kings Burton Gazette*—"BATHROOM BIRTH! MP turns midwife for baby boy in a hurry!"—over a colourful account of David taking instruction by phone from the paramedics who arrived just too late. In the photo, David was trying to look modest while cradling a sleeping Finn. She just looked knackered.)

Joy being Joy has the situation under control when Felicity finally manages to park the car and navigate her way to the right ward. Poor Mammy looks terrible. Tiny and frail and hanging on by a thread. Joy is positively brusque with her, practically tells her to pull herself together. (Just because she's the sensitive one! Her sister is so buttoned up it's not true.)

But what a relief she's made it there in time! Felicity holds her mother's hand and chats to her. At first, she doesn't know what to say, but then she finds herself telling Mammy all the news about the family and it's easier all of a sudden. Aware that hearing is the last sense to go, she does her best to come up with stories about the grandchildren that would make Mammy chuckle. Whether anything is getting through is another matter.

The hours yawn and stretch. After a while, Joy persuades her into the family room for a cup of tea. Disgusting, horrible stuff from a vending machine, but better than nothing. They sit on tired sofas that might once have been pink.

"I was just thinking," says Felicity. "She was a better Granny and Great Granny than she was a mother."

Joy grunts. "Oh?"

"I mean it. She really loved our boys. They still think she's a hoot. Remember just how chuffed she was when Henry was born? And the littlies?"

"You should have heard her on the subject of their names," says Joy.

"Really?" Felicity is briefly affronted. "What did she say?"

"Oh, something like *Summer! To be sure that's a season, not a name.*" Joy smiles at the memory. "She's become quite unfiltered in her old age, have you noticed? Not afraid to call a spade a shovel."

Felicity laughs, in spite of herself, before becoming serious again. "I still can't help wishing . . . "

"What?"

"That she'd been . . . *there* for us. You know. Kept us safe."

"I don't think she knew how. You know what Father was like. He was a brute."

"A strong personality, anyway." Felicity takes a sip of tea. "You know, I was so *angry* with her for that. I've had to work really hard on that with my counsellor. You know, I still think—"

"No thanks," says Joy resolutely. "No need. Told you before. I'm fine. End of subject."

Felicity sighs. She sought counselling when the sole relationship since her divorce ended in tears. To her surprise, rather than talking about her failed romance—a classic rebound fling, she now sees—she found herself spilling out the deep, unfathomable pool of regret around her childhood. Anger and tears and sadness. Agony at the time, but she feels better for it. Unburdened. Able to let go of the past. Joy won't hear of it.

"Why on earth didn't we tell anyone?" she asks Joy now. "That's what I don't understand."

"You didn't in those days, did you? It's not like now where it's all in the open and everyone's trained to look for the signs."

"I'll tell you one thing. I wish we'd told each other at least. How come it took us decades before we talked about it?"

"Just too difficult? A conspiracy of silence?" Joy shrugs, then adds, almost as an afterthought, "Actually, I did once try to tell Mother."

"Did you? What did she say?"

"We had this massive row when I said I was leaving home. She demanded to know why I was off to Dolly's."

"Go on," says Felicity. "What happened?"

"She wouldn't hear of it. Literally, I mean. I can picture her now, putting her hands over her ears. *I won't hear another word of your nonsense*, she said, or something like it. So that was that."

"Oh *God*, Joy. That's *awful*! Do you think . . . do you think she knew all along what was going on?"

"I'm honestly not sure." Joy looks at her. "What about you? Did you ever confront her? If you were so angry?"

"God, no! I was far too ashamed. And confused. So confused. Because . . . because I loved him. I really *loved* him. Remember how charming he could be? When he wasn't being a bully?"

"If you say so," says Joy.

Felicity lets out a long sigh. "I just *couldn't*. I felt so embarrassed about the whole thing. Ashamed that I'd brought it on myself. And guilty as sin. I thought it was all my fault."

"Oh Flick," says Joy. "You were a *child*, for heaven's sake. It wasn't your fault."

Felicity smiles. "Sound familiar? *No blame should be attached to the driver*. Easier said than done, sometimes. Don't you think?"

"Fair point." Joy stands up and clears their paper cups into the bin. "Come on. I think we'd better get back to her."

"I'm running out of things to say," says Felicity. "I'd say she's entirely updated on the doings of the Hetherington family. She's probably had more than enough of me wittering on."

"Well, why don't you play something for her? Did you bring your harp?"

Felicity laughs out loud.

"What's so funny?"

"I can't believe it! Of all the times! The one time above any other when I need my harp, can you believe I left home without it?"

"Well, go and fetch it then. Or bring it tomorrow. She seems pretty stable. I suspect we'll be back in the morning."

"Are you sure you want me to play?"

Joy nods. "What do you call it? A song of farewell?"

So it really is farewell, then. Joy has made up her mind. And Felicity has attended enough deaths to know that she's almost certainly right.

"A vigil," she says. "It's called a vigil."

BRIDIE

2019

They're both here now. I hear the murmur of voices. It's a bit like listening to the wireless when you're about your housework. You tune in and out, and then along comes a song you know, and it jumps out at you. Interrupts your thoughts.

Sometimes the words are clear. *Listen to her breathing*, says Felicity. *Is it shallower now?*

Don't fret, I want to say. I hear Joy murmur a reply I can't catch, reassuring her sister. She knows her way around the dying, does Joy, being a nurse.

Just like Dolly. She could put those jumped-up doctors in their place with a glance, so she could. Built like a docker but soft as feathers inside, as Ron discovered. They made a right pair! Ron as tiny as she was large, but a picture of elegance on the dance floor. I don't know how they did it.

I was heart-sore for Dolly when we moved south, for all I was busy playing house. But she never forgot us, always wrote letters, and made a home for our Joy when she moved back to Liverpool. Buttoned her lips, even though she didn't approve. The sister I needed when my own were out of reach. I wrote home again, mind, when Felicity was born, posted snaps of both my girls. To Ellen this time, not Mary-Pat, and she wrote back at Christmas. So from time to time I had the O'Leary news.

I'm drifting now. It's back to the floating I am. Everything is muffled, as if I'm wrapped in cotton wool. My Mam comes in and gives me her shawl.

Oh, how I loved that shawl when I was a young thing! It was a purple-grey, the sort of colour you can't quite pin down. *The colour of heather*, my

Mam tells me. It was a kind of tweed and looked as if it might be scratchy and rough against your skin. But put the wool to your cheek and it was soft as silk. Sometimes she bundled me up in it and I'd breathe in her scent. Like bread, warm from the oven, mixed with onions and sweat and something else, indefinably sweeter. I'd feel safe in my cocoon.

Now she spreads the shawl over my shoulders to keep the draught from my neck and I feel myself smile. *Thank you*, I think. *Ack ooh*. She'll know what I mean.

I think it must be night-time because it's quiet, and somehow I know it's dark, even though my eyes are closed. My eyelids are too heavy to lift. I listen out for the church clock that drives my Da to distraction as it strikes the hour through the night. Nothing. Never mind. I wonder if there are stars.

Night used to scare me when I was a girl. Dark as ink in the countryside. No streetlights, to be sure. And not much better in the city, with the blackout and all. It was the vastness of it all that gave me the willies. The fear of what happens unseen under the cloak of darkness.

My Da staggering home, three sheets to the wind. His fists meeting soft flesh. The bed creaking, and the sobbing. My Mam, before she died. Mary-Pat and Ellen, after. Then me. We all took our turn. His tread on the stairs, and you'd lie there holding your breath.

Waiting, sick with fear. Is it any wonder I went looking for love in all the wrong places?

But Joseph, my Joseph that was once Father Kelly, he loved the stars. Showed me what to look for, taught me about the different consolations, and that made me braver to feel I had some company in the darkness. Those were the nights when he still held me close to his heart. I lay with his arms around me and it felt as if nothing bad could touch us. I wondered then and I wonder now if there's another Mrs Kelly on one of those stars living my life, only not my life. Making a better fist of it, for all I know.

Not *consolations*. Another word for it, though perhaps that's not such a bad name because the stars brought me consolation. The stars in the bright sky looked down where he lay on my naked breasts. Where I lie now with my Mam's shawl around my shoulders. Heather. The softest wool against my skin. I'm glad she's here.

A hand holds mine. Strokes my hand gently. *A little stroke.* Another *little stroke.* Which of my best beloved girls? Joy's hands are bigger. Strong, practical hands, like her father's, I suppose. Felicity's are more delicate and can weave spells on her harp. Both bring comfort.

They've not deserted me at the end, my girls, for all I closed my eyes to what I didn't want to see. It fair breaks my heart to think of that now. How can a body know a thing yet not know it, all at the same time?

There's none so blind as those that will not see, says my Mam. But you could just as easily say the same to her.

Best beloved girls. When they were wee things, it was for me to soothe their hurts. Now the tables are turned. The tables are turned over in the temple, in rage. Everything spilled out on the stone floor. That was Our Lord Jesus Christ himself, was it not? And I thought the Lord was supposed to be merciful and gracious, slow to anger and swift to love?

Will I be feeling the force of that anger myself when I meet my Maker?

Be not afraid, says himself. *Be not afraid.* But I know he was. Afraid, I mean.

JOY

2019

Four days after the phone call that summoned her, she is washing up her breakfast things at the sink of her mother's narrow kitchen and mulling over possible future living arrangements for Bridie.

Bridie has regained consciousness. Although obviously weakened on her right side, she appears to be recovering. She is responsive and has spoken a few words. There's a long way to go yet, of course, but things are looking hopeful.

Remarkably, considering Bridie came from so little, her mother was able to buy Number 12 under the Government's right-to-buy scheme in the 1980s, so the little house that she's lived in for seventy years is all hers. (Good old Uncle Norman insisted on it, and almost certainly made a generous contribution towards the purchase price.) Much as Joy disapproves of Margaret Thatcher and all her works—goodness, she had some barneys with David over the years—she's glad that Bridie has some financial security as a result. Her pension is tiny, but if she needs specialist rehabilitation, the capital in the house should make that possible. Not that Joy is sure about the nuts and bolts of the funding rules these days, but she'll do her homework when she knows what they're up against.

She's just wondering if there's any realistic prospect—or point, for that matter—of installing a stairlift at Number 12 when her mobile rings. She listens, and feels an icy calm descend. "Thank you, Sister. I'll be there as soon as I can," she says levelly. "If you speak to my sister, you may need to spell it out. But I'm on my way."

Bridie has deteriorated, badly, in the night. By the time Joy arrives, she has just returned to the ward after a CT scan. The quickest glance at her mother confirms that Bridie is no longer alert; the old spark has been snuffed out. She appears altogether absent.

A doctor they haven't met before ushers them into a quiet side room as soon as Felicity arrives. "The scan shows significant swelling on the brain," she says. "I've had a good look at all her results, and I'm sorry, but you need to prepare yourselves for the end now."

"But she was getting better!" cries Felicity. "You didn't see her. But she was, wasn't she, Joy? She was *fine* yesterday. Trying to talk. There must be something you can do."

"Flick, *please* . . ." starts Joy, at the very moment the doctor says, kindly but firmly, "I'm really sorry. There's nothing we can do, except keep Mrs Kelly comfortable and let nature take its course. The brain damage is too severe."

Felicity hiccups a sort of sob in acknowledgement and collapses back on the hospital chair in defeat. The doctor takes her leave, closing the door gently behind her.

Joy looks at her sister. Somehow, she manages to look both a decade older than her years and as vulnerable as a little girl. "Come on, Flick," says Joy as kindly as she can. "She's a very old lady. She's had a long life. Let her take her leave."

"Sorry. I know I'm being silly." Felicity blows her nose. "I can see perfectly well she's near the end. But it's different when it's your own mother. My heart's out of sync with my head. Let me have a breath of fresh air and then I'll play again, if that's OK with you."

"Yes please," says Joy. "It's been very . . . calming. More than that. Healing."

Felicity looks up with surprise. "I thought you thought it was a load of baloney."

"When did I ever say that?"

"You didn't need to," says Felicity, but her eyes are laughing. "It's the way you purse your lips whenever I talk about it."

"Stuff and nonsense! Just because I don't have your *artistic* sensibilities . . ."

They giggle again. Felicity hugs her briefly, then stands up with a renewed spring in her step. At the door, she turns back to her sister. "You know what, I've just realized. We're two sides of the same coin, us two. If your job's the body, mine's the soul."

She's right, thinks Joy, watching her go. *Birth and death . . . beginnings and endings. We're cut from the same cloth.*

"Now Mammy," she says in her very gentlest voice, taking Bridie's hand in her own. "It's time to say goodbye."

BRIDIE

2019

Music again. Like the boy David, Felicity tells me when she goes away to study. Music to soothe a troubled King. Not her man David. Nothing soothing about him.

Does that make me a Queen, then? Am I troubled, so? *It's about helping people to let go*, says Felicity.

Let yourself go. I was sure not to let myself go whatever my husband might tell you. I kept my figure and took trouble with my clothes, for all they were homemade and many times mended.

If he turned his back on me, it wasn't my fault.

Just you ask Norman. No complaints from him. Tears of gratitude, more often than not.

Beautiful Bridie, says he. *He didn't deserve you.* Who knew a man could be so tender?

Let go, let go, let go, says Felicity.

Let go, says Joy, when I hug her too close. My Joy, my firstborn, fed at her mother's breast for all it looked to the world otherwise. My secret love child. Even Dolly only knew half the story. The truth lay buried deep in my soul.

Let go, *Bridie*, says John-Joe. *Jump!* And I know my legs aren't long enough, and I know I'll end up in the stream, but because it's John-Joe and he's my favourite, I let go of the rope anyway.

And now Mary-Pat comes running and she's calling John-Joe a little tinker, and I'm crying, and she scoops me out of the stream and runs all the way back down the lane to our house, me with my dress dripping and my legs blue with cold, knowing our Mam will be cross because she's cooking our tea, and doesn't want to heat a tub of water, too.

Let go. I'm holding on, just. But the rope is fraying at the edges. The twists of hemp are beginning to unravel. Soon it will unwind into a single thread, and maybe I'll float out to sea, leaving my girls on the dockside.

Will they wave, so?

Like those ships that sailed for America and no one back home ever heard from their loved ones for all their promises of sending for their family.

Another voice. The coloured nun, not laughing today. Whispering. Words I can't follow. So very tired; I take refuge in sleep.

Holy Mary, Mother of God. Holy angels of God, pray for our sister Bridget. A man's voice, soft. *May holy Mary, the angels, and all the saints come to meet you as you go forth from this life.*

I look up to the heavens. No angels, that I can see. No stars in the bright sky.

Just seagulls, circling in a clear blue sky. Keening high above the dock.

The tang of salt-water.

A voice on the breeze.

Bridie! Bridie! Let go, now. Let go. Let go!

EPILOGUE

September 1941

"I know it sounds extraordinary . . . but would you at least *think* about it?"

Bridie is struck dumb. What can she possibly say? She is trembling with fear or maybe relief that rescue might be at hand. Or perhaps it's plain and simple hunger. She hasn't eaten since breakfast. She daren't, now Sid, the one-eyed foreman at the fish-market, says they don't want her back.

It's a mercy, at one level, because it's a vile job, sweeping up after the market and mopping down the quayside of fish scales and guts and blood, and it makes her want to vomit, though she thought she was over the worst of that now. But she needs every hour's work she can get if she's to find a room to rent and put something by for the future when she'll be forced to put her feet up.

"I . . . er . . . I mean . . . " she stutters, and then feels her legs give way underneath her. Veronica Morris steps forward and catches her before she falls.

"You poor little thing!" she says. "You look like death, darling! When did you last eat? How about a piece of toast? Let me make you a cup of tea, at least." Veronica installs her on an upright chair and lights the gas under the kettle. The kitchen is in chaos: the draining board is stashed high with dirty crockery and wine glasses smudged with lipstick. Flies are buzzing around the remains of a meal left carelessly on the kitchen table.

"I'm pretty much all done in, myself." She yawns extravagantly. "We're all simply holding our breath. When morning comes after another quiet night, you don't know whether to be relieved or plain cross you've had nothing to do. Honestly! Of course I don't want another Blitz, not really. But there's no pleasing some of us, is there?"

Veronica rolls her eyes in self-mockery. Her wide smile—a slash of scarlet in her pale face—is dazzling. She looks like a bird of paradise in gold and green brocade. She's wrapped in a garment unlike anything Bridie's ever seen before. A gown? A dressing gown? For all her declared exhaustion, Veronica sparkles with energy. She is the sort of woman, thinks Bridie, who is enjoying the War for the sheer adventure of it.

Is she never frightened, when she drives that great lumbering ambulance through the scarred streets of the city in almost total darkness? How in heaven's name does she find her way, when Bridie still gets lost in broad daylight?

And where does she find the stamina to keep going, night after night after night? But perhaps that explains the appalling mess in the kitchen. She's at least twice Bridie's age, and so far out of her orbit that Bridie can only gaze in wonder. The sole reason Bridie is in Veronica's kitchen at all is that Dolly has sent her. Veronica and Dolly struck up an unlikely friendship during the Blitz when Veronica delivered casualties into Dolly's care at the Royal Infirmary.

Now Dolly has altered a dress for Veronica, and Bridie's agreed to deliver it while her cousin is at work. That was before Sid delivered his bombshell. It shouldn't be a surprise, because Bridie was only ever filling a gap while one of his regulars was in hospital with tuberculosis, but still, it's a nasty shock.

Veronica offers Bridie a Lucky Strike, but she shakes her head. Cigarette smoke only adds to the nausea. Her head is still spinning, and there's a tightness in her neck, as if a pair of unseen hands is wrapped round her throat. It's hard to catch her breath. The numb terror that's gripped her ever since she stepped off the boat shows no sign of lessening with time.

"So," says Veronica, lighting her own from the gas flame under the kettle. "Spill the beans, chum. All I know is that you're Dolly's baby cousin, run away from home to the mainland. No prizes for guessing why." She nods at Bridie's distended belly. "Don't, if you don't want to, of course. But it might be easier to tell someone outside the family. No skin off my nose."

Bridie hesitates for a mere heartbeat. Then suddenly there's no reason to hold back, and it all comes pouring out. She finds she can tell this exotic creature what she couldn't bear to burden Dolly with. Veronica doesn't look like a Catholic—she might as well be from outer space, so alien is she—and doesn't look likely to mention hell and damnation.

Once she starts, she can't stop. A jumble about her family: Mary-Pat and Ellen, Darragh and John-Joe, herself the youngest. How they'd scraped by on her father's erratic earnings until he fell off a ladder and broke his back and was never quite the same again. How her Mam had somehow held it together, until she took to her bed with the pleurisy, and never left it, and that was when her Da's drinking reached a new peak.

About Mary-Pat packed off to the Laundry with the Magdalenes when Da found out she was expecting and Tommy O'Brien disappeared into the sunset instead of making an honest woman of her. The fistfights between Darragh and John-Joe. The crashing footsteps on the stairs at night. Her racing heart, the sweat that broke out on her body as she heard the turn of the doorhandle and no Mary-Pat there to protect her anymore. The dreadful knowledge when she missed her curse. The prospect of public shame and humiliation. The raiding of the housekeeping jar, the headlong flight to Liverpool.

"I wasn't going to the Sisters of Mercy, that's for sure," she says, tears streaming down her now flushed cheeks. "When I saw how Mary-Pat suffered, I thought I'd take my chances in England. Tell the truth, I hoped the journey might shake the baby out of me, but no luck there. The wages of sin are death, and death's the best I deserve, so it is.

"So here I am, the Lord have mercy. I have to find somewhere to live, or to be sure I'll be bringing terrible shame on poor Dolly when the baby comes. There's barely space enough for me as it is. And she's been so good to me these last weeks, bless her soul. It's bad enough that she thinks I've a boyfriend who's away to the War and let me down. I daren't tell her the truth."

"Have you thought about afterwards?" asks Veronica. "How you'll support yourself and the baby? Or . . . are you thinking of adoption?"

"No," says Bridie, and begins to sob noisily. The stark reality—which she's worked so hard to bury these last few weeks—rears its ugly head all over again. "I can't let the wee mite go. But what can I do?"

That's when Veronica makes her extraordinary suggestion. "Look, darling, I know we've only just met, but I've a room going spare, if you don't mind living under the eaves. Ivy, who used to look after me, fled home to Cheshire once the bombs started falling. Couldn't stand the noise. Can't blame her, really, poor lamb. And while Howard's away . . . well, it's been fearfully quiet. I'd enjoy the company, as well as needing a bit of help around the place."

She pauses for a moment, as if she's considering something. Then, taking a long drag on her cigarette, she says, "I think I just might be able to help with your other little difficulty, too."

And she tells Bridie that she is eaten up by longing for a baby, but two years into marriage, there's no sign of it happening. "Not that we're not giving it our very best shot," she says, with a mischievous wink. "There's no problem in *that* department, sweetie, rest assured. Howard is *most* attentive."

She takes a drag on her cigarette, and sighs. "I never thought I'd mind so much. But I can tell you, I'd give my right arm to be a mother. I'm nearly forty and not getting any younger. Poor Howard had the most frightful dose of mumps as a young man, so chances are, it's simply not going to happen for us. Whereas you . . . you'll have other babies, darling, trust me. When you're better placed to manage. Not such a child yourself. This way . . . well, it'll be like Moses in the bullrushes!"

Bridie stares at her blankly. "Oh darling, I'd have thought those frightful penguins would have taught you your Bible! Remember baby Moses? Cast into the Nile in a basket to keep him safe from the murderous Pharaoh? Fished out by the Pharaoh's own daughter. And if memory serves, Moses' sister wangled a way of procuring the baby's own mother as a nursemaid, the clever little thing."

Suddenly, the penny drops, and a tiny spark of hope ignites. Can Veronica really be suggesting what Bridie thinks she is? That she can exchange the nest of cushions and grey hospital blankets on Dolly's cold floor for her very own attic room in Upper Stanhope Street? That there's a way of keeping the baby, at least to start with?

Until some sort of adoption, presumably. But Veronica will always need domestic help, if the kitchen is anything to go by. Someone like her won't have been brought up to be their own housekeeper, that's for sure. Bridie will work her socks off, proving her worth. Maybe she can stay for ever. Never have to say goodbye.

"So . . . " says Veronica, almost casually. "When do we expect the happy event?"

We, thinks Bridie.

"Oh," she replies. "Christmas time, if Dolly's right. And why shouldn't she be, her being a nurse and all?"

"A Christmas baby! What *joy*! *Joy to the world*, and all that. My favourite carol. How simply marvellous, darling!"

And for the first time in months Bridie feels something approaching happiness. The layer of icy fear around her heart melts, just a little.

Yes, she thinks. *Joy. That's the word for it, and so it is.*

ACKNOWLEDGEMENTS

With my thanks, as always, to those who have helped me in the writing of this book.

This is a work of fiction though certain aspects of the storyline have been inspired by conversations over the years. I'm grateful to Dr Jo Russell and Alice McGarvie for generously sharing their professional expertise with me; any errors are, of course, my own. Thanks, as always, to my early readers for helpful feedback: Imogen Alexander, Lorna Fergusson, John Pritchard, Janet Russell. Above all, my enduring thanks to my husband Ben and family for their love and support in this and all things.